ALSO BY CRESSIDA COWELL

How to Train Your Dragon

How to Train Your Dragon
How to Be a Pirate
How to Speak Dragonese
How to Cheat a Dragon's Curse
How to Twist a Dragon's Tale
A Hero's Guide to Deadly Dragons
How to Ride a Dragon's Storm
How to Break a Dragon's Heart
How to Steal a Dragon's Sword
How to Seize a Dragon's Jewel
How to Betray a Dragon's Hero
How to Fight a Dragon's Fury

The Complete Book of Dragons: A Guide to Dragon Species
A Journal for Heroes

The Wizards of Once

The Wizards of Once
Twice Magic
Knock Three Times
Never and Forever

This book is dedicated to ANNE
my wonderful editor
for the past seventeen years

It's been a journey...

Little, Brown and Company
Hachette Book Group
1290 Avenue of the Americas, New York, NY 10104
Visit us at LBYR.com

Originally published in 2020 by Hodder Children's Books in Great Britain
First U.S. Hardcover Edition: November 2020
First U.S. Trade Paperback Edition: November 2021

Library of Congress Control Number: 2020945244

ISBNs: 978-0-316-59276-5 (pbk.), 978-0-316-59274-1 (ebook)

Printed in the United States of America

CW

10 9 8 7 6 5 4 3 2 1

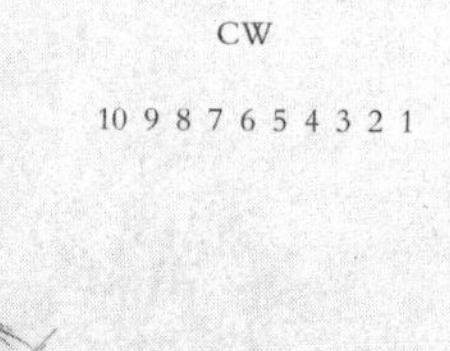

Never and Forever

written and illustrated by

Cressida Cowell

Little, Brown and Company
New York Boston

This is a story with two heroes.

The girl, Wish, is a Warrior, BUT she has a strange and powerful Magic-that-works-on-iron.

The boy, Xar, is a Wizard, but he has a Witch-stain on his hand that may be impossible to remove...

N
E
S
W
OG
THE GIANTS' FOOTSTEPS
a road to Giants' Last Stand
Sea road
Cliffs of Eternity
GIGANTICA
WITCH MOUNTAINS
The Sweet Track
SLODGER TERRITORIES (THE OOZE)
Breedling Fort
Beware of the Breedlings
WINDWARD
Pook's Hill
The Frozen Lak
THE ISLE OF THE NUCKALAVEE

This way to the Warrior Capital

The Mine of Happiness

Ghost Mountains

WARRIOR EMPIRE

The Sweet Track

Iron Warrior Fort

The QUEENDOM OF SYCHORAX

THE BADWOODS

Sinister little Clearing

LD WOODS

Wizard Fort

Ragged River

ENCANZO'S KINGDOM of the Lost

The Witches were winning...

Prologue

A curse had come upon the wildwoods.

The Witches were taking over the forest, and Witches were bad Magic, the worst sort of Magic, the kind of Magic that tore wings from larks and killed for fun and could end the world and everyone in it.

It had all begun a long time earlier.

The Wizards and the Witches had lived in the wildwoods for as long as anyone could remember, and they were intending to live there forever, along with all the other Magic things.

Until the Warriors came.

The Warriors invaded from across the seas, and although they had no Magic, they brought a new weapon that they called IRON ...and iron was the only thing that Magic would not work on.

From that moment on, Wizards and Warriors and Witches were fighting each other to the death in the wildwoods.

Until one day ...

A young Warrior queen called SYCHORAX fell in love with a young Wizard king called ENCANZO.

Wizards and Warriors should NEVER fall in love, so that was the beginning of the curse.

Sychorax had taken the Spell of Love Denied to make her love die...and the love had died indeed... and Sychorax had married a Warrior, like she was supposed to.

And Encanzo had married a Wizard, just as a Wizard should.

The danger of a curse ought to have been avoided.

But...

Thirteen years ago, Sychorax had a daughter, whose name was WISH.

And Wish had a terrible secret. The lingering true love's kiss of the Wizard Encanzo had made Queen Sychorax's daughter Magic. And for the first time in human history, Wish had a Magic-that-works-on-iron.

And thirteen years ago, Encanzo had a son whose name was XAR.

And Xar had a terrible secret. Xar stole some Magic from a Witch, and the stain of the Witch Magic was beginning to control him.

So now the curse really had come upon the wildwoods.

Wish's extraordinary and dangerous Magic had accidentally released the king of the Witches from a stone where he had been safely confined for centuries, and though she imprisoned him once more, this time in a ball of iron, the Kingwitch was now in alliance with the Droods, unrelentingly merciless Wizards who ruled over the southern wildwoods.

And he had a captive. Xar's sweet little sprite Squeezjoos, who would die if Wish and Xar did not get to him in time.

There was only one hope.

Xar and Wish, and Wish's bodyguard, Bodkin, had found the ingredients for a spell to get rid of Witches. Could they make the spell, and use it to eliminate the Witches now and forever?

Only I can see the Kingwitch, now, confined in the ball of iron, only I can hear what he is thinking, in the heart of the Drood stronghold at the Lake of the Lost, and it is not good news for our heroes.

Hear me, O boy-who-is-very-nearly-mine, thought the Kingwitch, in cramped wicked thoughts. *And bring me the girl-who-has-Magic-that-works-on-iron, for when I have all her Magic I shall at last be invincible.*

The Kingwitch knows about the spell that is supposed to get rid of Witches, and he is not afraid of it, and that is not a positive sign.

He still wants them to come to the Lake of the Lost to find him.

So maybe the spell isn't a real spell after all, and they

should stay as far away from the Kingwitch as possible, for if the Kingwitch gets hold of Magic-that-works-on-iron, he will unleash dark destruction on the whole of the wildwoods.

But on the other hand, oh, I wish I could not, but I can see Squeezjoos too.

He is crouching, forced to touch close to that ghastly ball of iron with the Kingwitch in it, and he is in utter misery. Terrified, pitifully racked with shivers, whispering to himself in that petrifying darkness:

"Xar…please save me…Master, I need you, time is running out, please save me, Xar…"

They have to save poor innocent little Squeezjoos, for no one else is going to.

So now I really don't know what I want them to do.

Can Wish and Xar and Bodkin save Squeezjoos? Can they save Xar? Can they lift the curse that had descended on the wildwoods? And, I am sorry to say this, but what might be the sacrifice and penalty for lifting such a curse?

For a price must be paid for a world without Witches.

Or would the Witches take over FOREVER?????

I am a character in this story
Who sees everything,
Knows everything,
Have you guessed who I am yet?
You will find out at last, for this is the end.
But DO NOT CHEAT and look ahead, just
follow me ...
I should warn you, however, before we start,

Someone in this story
is going to die.

I see it and I know it. There is nothing I can do.
I told you these woods were dangerous.

The Unknown Narrator

Part One

The Mine of Happiness

1. This Isn't Going to Help Wish's Fear of Small Spaces

Deep in the heart of the Emperor of Iron Warriors' territory, there was a mine.

This mine was called the Mine of Happiness, but there was very little happiness going on in this particular mine. In fact, absolutely the opposite, there was quite a lot of misery.

Nearly a mile underground, deep in this dreadful iron mine, three children were crawling down tunnels so narrow they had to wriggle wormlike on their tummies.

These tunnels were just above the water table, and only children were small enough to squeeze into spaces this tiny. So it was children who were braving the terrors of the deepest darkness. It was children who were taking out their hammers and their tools, and scraping out the rocks that contained the iron ore that would later be smelted. It was children who were loading the carts, and pulling them behind them on their hands and knees, up to the upper levels.

It was dark, very dark. A kind of dark that choked around you and suffocated you, and felt like it was going to swallow you up.

The three ragged, hungry children who were currently squirming through these terrible tunnels, trying not to panic, were Xar, thirteen-year-old second son of the king of Wizards; Wish, thirteen-year-old daughter of the queen of Warriors; and Bodkin, thirteen-year-old Assistant Bodyguard to Wish.

Let me introduce you to these three unlikely heroes.

Xar, as I said, was the thirteen-year-old second son of the king of Wizards. His name was pronounced "Zar"—I don't know why, spelling is *weird*. Xar was the kind of boy who *meant* well, but acted first and thought later, and he was partly the reason why the three children were in all this trouble in the first place. Wizards aren't born with Magic—their Magic comes in when they are about twelve years old. Xar's Magic had not come in yet, and so he had set a trap to catch a Witch and use its Magic for himself. As you can imagine, this was not a very good plan, and as a result of this, Xar had a Witch-stain on his hand that was beginning to control him.

Xar had a number of companions. Six sprites, and three hairy fairies, who were buzzing slow and sad around Xar as he wriggled forward, and the glow from their stick-insect bodies provided some light in that dark place. But this was an iron mine, and Magic is allergic to iron. So the iron that surrounded the sprites and the hairy fairies was making them fly sluggish and sad, weighing down their wings and confusing them so much that Ariel, the largest of Xar's sprites, couldn't even fly at all, and he was hopping along after them, like a bright glowing grasshopper, his lovely leaf wings dragging slowly in the mud.

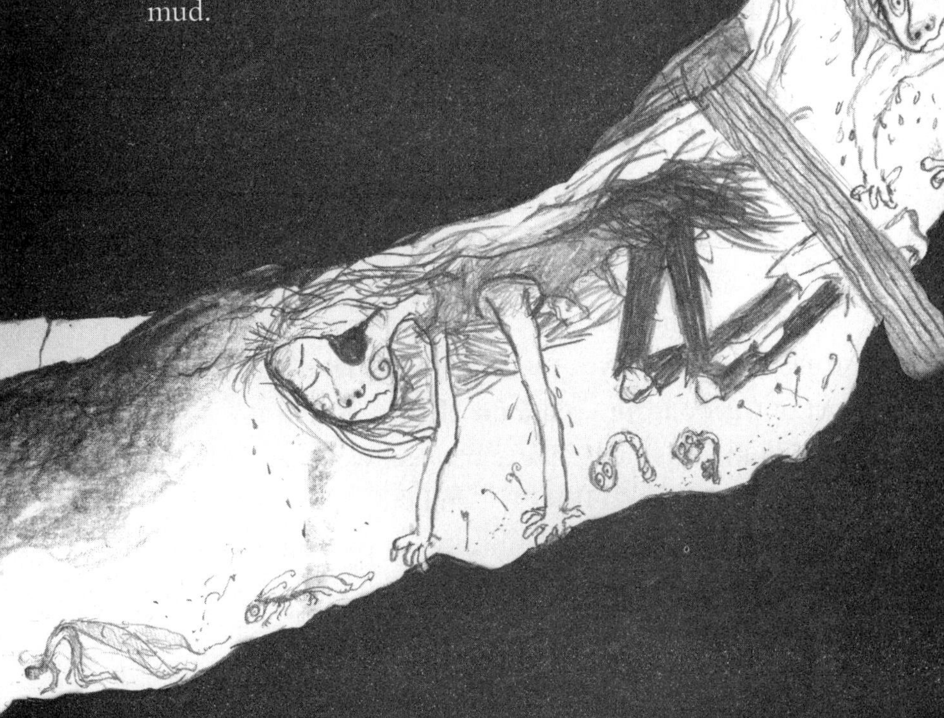

Xar also had a talking raven called Caliburn. Caliburn was supposed to keep Xar out of trouble, and the worry and the general impossibility of this task meant that Caliburn's feathers were falling out.

Xar had other companions, too large to join this secret operation, so three snowcats, a werewolf, and a great Longstepper High-Walker giant called Crusher were hidden outside in the forest, anxiously waiting for the return of the three heroes.

The last of Xar's companions, and his favorite, was an eager little hairy fairy called Squeezjoos, and he had been captured by the Kingwitch, so nobody knew where *he* was.

The eyes of the sprites were lit up green as emeralds, blinking on and off as they hissed "danger danger danger" to themselves, sometimes varying to "get out, get out, get out" or even more alarmingly, and at a dreadfully high pitch, "We're trapped! We're trapped! We'llnevergetoutofHERE!"—and this didn't really improve the mood of the situation, as you can imagine. It made it hard to relax.

Xar was whistling and trying to pretend that he wasn't frightened at all.

The second hero was Wish, who was the thirteen-year-old daughter of Sychorax, Queen of the Warriors. Wish was a curious little matchstick of a girl, with a kind but extremely determined expression on her face. She had hair that stuck out too wispily, as if it had hit some unnoticed spot of static electricity, and a black patch over one eye. Warriors, of course, are not supposed to be Magic. But Wish had a secret. Hidden behind her eyepatch, Wish had an extraordinarily powerful Magic eye, and this eye had a Magic-that-works-on-iron. Wish was a person of great destiny, for nobody had ever been born before with this kind of Magic, and the Witches were desperate to get hold of it, for it would make them all-powerful.

Wish had companions too.

Wish's Magic was so strong that it made things around her come alive, and she was currently accompanied by a number of enchanted objects, all made out of iron. An Enchanted Spoon, who was her oldest, and indeed *only* friend, when she was living in her mother's iron fort. The Enchanted Spoon was hopping along beside Bumbleboozle, helping the sprite along, and scooping up any little sprites if they were lagging behind.

And then there were an Enchanted Key and an Enchanted Fork, who were both in love with the spoon. And a sprinkling of Enchanted Pins, scattering and reforming, jumping and cartwheeling after them all in little prickly clouds.

Wish was scared of small spaces so she was finding their current situation particularly hard. She was singing the "Warrior Marching Song" under her breath as she squirmed forward, to give herself courage, so her song of "NO FEAR! That's the Warriors' marching song! NO FEAR! We sing this as we march along!"

was trying to drown out the sprites' rather unhelpful high-pitched cry of "We're trapped! We're trapped! We'llnevergetoutofHERE!"

I'm not really in a tunnel, a mile underground, Wish tried to think to herself, as the dark crowded in on her. She scraped her knees as she crawled forward, her hair all on end as if it were alive and brushing the ceiling. Wish could feel the rough surface of the rock above because something to do with her Magic meant that her hair seemed to have nerves in it like her fingers, especially when she was alarmed like this.

I'm not really so frightened I feel like I might be sick any moment...thought Wish to herself. *I'm in a wide open space*...*the sun is shining*...*this is all fine*...*it's fine*...

The third, and perhaps most unlikely hero was Bodkin, the thirteen-year-old Assistant Bodyguard to Wish.

Bodkin was a skinny long twig of a boy, who liked following the Warrior rules, and this was a bit of a problem, because for the last year he had been breaking so many Warrior rules it was difficult to know where to begin. He should not have let Wish join up with Xar, because Xar was a Wizard, and the first rule of being a Warrior was that Wizards and Warriors should never be friends. And he certainly shouldn't be helping Wish and Xar run away from their parents, and go down mines.

Bodkin had only been made Wish's bodyguard in the

first place because he had come out top in the Advanced Art of Bodyguarding exams, and her regular bodyguard had caught a nasty autumn cold. Every now and then, like when they got into an absolute skin-crawling *nightmare* of a situation like this one, Bodkin couldn't help wishing that this had never happened.

Bodkin had a slight problem as a bodyguard, which was that he had a tendency to fall asleep in times of danger, and although he had made great progress with this problem, he still had to concentrate very hard on keeping his eyes open. One of Wish's pins was helping him stay awake by jabbing him sharply in the bottom when it saw him yawning.

"Come on, everyone!" said Xar, impatiently looking over his shoulder as he crawled through the tunnel at the front of their little crawling procession. "You're lagging behind! Follow me...I'm the leader..."

"Oh dear...we shouldn't really be here...there are terrible creatures down here..." moaned Bodkin. Just then, he noticed a flickering light coming from a candle...with a helmet attached. He fastened it to his head, continuing behind Xar and Wish. "What about Bluecaps? What about Knockers? What about *the Tatzelwurm*?"

At the mention of that last name, the sprites gave little shrieks of horror and started flying around in desperate circles, like moths sent crazy by a light. The

Enchanted Spoon was so terrified he plunged headfirst into the ground, under the childish illusion that if *he* couldn't see anyone else, they couldn't see *him*.

"*Don't say that name!*" whispered Wish furiously. *"You're making everyone panic!"* And then she added, more loudly, "There's absolutely no evidence that any of these creatures actually exist..."

The sprites relaxed a little, and the fork and the key dug the spoon out of the ground and helped him to stand up on his stem again, very shaken, poor spoon, and wobbling from side to side.

"Okay, okay, but just remind me," said Bodkin, "how we have gotten into this mess in the first place? Why are we here anyway? Is this really necessary?"

"Oh for mistletoe's sake!" exploded Xar. "I told you all we shouldn't have come, but none of you listened to me! But now we are here, we just have to make the best of it, and get out of here as quickly as possible and—"

But Xar was interrupted by Bumbleboozle crying out, in a voice so screechily shrill that it shredded Wish's nerves like a cat having its tail pulled:

"STOP!" shrieked Bumbleboozle. "STOP!"

Everyone stopped.

Bumbleboozle was a sweet little dozy dormouse of a hairy fairy, who made a noise like a bumblebee when she flew.

"I *thinks* ..." whispered Bumbleboozle, putting five of her eight legs on her little fuzzy face in horror, "we mights be *lossssssst* ...bbbzzzz ..."

She ended this terrible statement with an attempt at a buzz that fizzled out miserably.

The fork did an emergency handstand onto the top of Wish's head and wound its prongs around her hair, tugging the individual hairs so exquisitely that she cried out with pain. Hinkypunk the sprite ran around in circles shouting, "Don't panic! Don't panic! Don't panic!" so hysterical with fear himself that he ran right up the walls and upside down across the ceiling, and back again.

"Bumbleboozle's right ..." hissed Tiffinstorm, drawing from her quiver a sharpened thorn, as if that tiny stab of a pinprick would protect her from the unholy horror of a Bluecap. "I can'tsss hardly hear the otherss anysmore ..."

It was true.

The mine was full of children and other magical creatures who were also working as miners, and only a few minutes ago the bouncing sound of axe on rock had filled the tunnel with bright ringing echoes. The sad songs of goblins, of kobolds and the smaller elves, lamenting the dimming of their Magic and the terrible heartbreaking toil of their work, had tumbled through the subterranean shafts, with haunting melancholy.

Now that sound was muffled and distant.

Wish and Bodkin froze deathly still, stretching out their hearing and their earsight into the darkness, longing, *willing* the noise to be louder than it was.

Xar turned around and crawled over to them.

"We can't be lost," said Xar crossly. "*I'm* the leader, and I'm brilliant, aren't I, Bumbleboozle?"

"Yes," whispered Bumbleboozle reluctantly, in a tiny and not very convincing voice. "You's brilliant..."

At this point the trumpet in Xar's backpack made a small but distinct raspberry noise.

Parp!

"I AM brilliant!" objected Xar.

PARP! replied the trumpet, a little louder, and even more impolitely.

Xar sighed. The Enchanted

Trumpet had been a present from Perdita of Pook's Hill, and it had a habit of making a rather rude raspberry noise whenever anybody lied, or boasted, or even exaggerated a little. This was very annoying, because Xar loved playing the trumpet, but he also had a tendency to garnish the truth. If the beastly trumpet kept on embarrassing him like this, he would have to get rid of it.

You see, this is why I miss the old Squeezjoos so much, thought Xar longingly. *SQUEEZJOOS would say I was brilliant, and Squeezjoos wouldn't have to lie. Squeezjoos would really mean it… I told them we shouldn't have come here… I TOLD them we should have been rescuing Squeezjoos instead, but did they listen to me? Oh no…*

The thought of Squeezjoos stiffened Xar's resolve.

They couldn't get stuck here; they had to get back to Squeezjoos.

"Look," said Xar briskly. He could just about sit upright in the tunnel. He got out the Spelling Book to show the others. The Spelling Book was a magical book with over a million pages in it, and Xar typed in the letters that would take him to the maps section.

"I've been following the map. I haven't been making this up," said Xar as he reached the page that showed the map of the meandering tunnels that were the Mine of Happiness. Their own route was marked in bright gold, blinking on and off helpfully, and they were quite clearly going in the right direction. There were even little illustrations of themselves, delightfully animated and cheerful, crawling steadily through the illustrated passages to where they wanted to be.

It was all very cheering.

"Oh thank goodness for that..." said Wish as she peered over Xar's shoulder. "The map's saying we're going in the right way..."

"I's *so* glad I's didn't panic," said Hinkypunk to the other sprites, all letting out whooshes of breath in relief.

"Of course we're going the right way," said Xar. "I told you we were, didn't I? I'm very good at map-reading because I've spent such a lot of my life running away and—"

Xar broke off, not just because the trumpet in his backpack was making a succession of rude and musical noises, but also because he had a sudden, particularly sharp twinge of pain in his right hand, the one with the Witch-stain on it.

This hand had a continual dull aching agony to it, painful as a burn, and it seemed to have a spooky life of its own. Something in the nerves of Xar's fingers was trying to pull him in its own weird direction, and it was deeply unsettling.

One of Xar's good qualities was that he didn't make a fuss about physical discomfort, so he tried to

The Spelling Book

A Complete Guide to the Entire Magical World

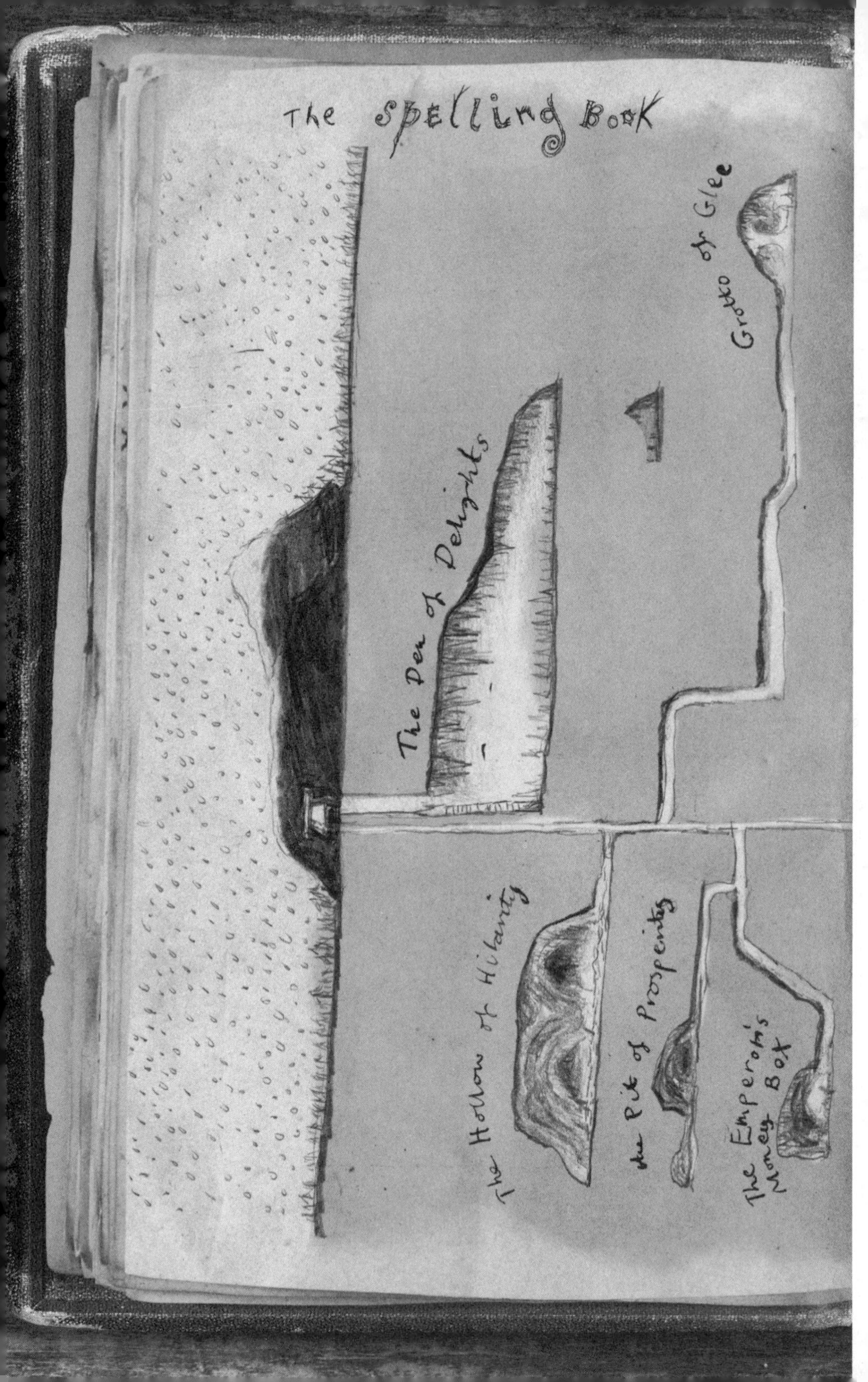

The Spelling Book

The Den of Delights

Grotto of Glee

The Hollow of Hilarity

the Pit of Prosperity

The Emperor's Money Box

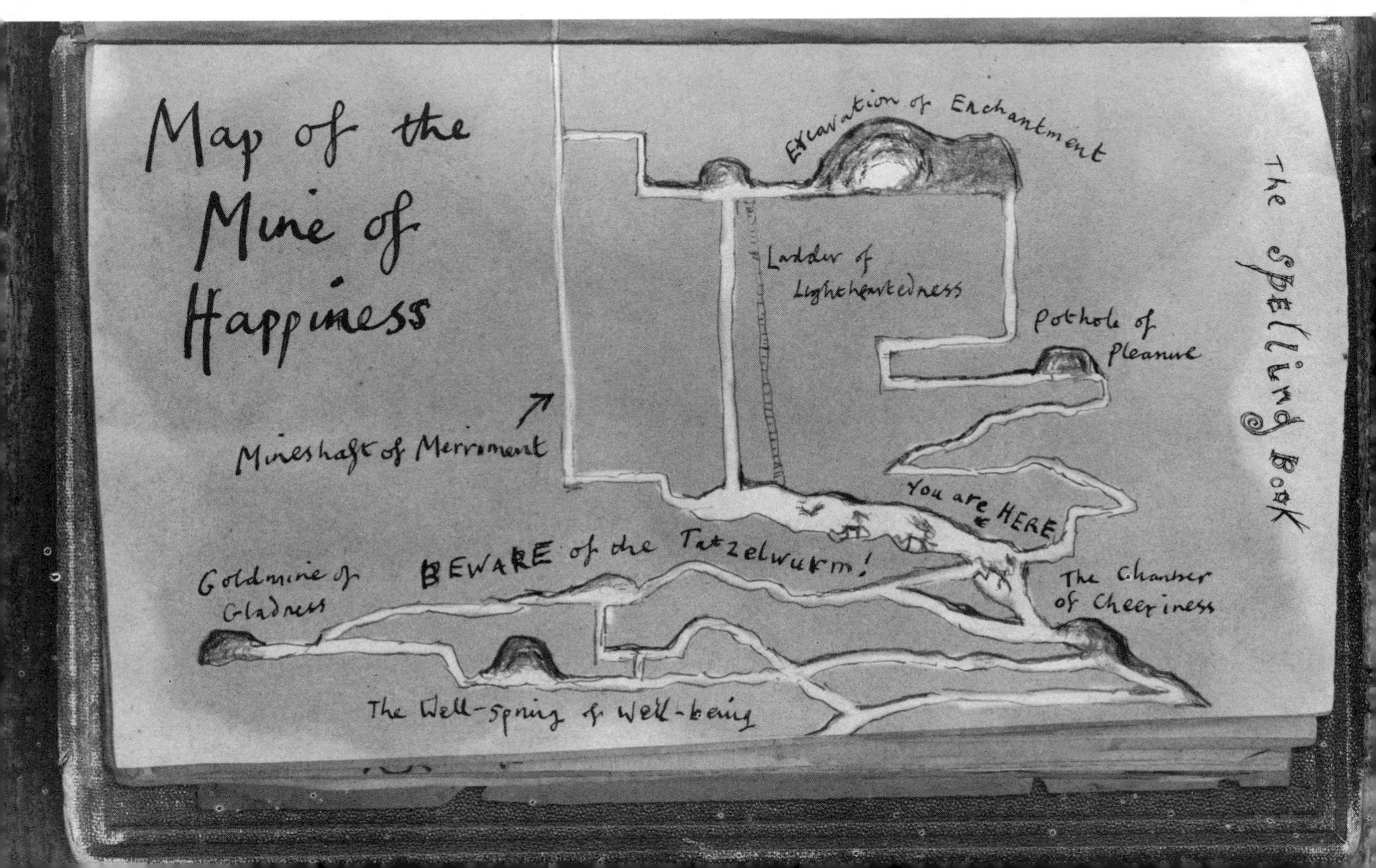

Map of the Mine of Happiness

Excavation of Enchantment

Ladder of Lightheartedness

Pothole of Pleasure

Mineshaft of Merriment

You are HERE

BEWARE of the Tatzelwurm!

Goldmine of Gladness

The Chamber of Cheeriness

The Well-Spring of Well-being

The Spelling Book

The spelling Book

Gobtrolls (also known as Battle Pigs)

Gobtrolls are creatures of the marsh. They are known for their fierce, warlike nature and impressive amounts of drool. They don't care whose side they are on, as long as they get paid.

Knockers

Knockers are experienced miners. Rarely seen, they are known for their ability to warn their comrades that a mine is about to collapse by making a distinctive knocking sound. Never insult a Knocker—they bear grudges.

The Spelling Book Thanks You for Reading,

and Would Gently Remind You That Things

Generally Turn Out All Right

IN THE END.

(Hopefully)

DIE!

Niteye eating Looter

SnOcats ForEVER

When my MAGIC
comes in I will bee
the MOST MAGIC ~~pursonn~~ purson
in the UNIVERSE

Spoons

This book has ben lent
to mee. Wish

ignore the constant spasms and twitches and he never complained, so the others did not know how hard this pain was to forget and how sorely it tormented him.

But now Xar's palm jangled with such a fierce, unignorable, biting throb that he looked down and realized for the first time that…

…while he was map-reading he had been holding the Spelling Book in the hand with the Witch-stain on it!

Oh dear.

Oh dear, oh dear, oh dear, oh DEAR.

Xar swallowed.

"Um, guys…" said Xar. "I'm so sorry, but I think we may have a bit of a problem."

Wish and Bodkin peered over Xar's shoulder.

Xar put the Spelling Book in his other hand.

It was just as he suspected. When the Spelling Book was in his left hand, the one *without* the Witch-stain, the illustrations on the map of the Mine of Happiness changed in front of their eyes.

Now the little images of themselves appeared to be crawling in entirely the wrong direction, and the crude cartoons of Wish, Xar, and Bodkin were no longer looking happy but extremely frightened and anxious. The blinking on and off of the trail they were making had a desperate urgency to it, and there was even an extra warning signal added, just behind them.

Bodkin read that signal out for them. "Beware... of the *Tatzelwurm*!...Oh for mistletoe's sake!!!" Bodkin grabbed the Spelling Book out of Xar's hands to make sure. There it was, clearly marked. *Beware of the Tatzelwurm.* "Why did we let Xar do the map-reading???" wailed Bodkin.

"We were trying to make him feel better," whimpered Wish.

But there was no time for recrimination.

"Whatt'sss that funny sssmell?" hissed Tiffinstorm.

Her little heart was lit up with such anxiety that you could see it, glowing with fear in her little matchstick of a chest.

A stink so noxious it made Wish's stomach heave came reeking and oiling out of the tunnel behind them.

It was accompanied by a scream, so loud and piercing in that narrow place that it pricked the eardrums like the nick of a knife.

In the tunnel behind them, two glowing eyes appeared.

The Tatzelwurm, part cat, part dragon, heart of darkness. They could hear the scrape of the claws on the tunnel floor, the long languorous flop of an impossibly huge serpentine body greasing its way through the passages.

"Let's get out of here!" yelled Wish, scuttling away on her hands and knees, going first down the tunnel. Bodkin followed, with Xar crying after them, "No, guys, no, don't run away. We have to face it!"

"We're not running. We're crawling," panted Bodkin, so frantic with fear that he did not notice the passages he was crawling down after Wish were getting narrower and narrower, and he had to crouch lower and lower until finally he was squirming on his tummy through the dirt, and the ceiling was pressing down on him, and oh my goodness...

...he could squirm no farther. He was stuck. He tried desperately to writhe forward. To wriggle backward. No. He was jammed tight, like a cork in a bottle. Wish was smaller and even skinnier than Bodkin was, so she had gotten through the particularly narrow bit, and she and Caliburn hauled on Bodkin's arms as hard as they could.

But it was no good. Bodkin would not budge.

Now Bodkin really *did* panic. At his back legs, Xar was panicking too, trying to thrust him forward. "Move!!!" screamed Xar. But Bodkin could not move.

Which left Xar having to face what was coming down the passages toward them, whether he wanted to or not.

The dreadful smell was now so sickly near that Xar had to put his hand over his face to defend his nostrils from the ghastly poison of it.

There was a horrible pause.

And then with startling suddenness a great clawed hand came shooting out of the darkness and trapped Xar beneath it.

Ariel
Bumbleboozle
Squeezjoos
The Baby
Hinkypunk

Xar's Sprites

Mustardthought

Tiffinstorm

Timeloss

the Once-Sprite

2. Four Hours Earlier

I'm afraid I'll just leave Xar and Wish and Bodkin facing that unknown creature a mile underground while I turn back time for a second to answer Bodkin's question about how on earth they had gotten into this mess in the first place.

It doesn't seem a very good time to leave them, but frankly, everything is so hectic in their lives at the moment that now is as good a time as any.

And I know that in real life turning back time is impossible, but I am the god of this story, so I have rather more Magic than is good for me.

Four hours earlier, Xar and Wish and Bodkin were hidden in the unforgiving prickles of a gorse bush outside the Mine of Happiness, trying to decide whether to go inside. Thick flakes of snow were drifting down on their upturned faces.

Although the climate was colder in the Bronze Age, it rarely snowed in October. But perhaps the freezing blood and breath of the Witches, returning to the wildwoods like dark feathery locusts, had had an effect on the weather, for this had been the chilliest autumn in living memory. It had begun to snow in early September, and a month later, the ground was hard as iron and the air was sharper than the bite of a Frost-sprite, so freezing that it hurt the children's noses to inhale it, and their breath misted out of their mouths as if they were three little dragons.

The three children were looking up in terror at a great cliff soaring up in front of them. Halfway up the cliff there was the entrance to the mine, gaping like the open jaws of a dreadful monster. Awful sounds were coming out of that abhorrent threshold. A cacophony of moaning and groaning, and terrifying and unexpected explosions, and the ring of axe on stone, for even though it was too early in the morning for the sun to even think about rising, all the poor souls caught up in the belly of that mine were already working, without a break or ever seeing daylight.

Huge, chained Climbing Lumpenogres were carrying the iron ore out of the mine entrance in immense sacks on their backs, and taking it down to the bottom of the cliff, and then on to the smelting furnaces, fires that burned with such ferocity that the snow all around had melted away and half the trees were scorched.

Scarier still, even though the children did not realize it, their gorse-bush hiding place wasn't doing its job, and a pair of malevolent eyes was already watching their every move...

"Why are we even *thinking* of breaking into this mine?" groaned Xar, shaking his arm convulsively, as if he could somehow rattle it right off his shoulder and get rid of the pain forever. "I thought the plan was to find the Kingwitch and say that if he takes away the last bit of Witchblood from Squeezjoos and me, Wish will use her Magic to let him out of his iron prison..."

"Yes, that's the plan," said Wish enthusiastically. "And then you and Squeezjoos will be saved, and then we can fight the Kingwitch with the spell to get rid of Witches, and we will expel those Witches forever and ever!"

"The plan is BRILLIANT!" said Xar, shaking his fist in excitement.

"The plan is TERRIBLE," said Bodkin, shaking his head in despair.

It was rather tough on poor Bodkin, as a feet-on-the-ground sort of person, to have to deal with Wish and Xar, who were both hopelessly unrealistic in their relentless optimism. It was like being dragged around by a couple of enthusiastic puppies with a death wish.

"Terrible or not, we need to GET ON WITH THE PLAN!" said Xar. "We've already GOT all the ingredients for the spell to get rid of Witches—we should just find the Kingwitch and fight him absolutely RIGHT THIS SECOND!"

"Patience, Xar, patience," said Caliburn, very harassed. "In order for the spell to work, the ingredients have to be mixed in a Cup of Second Chances, and you said your older brother, Looter, has the cup."

"Yes," said Xar moodily. "My father gave the Cup of Second Chances to Looter for his birthday last year. Typical. Looter gets all the best presents because *he* is my father's favorite."

"But are we absolutely SURE that Looter is here in this mine?" said Bodkin. Part of Bodkin was still hoping that someone was going to say, "No, Looter's not *here*. He's skipping through the Mystic Meadows on his way to your lovely old Wizard fort home without a care in the world; you can catch him if you hurry"—but now it was *Bodkin* who was being unrealistic, because the Witches had burned Xar and Looter's lovely old Wizard fort home down to a ring of burning tree stumps in an act of totally unnecessary maliciousness and vengeance.

"The great-chunking-brute-of-a-boy-called-Looter is definitely here," said Ariel, eyes glowing green. "The Droodsssss shut down the learning place at Pook'ssss Hill, so Looter and everyone else had to leave. And then they were captured by the emperor's guards and brought here."

"But even if Looter *is* in the mine, there's no guarantee that he'll give the cup to me..." Xar pointed out. "Looter hates me for some reason, I have no idea why..."

"Oh, I can't think either," said Bodkin sarcastically.

Xar's sprite Ariel

"Maybe it's your habit of doing things like turning him into a Graxerturgleburkin and not turning him back again for another three months?"

"Oh yes." Xar grinned. "I'd forgotten about that trick...that was a good one..."

That cheered Xar and the sprites up. They forgot they were in imminent danger and the gorse bush shook with their giggles so violently that snow came raining down off it in great fluffy clumps. "Ooh that wasss funny . . ." giggled Bumbleboozle. "And remember when we made Looter's spelling staffs go all floppy?"

"And when I's put Itchy-sprites in his knickers?" Timeloss grinned.

It became clear why Looter might not be all that fond of his annoying younger brother.

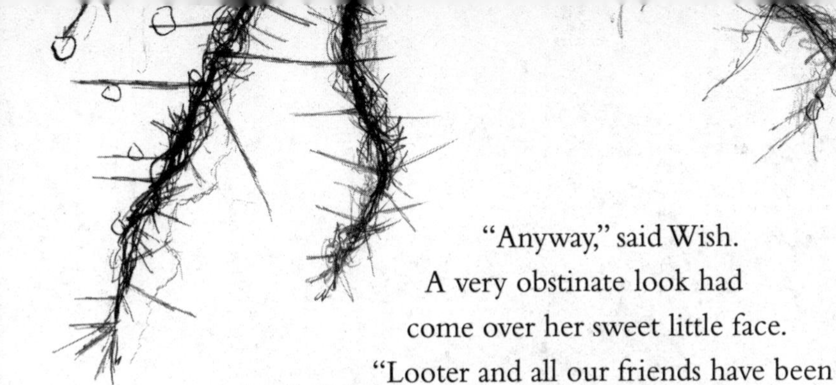

"Anyway," said Wish.

A very obstinate look had come over her sweet little face. "Looter and all our friends have been captured because of US, and it's our job to make amends and rescue them. And Looter is going to be so pleased to be rescued, of course he'll forgive you for the Graxerturgleburkin episode, Xar..."

As soon as Wish put the idea into his head, Xar had an image in his mind of Looter being pathetically grateful. Looter saying, "I always underestimated you, Xar." Looter hugging him, saying, "I was only ever mean to you all those years because I was jealous."

It was a good picture, and it made Xar pause.

Maybe it was worth doing this little detour, just to have the pleasure of Looter on his knees in front of Xar, thanking him for everything.

"Okay, then," said Xar thoughtfully, "we'll just nip in and quickly rescue Looter and then we'll get on with our original plan. So how do we get into this mine? It's heavily guarded."

"We volunteer!" said Wish enthusiastically.

"Brilliant," said Bodkin gloomily. "That's not hopelessly unrealistic and optimistic AT

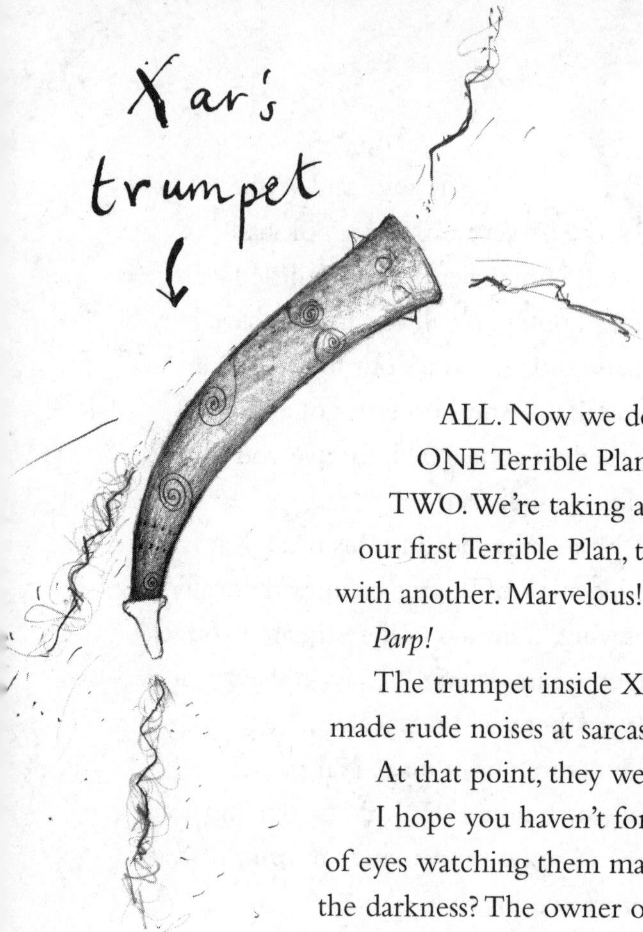

ALL. Now we don't just have ONE Terrible Plan, we have TWO. We're taking a detour on our first Terrible Plan, to kill ourselves with another. Marvelous!"

Parp!

The trumpet inside Xar's backpack made rude noises at sarcasm too.

At that point, they were attacked.

I hope you haven't forgotten the pair of eyes watching them malevolently in the darkness? The owner of that pair of eyes launched itself at them, in a screeching, spitting, blazing charge, screeching, "REOOOOOORRRRRRRR!"

3. An Unexpected Attacker

They were all taken completely by surprise.

Luckily the owner of this pair of eyes wasn't very large and it attacked the fur hat on Bodkin's head, apparently under the impression that it was a fierce animal.

Bodkin fainted, and whatever-it-was flew off with Bodkin's hat and tore it to pieces on the ground in what would have been a very distressing attack if the attacking creature hadn't been so small and the hat hadn't been so un-alive and—*hatlike.*

In about thirty seconds the hat was reduced to a hundred little pieces of fluff in the snow, and the minute attacking creature desisted, stomping on the last fragments with triumphant savagery. "Takess that, yous furry wickednesss!" said the tiny animal, and now that it had stopped stamping, and was still and turned its large, twitching eyes upward toward them, they could see for the first time who it was.

"Eye of newt and toe of frittering frog!" gasped Xar. "It's *Squeezjoos*! Wish, don't spell him!"

For Wish had lifted up her eyepatch ready to use her Magic eye on the tiny, unknown, but clearly vicious assailant.

"Oh, Squeezjoos, I can't tell you how wonderful it is to see you!" cried Xar, opening his arms wide in excited joy. "How did you escape?"

In answer, Squeezjoos just looked up at him from the mound in the snow of what-had-recently-been-Bodkin's-hat. A low growling came from his furry throat, and his top lip curled back, revealing his pin-sharp incisors.

"Squeezjoos?" said Xar, more uncertainly. "What's the matter? It's me. Xar, you don't growl at *me*..."

"Don't listen to Xar, keep your eyepatch up, Wish, and be ready to spell if necessary," said Caliburn. The old raven was shivering with horror. "I don't think Squeezjoos is quite himself."

Caliburn was right.

Poor little Squeezjoos was virtually unrecognizable. He was a hemlock green so nightshade poisonous it smoked with venom. Shaking, his eyes glowing a bright nauseous yellow, the sprite was followed by a hum of dark infesta-pests, sickening tiny menaces that bite insects to make them lose their own survival instincts, and serve as hosts for the infesta-pest larvae.

Xar was used to Squeezjoos looking up at him with loving hero-worshipping eyes. But those eyes now were hostile, sometimes without feeling, cold and dead as a shark's, sometimes singing and stinging with spitting hatred, sometimes crafty and calculating, assessing the situation, weighing the possible advantages and disadvantages. It was as if the Kingwitch himself were looking through the eyes of Squeezjoos.

But then—and this was almost worst of all—Squeezjoos's eyes cleared, and the old Squeezjoos seemed to come back for a second, very confused, very unhappy, and rattled his head as if he were trying to shake out some dreadful head cold that was infecting him, some dark intruder that had crept into his brain and was scrambling his thought processes. As if the infesta-pests that hummed around him in a stinking, malevolent cloud had gotten inside his head somehow and were buzzing inside his skull.

And then he turned to Xar, pleading desperately, poor Squeezjoos, drowning in misery, and reaching out for his old friend and protector to put out an arm to haul him out of whatever terrible trance the Kingwitch had put him in: "Help me, Masster…help me! I iss not myself…bring me home, I iss so unhappy!"

This last cry was so heartrending that instinctively Xar leaped forward, and Caliburn screeched, "Careful, Xar, careful!"

Quite rightly, for Squeezjoos's eyes misted over with rage again, and the sprite lunged at Xar in a blur of wings. Xar only just saw the attack at the last moment, leaping backward in the nick of time, so Squeezjoos's fangs shut viciously on the air rather than on Xar's arm.

"He tried to bite me!"

gasped Xar, very shaken, and Wish blasted a sliver of Magic toward the sprite who had so recently been their most faithful friend and companion. She was careful to miss actually *hitting* him, but the bolt was sufficiently close to stop Squeezjoos from attacking again. His face contorted in an ugly snarl.

"Yes," said Caliburn sadly, "he did try to bite you."

"You iss not my master *now*, boy-with-hair-that-looks-ridiculous..." hissed Squeezjoos furiously, lost in anger and taken over by the Kingwitch again. "I iss with the Chiwgink..."*

And then the little sprite seemed to remember himself. His eyes cleared and he looked around, confused, as if waking from a momentary trance, and he pleaded, "O, what did I do? I iss so sorry, Xar, I's didn't mean it...I didn'ts know what I's was doing..."

"Don't blame Squeezjoos, Xar," said Caliburn. "Witchblood is very powerful. It has poisoned him badly, and it is very difficult for a creature as small as a hairy fairy to fight an evil as great as that."

The wickedness returned to Squeezjoos's eyes and he hissed at them, "Why are you here? My master the

* "Chiwgink" is "Kingwitch" backward...Witches speak back-to-front, and it shows how far gone Squeezjoos is that he is using Witch-speak.

Kingwitch isss in the Lake of the Lost…he has made friends with the Droodsss…you should be finding him…you ssshould be rescuing me…before I become one of *them* entirely…before I am lost forever…before it is…*too late*!"

The little sprite charged again, but he was prevented from reaching them by an invisible protective spell Wish had now cast in an arc over them all, and he let out a screech as if he had gotten an electric shock when he hit it.

And then he seemed to turn back into the old Squeezjoos, pressing his nose to the glass of the spell in big-eyed, hopeless despair. "You don't love me…" said Squeezjoos. "If yous loved me you would be coming to the Lake of the Lost to save me…"

It was truly terrible to see dear little Squeezjoos in such a dreadful state. Squeezjoos, who was normally so cheerful, so enthusiastic and uncomplaining, who threw himself into every single quest, however crazily dreamed up by Xar, with total commitment, his tail wagging joyously.

Wish had a thousand happy memories of the little hairy fairy, sleeping with his legs up in a nest he had made in her hair, caressing her cheek, laughing himself silly at the love triangle between the spoon, the fork, and the key, or at some joke told to him by Bumbleboozle. And now to see him like *this*…it was unbearable.

Wish had tears pouring down her cheeks. "We *do*

love you, Squeezjoos...we just have to get the Cup of Second Chances so that our spell to get rid of Witches can work...and we can save Looter along the way, because he is being held in this horrible mine and—"

Squeezjoos's eyes opened even wider in outrage. *"You isss going to save that great-gurning-grunting-goon-of-a-boy before you ssavessss ME?"*

"No—I mean *yes*—but you don't understand," said Wish. "We're only saving Looter first because he has this cup that we need and—"

It was truly terrible to see Squeezjoos in such a state.

"Lies!" spat Squeezjoos. "Issss all LIESSS... you'ssss abandoned me forever..."

"No we haven't!" cried Xar. "I've changed my mind again! Let's forget about this whole mine plan. We need to get to the Lake of the Lost to fight the Kingwitch and save Squeezjoos *RIGHT THIS SECOND*!"

"It's a trick," said Caliburn. "The Kingwitch doesn't want you to make the spell properly; he's sent Squeezjoos to get you to come before we're ready."

"LIES!" screamed Squeezjoos, and this time he launched himself at the protective spell so violently that Wish was worried he was going to hurt himself, so she made the spell explode, which set fire to the gorse bush. Screaming, the other sprites ran away, the key and the fork and the pins hopping through the snow and the spoon rolling the baby-in-his-egg to safety.

"I don't care!" shouted Xar. "We still have to go to the Lake of the Lost RIGHT NOW! Squeezjoos is my most faithful sprite, I reared him from his egg myself—OW!" said Xar, for without the spell protecting them, Squeezjoos had gone on the attack again, shrieking "*Come with me!*" and sinking his jaws into Xar's arm with the Witch-stain on it.

"He's just not quite himself! He's gotten a bit carried away! He's very sweet really," said Xar, "Ow! Ow! Ow! Ow!" as he tried to shake off Squeezjoos, who only bit harder into Xar's poor arm. "He'll calm down if we do what he says...Drop! Squeezjoos, drop!"

However, their decision about whether to go to the Mine of Happiness or to the Lake of the Lost first was about to be made for them.

If you want to sneak away quietly from a heavily guarded mine such as this one, you really shouldn't set fire to the gorse bush that is hiding you. It rather draws attention to yourself.

A great two-headed Lumpenogre dropped the sack of iron ore he was carrying on his back to the furnaces of the smelting place and came bounding over toward them.

The Lumpenogre stopped in surprise.

Lumpenogres are not the brightest ogres in the wildwoods.

One head said to the other, very slowly, "What...is... going...on...here?"

Wish was quick at thinking on her feet. "We're volunteering to come and work for you in the mine!" she said.

"No we're not!" howled Xar. "We're on our way to the Lake of the Lost! OW OW OW OW OW!"

"Volunteering?" said the second Lumpenogre head to the first one. "That's weird..."

Both heads looked around to see if there was an iron

Warrior anywhere nearby that might make the decision for them of what to do next. There wasn't. Bother. The Lumpenogre would have to make up its own minds. It hated that.

"Quick, everyone!" said the key, realizing they might get left behind if they weren't careful. "We're going for a ride! Hop onto Wish!" The spoon and the fork and the key gathered up all the sprites, the spoon carrying the baby in his bowl, and hopped just in time into Wish's waistcoat.

"I bet you get rewarded for bringing slaves to the mine," said Wish cunningly up to the Lumpenogre.

"We do get rewarded," said the second head.

"With actual *food*," said the first head, licking its lips. Both heads were in agreement on the importance of food, so their minds were helpfully made up and the Lumpenogre reached out his long arms surprisingly quickly for someone who had a couple of such small brains, and gathered up Wish and Bodkin in one hand and Xar in the other. He had a bit of trouble catching Xar, because Xar was good at not being caught if he didn't want to be, but he caught him eventually because Xar was rather distracted, running around in circles shouting, "OW OW OW OW OW!!" with Squeezjoos still biting on his arm.

The motion and the surprise of being suddenly and

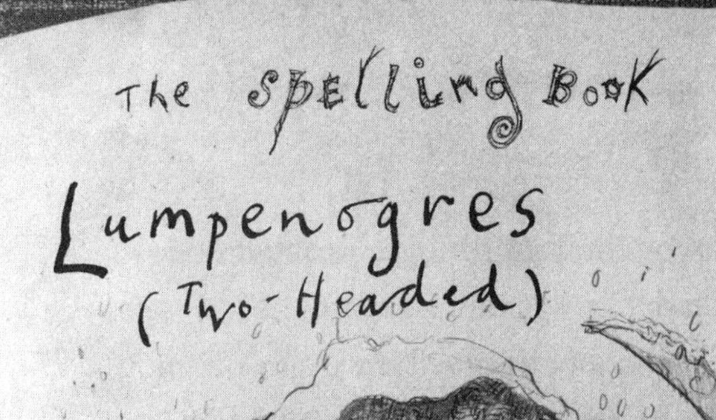

Lumpenogres are not the brightest big guys in the business. Their heads often disagree with each other, which makes decision-making difficult, and therefore they are easily led by others.

page 24,521

ruthlessly picked up by the Lumpenogre finally dislodged Squeezjoos's jaws, and Xar was carried up in the Lumpenogre's fist, and Squeezjoos fell back into the snow.

"NOOOOOOOOOOO!" cried Xar as he felt Squeezjoos's grip loosening, but it was no good. They were being carried inexorably toward the cliff that led up to the entrance of the Mine of Happiness, and there was absolutely nothing that Xar could do about it.

When he reached the bottom of the cliff, the Lumpenogre stuffed his prisoners into one of his pockets, so that he had his hands free for climbing.

So Xar and Wish and Bodkin and the magical creatures found themselves slipping and sliding in a jumble of arms and legs and wings into the bottom of the Lumpenogre's pocket, and the darkness closing over them as the Lumpenogre did up the buttons on his pocket so they couldn't get away.

"Is everybody here?" gasped Bodkin as they disentangled themselves.

"*Squeezjoos* isn't here," said Xar, angrily wiping his eyes with his ragged sleeve.

"I'm so sorry, Xar," said Wish guiltily. "But Caliburn is right, this is the best way; it's no good trying to rescue Squeezjoos if the spell doesn't work. How is the bite he made on your arm? Perdita taught me a healing spell that might help..."

Xar thrust his arm behind his back so she couldn't see it. "Don't touch me!" growled Xar. "That arm is so full of Witchblood it doesn't matter anyway."

There was a tense silence.

"If *this doesn't work*," said Xar with grim fury, "if we *get stuck in this stupid mine*, if *we are too late to rescue Squeezjoos in the end*, I will *never forgive you*, Wish."

Silence again in the swaying darkness of the Lumpenogre's pocket, everyone alone with their own thoughts. *I'll never forgive myself, either,* thought Wish sorrowfully to herself as the enchanted objects tried to cheer her up.

Down below in the snow, Squeezjoos picked himself up, aching all over from the fall. And then he lifted up his head to the stars and howled, like a tiny wolf, his tail tucked miserably between his many legs.

Squeezjoos issss alone again, thought Squeezjoos. *And whats do I do now? I's can't fly so clossse to the mine, and it wills takessss me a year to walk after them…*

His brain clouded over again. *Iss go back to my masster the Chiwgink*, thought Squeezjoos, *buts the master is going to be SSSSSO angry with Squeezjoos*…He gave a few little bleats of fear at the thought of the Kingwitch's anger.

The infesta-pests buzzed sickeningly around his head, biting him into action. Sadly, and unsteadily, he got to his eight feet. Slowly he turned away from the Mine of Happiness and back in the direction of the Lake of the Lost. He would have to walk until he got out of the iron-orbit of the mine, and it would be a long, weary plod through the snow for a poor little all-alone hairy fairy, with only infesta-pests for company.

4. The Second Terrible Plan Begins to Go Wrong...

For the next five minutes, Xar and Wish and Bodkin were silent in the darkness, concentrating on not throwing up because the Lumpenogre moved in a very jerky way as he climbed the cliff.

Wish found a hole in the Lumpenogre's pocket so that she could see what was going on, and what she saw down below her as the Lumpenogre bounded into the main hall of the Mine of Happiness made her heart beat quick and her stomach sink.

This was the deepest, most dreadful mine in the whole of the Warrior territory, and the mine was *busy*, for the emperor needed IRON for his war against the Witches. And for that he used slave labor. So huge, weary giants with their titanic arms in iron chains were loading the ore out of the mining carts and into packs on their backs. And crowds of ragged, hungry children were huddled in front of a dark cloaked figure, the Warrior who was in charge of the smooth running of the mine. Wish had never met him before, but she knew he was Brutal the Heartless, one of the emperor's most trusted men, known throughout the Warrior empire for his ruthlessness and cruelty.

For the emperor wasn't going to climb down the

endless, miserable suffocating tunnels of the mine *himself*, was he? No, he might get his cloak dirty. Or scuff his fingernails. And the emperor didn't even *like* the Ghastly Mountains—they were far too gloomy and provincial.

So the emperor stayed in his nice cozy capital and sent Brutal the Heartless and his Warriors to look after the mine, and Brutal the Heartless and his Warriors looked after it by shouting orders at the poor Wizards and Magic creatures who were doing all the work. Climbing down into the mine to dig out the ore that contained the iron were Wizards captured in battle, iron chains on their wrists so they couldn't perform any Magic.

This was what made the task so particularly miserable for the Magic people. Descending into the darkness of the center of the earth and doing the back-breaking, sweat-pouring, heart's-blood-weeping work of digging out the rock way, way down below without ever seeing daylight was bad enough. But when you are allergic to the thing you are actually tasked with collecting, it makes it far, far worse, and a low moaning hum was coming off the Magic people, their auras shriveled with despair, their gloved hands blistered, their breath wheezing, their backs bent over.

Yes, the Mine of Happiness was a place of dreadful misery indeed.

The little huddle of children being herded in front of

Brutal the Heartless

the Warrior in charge of this mine were about to be sent down into the lowest, scariest, most dangerous tunnels, for adult humans could not fit in these narrow places.

Oh dear, oh dear, oh dear, thought Wish to herself. *Maybe Xar was right, and we shouldn't have come...*

But it was too late now.

Brutal the Heartless was about to give the children a rousing pep talk, because they were looking ridiculously wimpy, he thought, before lighting a fire to scare them into going down there, when he was interrupted by the Lumpenogre.

"Yes, what is it, Lumpenogre?" snapped Brutal the Heartless. "I hope this is important..."

"We've brought you some volunteers, Your Honor," cringed the first head of the Lumpenogre, bowing low to Brutal. "And we claim our extra rations as a reward," added the second head nervously.

"*Volunteers?*" barked Brutal the Heartless in astonishment and suspicion. Who on earth would be foolish enough to *volunteer* to go down to the bottom of the iron mines? In twenty years of doing this job, Brutal the Heartless had never had a volunteer. Could this be a trap?

Trembling, the Lumpenogre reached into his pocket, pulled out Wish, Xar, and Bodkin, and put them on the ground.

Wish stepped forward.

"We are hungry, sir," said Wish humbly. "We will work with you for food."

Brutal the Heartless relaxed.

Ah. The wildwoods were full of hungry children, what with the fight between the Warriors and the Wizards, and the war with the Witches. These must be orphans. That made sense. Orphans would do anything for food.

Brutal the Heartless jerked his thumb in the direction of a large cauldron being stirred by a very sad-looking Warrior.

"Quick, then, quick!" barked Brutal the Heartless. "Get yourselves a bowl of stew and you can be in time to join the others for my morning pep talk!"

The three children and the Lumpenogre went to the cauldron to fetch their bowls of stew. Xar was still boiling with annoyance, but his stomach was rumbling, and food was food, after all. The smell of that stew was irresistibly delicious to the children, who had been surviving on wild berries and herbs. Listlessly, and grumpily, the Warrior sitting by the cauldron dumped a helping into a large bowl for the Lumpenogre, and one, two, three more dollops into three smaller bowls, handing them to the three children. He didn't look at their faces. This particular Warrior was feeling very sorry for himself, and he wasn't interested in three unknown orphans.

Until Xar couldn't help himself, and whispered, "Call that a helping? Give us some more!"

The Warrior looked up…

And thundering thistles and stingrays of stinging nettles and murmuring mistletoe and oh my goodness gracious me!

Wish stiffened in absolute horror.

It was the Witchsmeller.

What were the chances? How could this be?

What was *he* doing here in the Mine of Happiness?

The Witchsmeller knew them well.*

And the Witchsmeller hated all three of them, particularly Xar.

His sharp little eyes looked straight into Xar's.

His long, pointed nose started snuffling.

"Brutal the Heartless, Your Honor!" cried the Witchsmeller. "Permission to speak!"

"Permission to speak *not granted*!" yelled Brutal the Heartless. "Why do people keep interrupting me?"

"But Your Worship," whined the Witchsmeller, running crablike to Brutal the Heartless and tugging at his cloak. "This is important!"

* From *Twice Magic*.

their old enemy,
the Witchsmeller

Wish and Xar were *both* very good at quick thinking in a crisis situation.

With the Witchsmeller leaving the cauldron and the food unattended, Xar put huge ladlefuls of the stew into their three bowls, and the Enchanted Spoon hopped out of Wish's waistcoat to help him. Wish shoved bread into her pockets, and she got Bodkin to do the same. They were going to need every ounce of energy they could get.

"SHUDDUP!" roared Brutal the Heartless at the Witchsmeller, who was groveling before him. "You're not supposed to be talking! You lied to the emperor about having defeated the Witches, so *your* job now is to *stir the soup*! You were lucky to get away with your life. Sit back on your stool."

Okay, so whoever this Brutal the Heartless was, he was clearly very scary indeed, for when the children last met the Witchsmeller, he had been pretty frightening himself. And now the Witchsmeller had more than met his match. He went back to his stool and sat on it, like a sad, cross little five-year-old.

"Now, children, I am going to give you a short lecture about Doing Your Best," said Brutal the Heartless. "Us Warriors need as much iron as we can get our hands on in order to fight the Wizards and the Witches, so if you all work hard you will get double helpings at the end of the week. You may have heard," continued Brutal the Heartless, "of the Tatzelwurm..."

There was a murmur of horror and alarm among the children. They HAD heard of the Tatzelwurm. The Tatzelwurm was a dreadful catlike dragon of a creature that was rumored to live in the very deepest tunnels of the mines. It was supposed to carry a deadly venom and to kill with its poisonous breath.

"RUMORS!" roared Brutal the Heartless. "All lies and gossip...There is no such thing as a Tatzelwurm... but if you *do* happen to hear a sudden high-pitched hissing sound or smell anything a little peculiar, I advise you to crawl as quickly as possible in the opposite direction. We don't want to lose too many of you in one go."

"Oh dear." Bodkin swallowed hard. "This doesn't sound good..."

"Which brings me to the Knockers," said Brutal the Heartless. "This is very important. Knockers are said to be little creatures that haunt the mine, and if you hear knocking in the mine at any point, you need to get to the surface as fast as you can, for it is a sign that the walls are about to collapse. Very helpful of these totally imaginary creatures, if you think about it. Any questions?"

Bodkin put up his hand.

"Your Heartless Worship," said Bodkin politely, because you should always be polite to ferocious lunatics, "could you tell me whether a Wizard boy called Looter is currently working in this mine? He is my friend's brother, and we were wondering what had happened to him?"

"Permission to speak, sir!" interrupted the Witchsmeller with whining urgency from his stool.

"PERMISSION NOT GRANTED!" yelled Brutal the Heartless, now purple in the face with irritation. "And, ridiculous boy with legs like matchsticks, do you think I know the name of every single lowly Wizard child who is working in this mine? I am far too busy and important.

"Enough of this nonsense...LIGHT THE FIRES!" roared Brutal the Heartless. "GET READY TO TAKE THE CHILDREN DOWN TO WORK IN THE MINE!"

Brutal the Heartless stomped off to shout at someone else, and while the children waited, and the soldiers lit a great brazier in the center of the hall, Wish and Xar and Bodkin shared the bread they had stolen with the ragged group of children who were standing around them.

"Is Looter that big, very-pleased-with-himself boy who thinks a lot of himself and tells everybody else what to do?" whispered a girl standing behind Wish.

"That's him," said Wish eagerly.

"He went down the mines earlier this morning," said the girl. "He was on the early shift."

"Did they say *where* in the mines he was going?" asked Xar.

"Early shift was the bigger kids, so they got to go to the upper chambers—lucky them—they don't fit in the bottom tunnels. I think they were heading for the Den of Delight," replied the Wizard girl.

Looking around the crowd of wretched children standing huddled together, Wish recognized many of them from the learning place.*

Seeing them in such a ragged, scared, and desperate state made her feel that they had made the right decision in coming, whatever danger they might be in.

"While we're here, we can shut down this mine," she whispered to Bodkin determinedly. "It really isn't a suitable place for children."

Bodkin sighed even further. This was even more hopelessly unrealistic and optimistic than rescuing Looter. "Wish," he said, thinking, *Give me strength*, "we're going to have our hands full just surviving here..."

"No, actually I agree with Wish," said Xar unexpectedly. Xar hated being shut up himself, and

* The recognition was not mutual, for at the time, Wish and Xar and Bodkin had been in disguise.

seeing the iron chains around the captured Wizards' wrists was reminding him of his own time shut up in the terrible prison of Gormincrag. "While we're here, we might as well shut down the mine."

"Well done, Xar," whispered Caliburn, hidden inside Xar's waistcoat. They were in a terrible spot here, but still it was worth recognizing that despite having the Witch-stain, Xar was making some real advances. Xar wasn't great at seeing things from other people's point of view and doing things to help them, so this was a real step forward in growing up for Xar, however mad the idea.

The guards now advanced toward the little huddle of children, pushing them toward the ladders at the entrance of the mine.

Down, down, Xar and Bodkin and Wish climbed, descending long ladder after long ladder, until the entrance up above was just a blink of light and then *poof*! It was gone, and they had dropped into darkness.

Deep in the murk of the tunnel of mines, it was hard to see, for the world was very dimly lit by the flickering light of the candles worn on the helmets of the goblins, but from a hearing point of view it was bouncing with life, echoing with the ringing sound of the child miners working all around them.

"Follow me!" ordered the goblin in charge of their working party. "You little 'uns are small enough to go in the really deep tunnels..."

The goblin charged off, assuming that they would all follow her, because she was the only one with a candle on her head, and nobody would want to be left alone in the darkness.

Xar and Wish and Bodkin waited till the little line of children disappeared, and then the sprites crept out of their pockets, queasy with anxiety, wings hanging like limp rags, hissing, "Itt'sss creeeeepy downs here..."

"Okay," whispered Xar. "We need to find Looter, shut this mine down, and get out of here as quickly as possible, and I'LL be the leader, because I'M THE BEST at this sort of thing."

Normally, Wish would have argued with this. But she was feeling guilty about overriding Xar about leaving Squeezjoos, and she was relieved that Xar was going to help her shut down the mine. And it had to be said, Xar was good at escaping from places—he had had a lot of practice at that.

So she and Bodkin let Xar be the leader, this time. And Xar took the Spelling Book out of his waistcoat, and spelled out the way to the maps section, where he found the intricate and detailed study of the complete network of tunnels in the Mine of Happiness.

"This is easy-peasy!" crowed Xar, holding the Spelling Book firmly in his right hand, which had the Witch-stain on it, and showing it to the others. "Look, here, I've found it, the Den of Delight! And it looks fairly close.

"Follow me, everyone! *I'm* the Leader!" said Xar confidently.

So off Xar set, full of hope and optimism and belief, thinking he was leading his little crew in the direction of the Den of Delight, while in fact the Witch-stain was leading them deeper and deeper and lower and lower into the narrow splinters and wormholes of tunnels that snaked through the depths of the Mine of Happiness, where lurked the very creatures they had been most warned about, and most dreaded to meet.

And *that* was how they got into this mess in the first place.

5. The Second Terrible Plan Has Gone VERY WRONG...

Unfortunately, we've had to return to the present, two hours later. I would have loved to stay in the past where everyone was so much more cautiously hopeful, but time has this relentless way of moving onward, however hard we may wish it otherwise. So...

"DON'T BE FRIGHTENED!" yelled Wish.

The situation the heroes were presently in would have been amusing if it wasn't so absolutely terrifying. Wish and Caliburn and the sprites and the fork, key and pins and the Spelling Book were on *one* side of Bodkin's body jammed in the tunnel, where Bodkin's head was. And on the *other* side, the side where Bodkin's legs were flailing madly as he tried to wriggle free, Xar and the Enchanted Spoon were facing the dreadful nightmare of the Tatzelwurm on their own.

And the problem with *this* was, that even though Xar had been given many lessons about "Magical Creatures, Their Powers, Disadvantages, and Weak Spots"—both back at the Wizard fort where he grew up and in Perdita's learning place—Xar had never paid any attention whatsoever. He had been concentrating on the far more important task of messing about and showing off in front of his classmates.

Which meant he hadn't really got the foggiest idea about what to do when faced with a hungry Tatzelwurm in a very small tunnel.

Wish and Bodkin were trying to tell him some facts about Tatzelwurms—they were shouting at the tops of their voices—but Bodkin's whole body was in the way and Xar couldn't hear what they were saying.

"DON'T BE FRIGHTENED!" Wish and Bodkin were yelling, and though this might seem rather ridiculous and vague advice, it was in fact very specific. The Tatzelwurm only likes eating frightened food. I'm not sure why. Fear tenderizes the meat, or something.

An overpowering waft of disgustingly poisonous vapor made Xar gag. The glowing eyes were coming nearer, nearer, and he could hear the revolting sludge of the creature's great body slithering against the tunnel walls.

The Enchanted Spoon HAD been concentrating in those magical creatures lessons in Perdita's learning place, but unfortunately he couldn't speak, only make vague humming noises, so he was trying to be helpful by acting out "DON'T BE FRIGHTENED" in spoon body language.

So the spoon was dancing about, trying to swagger in an unconcerned sort of way and making his eyes look as *un*-scared as possible, which was quite tricky

when the Tatzelwurm was slithering nearer, now hissing and spitting like a malevolent serpent/boiling kettle: "Tresspassers…tressspassssers…the penalty for tressspasss is to *be…my…FOOD…*" And following up this thoroughly alarming statement with a high-pitched scream deliberately intended to scare the living daylights out of whoever heard it.

Xar put his hands over his ears.

Xar hadn't the faintest idea what the spoon was trying to communicate, as the spoon bounced up

and down in front of Xar with his eyes as big as he could make them, and then the spoon flopped about, elaborately casually, before jumping up and down again urgently...*Is the spoon drunk?* thought Xar irritably. *What is wrong with him?*

"Oh for mistletoe's sake...what are you trying to say, you ridiculous dining implement?" snapped Xar. "Are you trying to tell me what could be the Tatzelwurm's undoing? Is it allergic to onions? Has it got a weak spot on its nose?"

The spoon frantically shook his bowl of a head from

Spoon hopping through the Mine of Happiness without a care in the WORLD . . .

side to side to say *No!,* and then mimed a person totally unconcerned, humming to themselves while strolling about the tunnels of the Mine of Happiness without a care in the world.

It was rather a good impression, the spoon thought, but Xar still hadn't a clue, guessing, "The Tatzelwurm is afraid of music? It's defeated by weird vague humming noises?" before losing his patience, and flapping the spoon off his chest, snapping, "I'm never going to guess this, and you're getting in my way, I'm trying to *think*..."

But the spoon being distracting had brought out Xar's irritability, and that helped him focus on his own strengths when facing an implacable foe. Xar was tricky and quick-witted.*

Start a conversation, thought Xar. *Always keep the enemy talking...*

"TATZELWURM!" shouted Xar. "WE NEED TO TALK!"

The glowing eyes moving slowly, carefully toward him, narrowed to little splinters, and the creature stopped.

---

* This was a strength Xar shared with his father Encanzo, as you will find out if you read Book 2, *Twice Magic*. It's really rather good.

The Tatzelwurm was never going to admit it, of course, but she was already surprised. She had given her really most terrifying high-pitched death screams, and normally the food would have been mouthwateringly petrified by this time. It wouldn't have been lying on its back trying to start an interesting chat.

She knew better, however, than to let the food talk itself into a stay of execution. The only reason she hadn't dispatched it so far was that for some mysterious reason she didn't seem to have frightened it yet.

"I haven't decided whether I am going to tear you limb from limb...or whether I should suck you out of your wrapping like a limpet out of its shell and swallow you whole..." hissed the Tatzelwurm, and she sniffed the air hopefully. No sign yet of the delicious sweet smell of fear, which would make the meal as scrumptious as hazelnuts dipped in honey. How disappointing. That last threat really should have had the food in an exquisite quake of anxiety, wobbling with the scrumptiousness of a toothsome little jellyfish.

The Tatzelwurm slithered forward, slowly, thoughtfully, so close now that Xar could begin to make her out in the light of the bowl of the spoon, which was glowing bright like a candle, for the spoon was terrified, even if Xar wasn't.

Xar could make out her eyes first, and then her

glittering smile, for one of the dreadful things about the Tatzelwurm is how it smiles even when it attacks.

The Tatzelwurm is a kind of dragon, so there was something lizard-y in this particular Tatzelwurm's catlike face, as well as a keen, crafty intelligence in her calculating eyes. But the wings on her serpentine body were long withered and ruined, for she had chosen to live in an iron mine, and that choice would have taken away her Magic. What desperation would have made this creature willfully choose to live somewhere that would inevitably mean the destruction of the thing that made her so special? That

meant she would forever no longer be able to fly up, up, and join her ancestors in the sky, when her dying time came?

"I don't need to talk," hissed the Tatzelwurm, and her grin was truly awful to behold. "I need to *eat*."

When the Tatzelwurm had come into seeing-distance of her next meal, she was intending to eat it anyway, whether she could make the food delicious by making it frightened or not, for the Tatzelwurm was really very hungry indeed. Normally a stray child or goblin or Bluecap would get lost and blunder their way into her territory every now and then, but for some reason for the past three weeks, nothing like that had happened—not even a Knocker or two had come her way, not that a Knocker filled the belly much, there was no meat on the bony little creatures at all.

So the Tatzelwurm was starving.

But as she slid forward, grin becoming a little wider as her teeth ached for the meal, her clever cat eyes took in the spoon. And that made her pause.

The spoon had fainted dead away with fear as the Tatzelwurm approached, but now he staggered onto his stem again, remembered the Tatzelwurm, jumped in the air, and in one, two, three bounces, jumped onto Xar's head, where he hid quivering in Xar's hair.

Xar was watching his enemy carefully (you should always watch your enemy carefully), and he noticed the slight halt in the Tatzelwurm's slither, the slight check of surprise in her clever yellow eyes as they took in the spoon, and he exploited that knowledge. Up until that moment, Xar hadn't really had any idea what he was going to talk to the Tatzelwurm about, he was just playing for time. Now he knew.

"I want to talk to you about *spoons*," said Xar firmly.

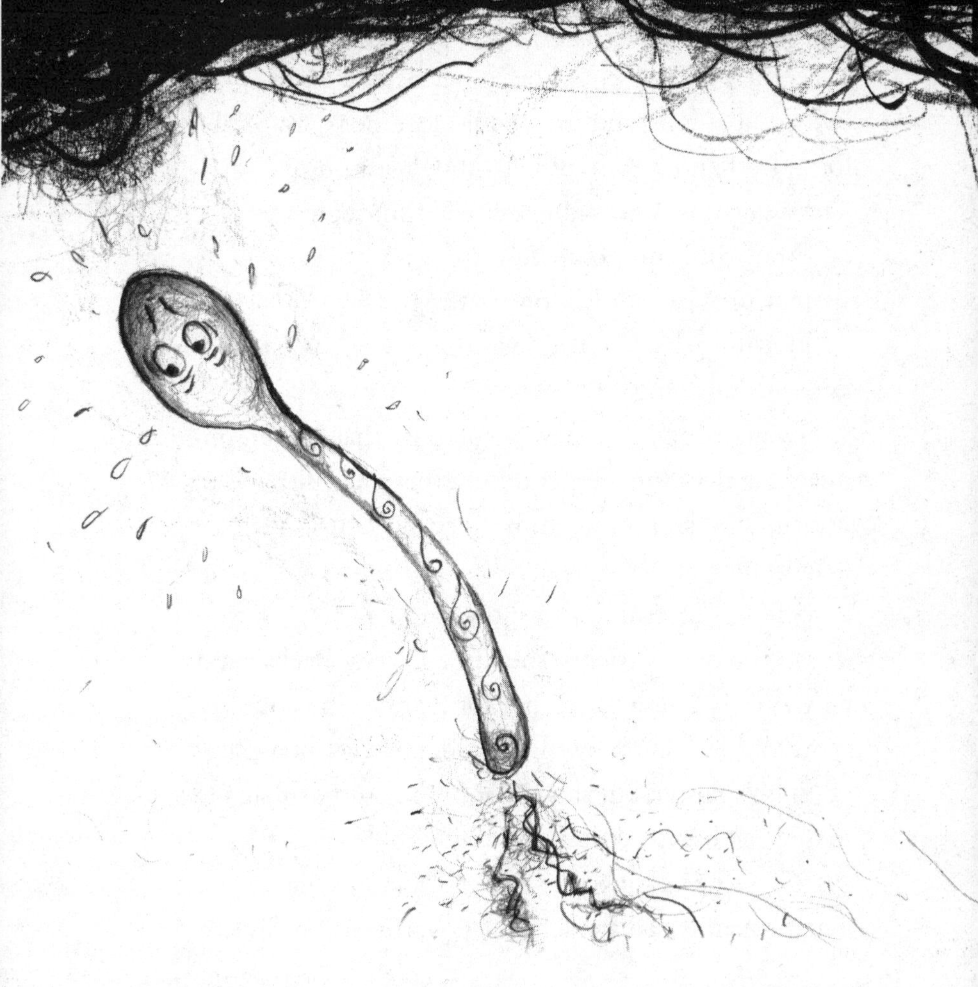

6. Spoons?

Spoons?" replied the Tatzelwurm, consideringly. "Spooooooooons????"

Now *she* was playing for time too.

She was already regretting hesitating, for even a second. This boy could be in her belly by now, *and* his two companions, and that would feed her comfortably for at least another month, for the digestion of a Tatzelwurm is slow and extremely thorough.

And words fill no bellies.

A wurm cannot live on chatting.

But now that she had seen the spoon, she *had* to know its meaning.

Dragons, and cats, have a curiosity that is even more insatiable than their appetite, and this particular spoon was sufficiently unusual to be very, very curious to a dragon indeed.

She was careful not to show this.

This boy was tricksy, she knew he was tricksy, and he was only going to tell her for a price. She could *pain* it out of him, she knew she could, however bravely he might bluster, but this situation was so peculiar she sensed she had to slither carefully.

There was a long pause, while Xar and the Tatzelwurm gazed at each other, warily. You really are not supposed to look a dragon straight in the eye, it can hypnotize you within minutes, but Xar was discovering another unusual quality of his. Staring into a dragon's eye had no effect on him whatsoever.

The pause became so long it was almost embarrassing.

If the spoon could have talked, he would have filled it himself.

The Tatzelwurm snapped first. And that was how Xar knew he had an advantage. It was just a question of how he was to play that advantage to get them all out of there, whole and alive. She wanted something out of him, or she would not have spoken.

"The spoon," hissed the Tatzelwurm, so furious that it was she who was unable to resist speaking first, that it was as if each word was a hornet and she was spitting it out, "is alive and *it is made out of iron.*"

There was another pause, where Xar was still young enough to show a brief little flicker of triumph on his face. An older, more experienced Wizard would have known not to allow that.

Foolish, for it made the Tatzelwurm even angrier.

She slithered forward, her dark, ruined countenance so near to Xar, steam coming out of her ears, biting out the words through her ghastly fixed smile:

"How can an Enchanted Spoon be made out of iron???"

So infuriated was she that she accidentally let her poison gas glands open, and a great billow of sulfur-greeny-yellow gas poured out like vaporous pus, smothering Xar's face. He coughed. His eyes bulged. For the first time, he was truly frightened, for he could feel the poison screaming down his nasal passages as if it were chili peppers, and he couldn't breathe.

Oh by the ear-hairs of the great green gods...thought Xar in absolute horror, *I'm going to die*...He tried to breathe in lovely, fresh, life-giving air, but with every inhalation his lungs were drowning further in the fumes.

The spoon went completely mad at this.

In a frenzy of anxiety, he bashed his bowl of a head repeatedly on the Tatzelwurm's poison glands to get her to close them.

The Tatzelwurm had a brief delicious fantasy of eating them all up because the fear of the boy was now making him smell quite scrumptious. She could sniff it even over the cloud of her own stink, but she unfortunately really did need to know the secret of this mad little spoon, however stupid it was, for mistletoe's sake, didn't it even know that spoons shouldn't attack dragons as scary as she was?

So the Tatzelwurm closed up her poison glands and Xar gasped in huge gulps of air like gloriously cool water.

The Tatzelwurm strummed her fingers on the tunnel floor.

"*Now*, boy...you haven't told me yet," she said a little more calmly than she had earlier, her poison glands under control now and firmly shut. "Why is the living spoon made out of iron?"

Xar struggled to get the words out. He had a little more respect for the Tatzelwurm now that she had nearly killed him, and also a sliver of fear, which was all very well. You should always respect your enemy, and that may keep you alive.

"We are extremely powerful Wizards," said Xar. "And we have a Magic-that-works-on-iron."

There was a very long pause indeed, as the Tatzelwurm absorbed this amazing information.

"Impossible!" hissed the Tatzelwurm in astonishment. "Anyone born with an extraordinary talent such as that would be the most unusual person of destiny ever to walk the wildwoods...No Wizard has EVER had Magic-that-works-on-iron.

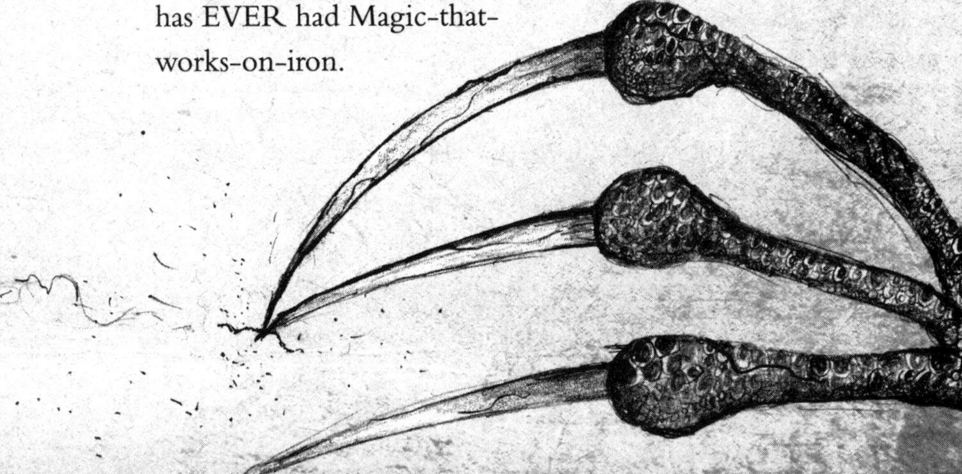

That's why we creatures of Magic have been beaten back by those hulking clods of Warrior barbarians. That's why *I* have chosen to be *here*, wingless, heartless, skulking in this prison of earth…I would rather be here, than defeated by Warriors."

The Tatzelwurm's bitterness was edged with a hint of hope, as her intelligent dragon brain sifted through the possibilities that such an incredible development in the powers of Magic might bring to the world.

The living iron spoon was proof that there must be some truth to what the boy was saying. And yet her acute dragon eyes could see how easily the boy lied, how tricksome he was. Perhaps it was all a ruse, a snare, to catch her unawares.

The uncertainty made her cruel.

"But do you expect me to believe that such a precious gift belongs to YOU?" jeered the Tatzelwurm contemptuously.

"No, not *you*, my friend, I think not," she said with delicate scorn.

"Not me," admitted Xar, stung.

"But it COULD have been me!" objected Xar. "*I* could be the child of destiny, why not? I'm brilliant, I'm marvelous, I'm a born leader of people!"

To add insult to injury, Xar had forgotten not to exaggerate, so the trumpet on his back made a derisive

PARP! And that only made the Tatzelwurm laugh even more mockingly.

It took being confronted by a scoffing dragon and a teasing trumpet while stuck in a tunnel half a mile underground for Xar to FINALLY admit that it really *was not he* who was the child of destiny.

Bother it.

Bother, bother, bother, bother, BOTHER.

"Okay, it's not me," sighed Xar grumpily. "It's my friend, Wish. She's on the other side of the boy who is stuck in the tunnel, and *she* is the child of destiny who has the Magic-that-works-on-iron."

The spoon hopped onto Xar's shoulder and nuzzled his cheek, because he knew this was a difficult moment for Xar.

"Ahhhhh," said the Tatzelwurm, thinking hard. She longed, needed, HAD to see the child of destiny for herself.

"But if I help unstick the stuck boy, the magical child of destiny might hurt me...she will have powers that work down here," said the Tatzelwurm.

"Oh no," cried Xar, "Wish isn't like that! She will only use her powers for protection..."

"More fool her," whispered the Tatzelwurm.

"Yes, she's too soft," said Xar. "If *I* had that power, I would be a lot tougher. I don't know what destiny was thinking about, giving it to her."

"Destiny generally knows its business," said the Tatzelwurm. "And it's up to us to work out exactly what that business is."

The Tatzelwurm turned to the spoon.

"Do I have your word, spoon," she hissed, "that your mistress will not attack me if I help release her?"

The spoon made a little old-fashioned bow of assent.

The Tatzelwurm stretched her arm past Xar—there was barely room—squirted something slick all around Bodkin, took a good hold of one of his legs, and pulled, hard.

There was a revolting squelch and Bodkin shot out of the tunnel with such violence that he skidded past Xar. Wish crawled at top speed after him, shouting, "Xar! You're alive! I thought you were dead...thank goodness you're safe!" and throwing her arms around him in relief.

The Tatzelwurm had retreated to a little distance away, so they could only see her eyes. Her poison glands were up, her talons were out, long as kitchen knives, pointing quaveringly toward the three of them.

"He is not safe." The Tatzelwurm smiled through gritted teeth, shaking with fear and suspicion. "None of you are safe. *You* may have promised not to harm me, but *I* did not promise not to harm *you*. I need to question the girl, now, and trust me, your lives depend on her answers."

"Careful, Wish, careful," warned Caliburn. "You must be very careful when talking with dragons. Dragons are treacherous."

"She will be fine," said the Tatzelwurm, "as long as she tells me the truth."

The Tatzelwurm crept gingerly toward them.

"So, child," whispered the great serpent, "do you have Magic-that-works-on-iron?"

Oh my goodness, thought Wish, as the ghastly ruined face of the dragon drew nearer, *she's shaking...the dragon is actually SHAKING.*

Much, much worse than her own fear of the dragon was a cold realization, suddenly occurring to Wish, like icy sludge in the pit of her stomach.

The dragon is frightened of ME.

Up until that moment, Wish had not really absorbed the implications of being this extraordinary child of destiny. Now the horrible reality of what that really meant was finally burned into her consciousness.

"Don't look away!" snapped the Tatzelwurm harshly. "Put up your eyepatch!"

Obediently, Wish put up her eyepatch, and she winced at the dragon's obvious start of alarm when it looked into her Magic eye. Trembling all over, she carried on exchanging the hypnotic gaze of the dragon, even though she was drowning in the horror of the dragon's evident fear.

Eventually the dragon released her, saying drily, "You will have to learn NOT to obey orders, child, even from someone as persuasive as me.

"So, child of destiny," said the Tatzelwurm. "I can see you do indeed have Magic-that-works-on-iron, which makes you the most powerful Wizard that *I* have ever met, and *I* was born over ten thousand years ago. But power is dangeroussss." The Tatzelwurm's grin turned momentarily into a snarl before turning back into a smile again. "What are you intending to do with this power, child of destiny?"

"I am going to expel the Witches from the wildwoods forever," said Wish. "And before that, I am going to shut down this mine."

"Why?" asked the Tatzelwurm.

"For kindness," said Wish.

And then she added, "This mine is not a suitable place for children."

"This mine is not a suitable place for dragons either," replied the Tatzelwurm.

The Tatzelwurm was still staring at Wish, but her eyes were not taking her in—they were looking back into the past and forward into the future.

"History goes in circles like the tides," said the Tatzelwurm dreamily. "Ten thousand years ago, when I was born, it was the age of

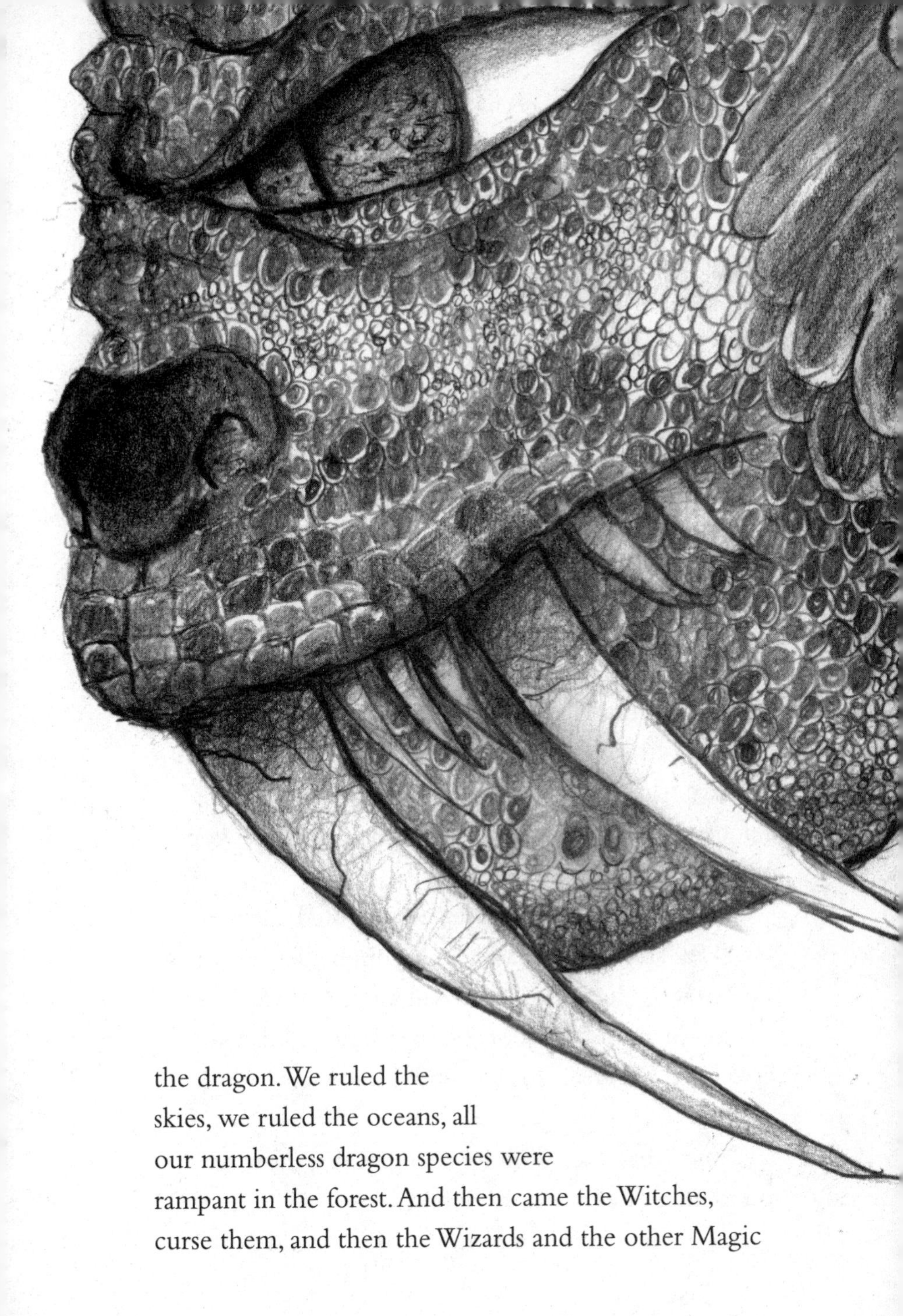

the dragon. We ruled the
skies, we ruled the oceans, all
our numberless dragon species were
rampant in the forest. And then came the Witches,
curse them, and then the Wizards and the other Magic

things. And now look at us…fled to the icy parts of the north…hiding under the ground like I am, all my Magic lost and gone…"

"Poor Tatzelwurm," said Wish, laying a hand on the dragon.

"A human touch…laid in kindness!" said the Tatzelwurm in astonishment.

The touch seemed to bring the dragon out of her trance and back into the present again.

"I am going to offer you some extremely valuable advice, that you do not know you need," said the Tatzelwurm, her eyes crafty, intelligent once more. "It is not enough to be GOOD, Wish, child of destiny. You also have to be STRONG. You have to ENDURE. You will have to be flinty as stone if you want to resist the Witches, who I imagine are after your power like dogs chasing a rat…

"Learn from this boy here." She pointed a talon at Xar. "He can teach you a lot about disobedience, just as you can teach him a lot about kindness. And I will let you continue on your journey, even though I can see there is a good chance it will end in utter apocalyptic disaster…"

"And what does Wish have to give you in return if you let us go free?" asked Caliburn.

"I ask only for a hair from the Magic child of

destiny's head," said the Tatzelwurm. "Given lovingly, out of her own free will. For kindness."

"Why do you want it?" said Caliburn suspiciously.

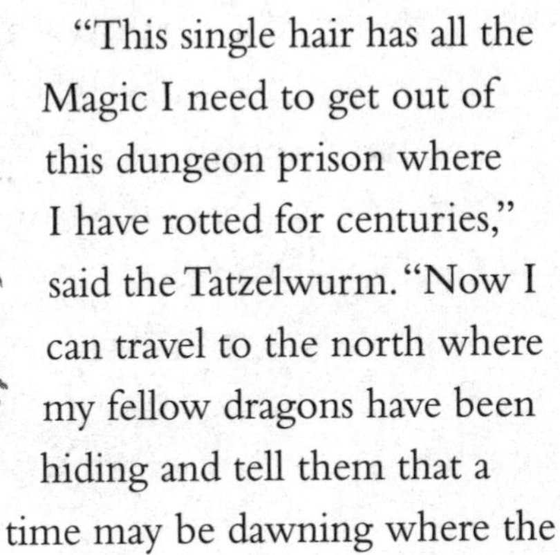

"This single hair has all the Magic I need to get out of this dungeon prison where I have rotted for centuries," said the Tatzelwurm. "Now I can travel to the north where my fellow dragons have been hiding and tell them that a time may be dawning where the dragons can come back."

"You can break out of this prison using just ONE HAIR?" said Wish. She was feeling a little sick. I *never ASKED for the weight of all this Magic. I don't WANT it…*

The Tatzelwurm nodded.

"That shows you how powerful you are. So beware," said the Tatzelwurm. "Avoid the Kingwitch like the plague if he has anything of yourself, no matter how small…"

"I'll bear that in mind," said Wish, thinking, *Oh my goodness, the Kingwitch has that tiny piece of blue dust that was once a part of me, and me doing battle with the Kingwitch is our ENTIRE PLAN…*

"And do not be so quick to give up your power, child of destiny," said the Tatzelwurm. "Know how uneasy you are with it. For if *you* do not want it, there will be plenty of others lining up to take it."

So Wish gave the Tatzelwurm a single hair from the top of her head, freely, lovingly. For kindness.

The Tatzelwurm took it, delicately, and it was so fine and hard to see in her huge talons that it was as if Wish were giving her nothing.

Nothing, and everything.

The Tatzelwurm shivered with pleasure, and apprehension and amazement, before putting the hair away.

"Can you let us go on our way now?" asked Wish politely. "We are headed toward the Den of Delights."

"It's not very delightful," warned the Tatzelwurm, "but I expect you knew that already. I will speed you on your journey before my hunger gets the better of me...

"Hold on to my tail," said the Tatzelwurm, slithering around on herself inside the tiny tunnel.

Wish took hold of the dragon's tail, and Xar took hold of Wish and Bodkin took hold of Xar. And the Tatzelwurm dragged them all with surprising speed through the darkest tunnels of the Mine of Happiness, the sprites hopping after, and Caliburn in the rear, losing feathers as he flew.

These were tunnels made by the Tatzelwurm herself, and so the floor beneath them was as sleek and glossy as the Tatzelwurm's belly. Wish hung on for dear life, and Xar, who loved speed of any sort, let out a whoop of excitement as they rocketed along.

Up, up, up, to the Den of Delights.

7. The Den of Delights

When they arrived at their destination, the Den of Delights, the Tatzelwurm's tail came off in Wish's hands.

One moment Wish was whooshing through the tunnels on her stomach at great speed, the next the tip of the tail she was holding snapped off, and she came to an abrupt halt, Xar and Bodkin slamming up behind her.

"The Tatzelwurm!" cried Wish in anxiety. "Her tail's come off!"

"Eeew..." said Xar. "Yucky."

"Don't worry," panted Caliburn, catching up with them at last. "Dragons are like lizards; they can drop their tails if they wish. She'll grow another one. It means we've arrived..."

They could hear
the echoes of the
Tatzelwurm slithering
creamily through the tunnels,
and she sounded healthy
enough, the slump and slodge
of her great body rocketing away,
two triumphant bursts of her piercing
whistle, and a hiss that echoed back to
them, saying, "You've gotten out of my
way jusssst in time...I wassss about to change
my mind and killsss you after all...but good
luck...good luck..."

Right beside where the Tatzelwurm had dropped her tail was the entrance to the Den of Delights.

The three children, the sprites, and the talking raven peered into it, and, as the Tatzelwurm said, what was going on in there was not very delightful.

The Den of Delights was the upper cavern where the iron ore dug out by the smaller children arrived

from down below on carts and was sorted before being hauled up to the surface. So great sad giants, arms in chains, were emptying the carts and loading up barrels that were then hauled up on ropes by ogres from up above. It was a chaotic scene, full of running children, goblins shouting, giants bellowing, axes chipping.

But even over all this noise, Wish and Xar and Bodkin could hear the loud, unmistakable

sound of Looter's voice
from the other end of the
cavern, and they made their
way in his direction. Looter was
part of a group of children who were working halfway up the main cliff face in the Den of Delights. He was balancing on a platform, hacking away at the rock, while very helpfully giving the other children a lesson in EXACTLY how to chip the iron ore out of the stone.

"Now," said Looter pompously. "You hold the pick like *so*—not like that, Sneering, do concentrate, do what I'm doing—and then you give a quick sharp blow like this, and—see how much I am getting out in one chunk?"

"Wow," said Sneering admiringly.

Looter's other cronies were similarly impressed, but quite a few of the other children looked thoroughly fed up with Looter, as if they felt they had quite enough to put up with in the Mine of Happiness, without Looter telling them what to do.

"Pssst..." said Xar, hissing up at Looter.

Looter wiped the sweat away from his forehead and looked down.

Xar's brother,
Looter

"Xar!" said Looter. "What are you doing here?"

He didn't look as pleased to see Xar as Xar was, in his hopeful way, expecting.

There wasn't a hint of thanks or gratitude, or any of the things Xar had been making up in his head. He didn't look like somebody who was going to go down on his knees to Xar, in pathetic gratitude.

"We're here to rescue you," said Xar.

"I don't need rescuing by a disobedient little out-of-control ruffian like *you*!" objected Looter. "*Our father* will rescue me…Our father told me *you* are a disgrace…but *I'm* far too important to be left in this mine."

"That's right," said Blister, another of Looter's cronies. "You're just a nobody who can't even do Magic, Xar, but Looter is the heir to Encanzo. Nothing must happen to *Looter*, he's vital to the future success of our tribe."

Xar reddened.

His hand with the Witch-stain on it shot upward automatically, fingers turned into claws, but Xar held on to it with his other hand.

What he wanted to say was, "Well jolly well stay here then if you're so bear-wettingly important, you great bloated bullying buffoon!"

But Looter had the Cup of Second Chances, and they needed that cup.

So what Xar *actually* said, through gritted teeth, was:

"We're going to shut this mine down. Follow us when we do it."

"You three little shrimps can't possibly shut down this whole great big mine, you absolute lunatic!" roared Looter in a frantic bellowing whisper, looking anxiously over his shoulder at the goblin and the Warrior in charge. "It's guarded by thousands of

-a-a-rp!!!

the emperor's most fearsome guards—look at them all! *Go away!!!* You're going to get us into trouble!"

But Looter's absolutely maddening younger brother did not go away. In one, two, three leaps, Xar bounded up onto a nearby cart, loaded with iron ore. The child who was pushing the cart stopped in surprise.

PAAAARRRRRRPPPPPP! The clear ringing sound of Xar's trumpet pierced through the clamor and the chipping and the shouting and the hacking.

"ATTENTION, EVERYONE!" cried Xar. "*WE ARE SHUTTING DOWN THIS MINE!* ANYONE WHO WISHES TO FOLLOW *ME* TO THE FREEDOM OF THE WILDWOODS, FOLLOW THE SOUND OF MY TRUMPET!"...PAAAARRRPPPP!!!

There was an astonished pause. And then a Warrior came rushing forward, spluttering, "Shutting down the mine??? TREACHERY!

INSUBORDINATION! WARRIORS, ARREST THAT BOY!"

"I knew it!" fumed Looter, in terrified fury. "He's going to get us all whipped! And I have very sensitive skin—I have to be careful and look after myself. The tribe needs me."

"I can't look..." said Caliburn, putting his wings over his face, for Warriors and giants and ogres and goblins were storming toward Xar...

Knock! Knock! Knock!

And then...

"*LISTEN TO THE KNOCKERS!!!*" yelled Xar.

Xar's yell was followed by a sound of:

Knock! Knock! Knock!

And this was the sound they most dreaded in the Mine of Happiness...

Knock! Knock! Knock!

A clear sound of knocking.

Now this knocking wasn't *really* coming from the Knockers, of course.

It was *Wish*, banging on a wall with the Enchanted Spoon, giving the impression of knocking so they would shut down the mine.

And Bodkin, over on the other side of the cavern, was knocking away too.

Knock! Knock! Knock!

Knock! Knock! Knock!

Knock! Knock! Knock!

So it wasn't the Knockers at all. But the effect on the inhabitants of the hall was electric.

The knocking of the Knockers on the walls of a mine was an indication that unknown tunnels in that mine were about to collapse.

"*Knockers!*" screamed the Warrior in charge. *"PUT THE EVACUATION PLAN INTO ACTION!"*

And then there was chaos in the Den of Delights.

Goblins shrieked down the caverns: "The Knockers have spoken! GET THE CHILDREN OUT OF THE TUNNELS! EVERYBODY UP TO THE SURFACE AS QUICK AS YOU CAN! WE DON'T WANT TO LOSE ANY OF THE WORKERS!"

Giants hauled screaming children up on ropes. Warriors, goblins, and Bluecaps swarmed up the ladders as the Mine of Happiness was evacuated for fear of the Knockers.

8. Encanzo and Sychorax

Meanwhile, up on the surface, fifteen minutes earlier, Brutal the Heartless had a couple of unexpected visitors.

Sychorax, Queen of Warriors.

And Encanzo, King of Wizards.

Encanzo had his hood over his head so that nobody would recognize him, because as Warrior and Wizard, and particularly as monarchs of their respective tribes, Encanzo and Sychorax should not have been working together. They were breaking the rules of the wildwoods in doing so.

But Wish and Xar were proving horribly slippery to recapture. Both parents feared for the lives of their children. And though both parents were bossy they were, in their own way, acting out of love. Encanzo knew that Xar's Witch-stain was taking him to the dark side and wanted to lock him up in Gormincrag, where the stain could be treated and controlled. Sychorax knew that the Witches were trying to get hold of Wish for her Magic-that-works-on-iron, so she wanted her safely locked up in one of her iron fortresses, where the Witches could not get her.

With Wish and Xar safely locked up, it would be easier to fight the Witches who were currently rampaging through the wildwoods, causing chaos in their wake.

So Sychorax and Encanzo had been forced to make a temporary alliance, on a secret mission to try and recover their disobedient children.

With his hood over his head, Encanzo looked like he was Sychorax's servant, and though this stung the pride of the great king of Wizards, in this heartland of the Warrior domain, disguise was necessary.

Sychorax, however, was instantly recognizable.

Heartbreakingly beautiful, tall and slim as a golden candle, just one look from her cold-as-an-icicle eyes had Brutal the Heartless bending in a bow so low his forehead nearly touched the ground, whispering:

"Your Majesty...what an honor..." as humbly as if she had been the emperor himself.

The Witchsmeller, still on his stool, squeaked even more urgently than he had done before: "*Permission to speak!!!*"

Sychorax swept magnificently around to face him, and one look at the Witchsmeller made her lips purse sour as lemons.

"Permission to speak NOT GRANTED," said Queen Sychorax, her golden pear-drop of a voice dropping several degrees below freezing. She turned back to Brutal the Heartless, one eyebrow splendidly raised in accusation, as if the Witchsmeller's presence was all Brutal the Heartless's fault. "What," said Queen Sychorax, with undisguised loathing, "is *he* doing here?"

"Um...I'm so sorry, Your Majesty...he was sent here by the emperor as a punishment...he lied to the emperor about having defeated the Witches...lucky to escape with his life...he's not supposed to be speaking..." gabbled Brutal the Heartless, terrified he might be offending Queen Sychorax but also knowing that even *she* was a subject of the emperor.

"Well, if he isn't supposed to be

speaking, why don't you make sure he doesn't?" said Queen Sychorax silkily.*

"SHUDDUP!" roared Brutal the Heartless at the Witchsmeller, and then turned back to Queen Sychorax, groveling deeply again and saying submissively, "To what do I owe the great privilege of this visit to the emperor's favorite iron mine?"

---

* Queen Sychorax didn't want the Witchsmeller to speak because the Witchsmeller knew that Wish was Sychorax's daughter, he had seen her perform Magic on iron, and he knew that something fishy was going on.

Queen Sychorax's foot was now tapping with temper, as she noted the miserable conditions of the inhabitants of the emperor's favorite iron mine. Queen Sychorax hated to be reminded that places like these existed, and her conscience was pinching at her like angry fairies.

"I am looking for an escaped child," said Queen Sychorax, looking at Brutal the Heartless with all the contempt she was trying not to feel for herself.

"A child?" said Brutal the Heartless. "There are many children here, for we need people small enough to mine the deepest and most fruitful tunnels...so we have lots and lots of children here...hundreds of children..."

I mean really, *how unreasonable*, thought Brutal the Heartless. *It's impossible for me as a busy leader to keep track of all of them. It's like knowing one particular horrible little cabbage in an entire* field *of horrible little cabbages.*

"This child is quite distinctive," said Queen Sychorax. "She has a black patch over her left eye."

Blithering brambles and cursed bits of bogs and whimpering warlocks, BOTHER it! thought Brutal the Heartless. *The child with the black patch over one eye was one of the three children who turned up this morning! I knew it was a bit suspicious that they were VOLUNTEERING to work in the iron mines—nobody in their right minds would do that. But how was I to know the wretched ankle biter was anything to do with Queen Sychorax?* He flicked a glance toward the

Witchsmeller, who was now staring at him fixedly with big bug eyes. He *knew*...thought Brutal the Heartless. He *knew*...*and he was trying to tell me*...

"Let me see..." said Brutal the Heartless, pretending to think. "A child with a black patch over her right eye... I'm not sure I've seen one of those—"

And at that moment, Brutal the Heartless's pretended ruminations were interrupted by the great cry of "Knockers!!! Shut down the mine!" coming from below, and waves of shouting, panicking Warriors, Wizard children, and Magical creatures storming up the ladders, ogres helping to tip them up and over the side.

Brutal the Heartless turned a little green. "Knockers..." he whispered. How unbelievably unfortunate for such a calamity to strike in the middle of a royal visit.

Sychorax tightened her lips, and Encanzo lifted his head.

Wish and Xar! the two monarchs thought grimly to themselves, for they knew that calamities were rarely coincidences where their children were concerned.

Encanzo vaulted over the edge of the shaft descending into the mine and climbed *down* the backs of the astonished Warriors and goblins who were clambering up the other way, as if he were descending a ladder.

"Show-off," sniffed Sychorax, as she swept to the

entrance of the shaft herself, clicked her fingers at a Lumpenogre with two heads, and ordered him to carry her.

"The mine is being evacuated, lady," said the first head of the Lumpenogre as he lifted her down to the Den of Delights.

"I am not a lady," sniffed Queen Sychorax, as the ogre set her on her feet. "I am a *queen*."

As soon as Queen Sychorax had disappeared, Brutal the Heartless hurried over to the Witchsmeller.

"Talk!" ordered Brutal the Heartless.

"So *now* you want me to talk, do you?" sneered the Witchsmeller. "You may not like what I have to say. You have just signed your own death warrant. The emperor is going to KILL you...The child that Queen Sychorax is looking for is her own child, and she is the most dangerous threat to us Warriors you could possibly imagine...for the child has *Magic-that-works-on-iron*...and Queen Sychorax herself must be in league with the Wizards..."

"Not possible..." whispered Brutal the Heartless. But nonetheless, he turned whiter than snow. *Was* it possible? Something very odd was going on.

Meanwhile, when Encanzo landed in the Den of Delights, Xar was highly visible, blowing on his trumpet in the middle of the cavern. Encanzo ran full tilt toward his son, hoping to catch him by surprise.

But over on the rock face, Encanzo's elder son Looter and his two cronies were in trouble. An ogre had stampeded toward the exit and accidentally nudged Looter on the way, knocking him off the platform he was balancing on. Looter's wrists were chained together, which made it hard for him to regain his foothold.

So Looter was dangling from his own mining pick, above a sheer, life-threatening drop.

"HELP ME!" yelled Looter.

"HELP HIM!" cried Blister and Sneering, Looter's cronies. "HE'S VERY IMPORTANT!"

"Don't worry, Looter, I'm coming!" roared Encanzo, changing direction and running toward his elder son.

"Bodkin! Get in!" yelled Wish, climbing into the cart at the front of the caravan of carts, and Bodkin climbed into the one at the back beside Xar. Wish pushed up her eyepatch, twitched her fingers ... and the linked carts rose in the air, over Encanzo's head, toward where Looter was dangling.

"Oh thank goodness, he's safe ..." breathed Encanzo, as Looter finally lost his grip, and landed heavily but safely in the cart in the middle of the flying caravan. "And at least he protected his spelling arm as well ... the boy is phenomenally gifted in the Magic department ..."

"Hold on tight, everyone!" yelled Wish, as she turned the flying carts around, back over the heads of the evacuating children and Magic creatures, toward the exit of the mine. Encanzo recovered his surprise and ran after the carts full tilt. The end one, where Xar and Bodkin were, was dipping in the air a trifle. Encanzo leaped upward, just managing to get a grip on the edge of the cart, which then carried him up into the air.

Queen Sychorax snapped at the Lumpenogre to carry her back into the entrance again, where she hoped to cut them off. "Make up your mind, lady," sighed the Lumpenogre, lifting her up.

"Wish! My father is trying to get on board!" warned Xar. The train of mining carts sailed off, with Encanzo dangling from the end of it, out of the Den of Delights, and into the main entrance of the mine.

Where there was absolute chaos.

The flying caravan of mine carts, with Encanzo and Sychorax dangling from the end of it, sailed over the heads of a stream of Wizards and Magic creatures and ogres and goblins and Warriors who were flooding out of the mine, panicking like crazy.

"Trillions of traily bits of twiddly green jungle!" cursed Brutal the Heartless, staring upward, unable to believe his eyes. "Queen Sychorax IS in league with the Wizards!"

"I have never been more disappointed in you, Wish!" scolded Queen Sycorax.

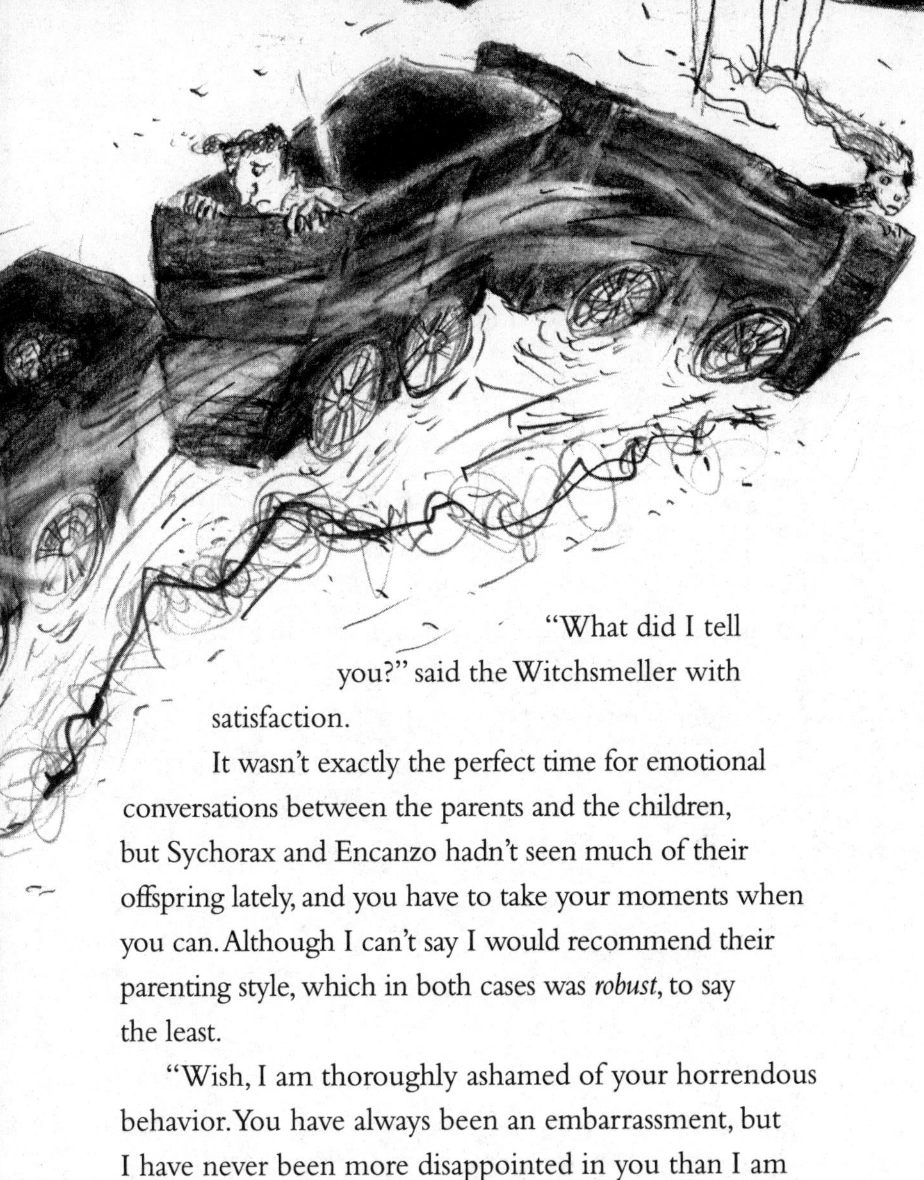

"What did I tell you?" said the Witchsmeller with satisfaction.

It wasn't exactly the perfect time for emotional conversations between the parents and the children, but Sychorax and Encanzo hadn't seen much of their offspring lately, and you have to take your moments when you can. Although I can't say I would recommend their parenting style, which in both cases was *robust*, to say the least.

"Wish, I am thoroughly ashamed of your horrendous behavior. You have always been an embarrassment, but I have never been more disappointed in you than I am right now!" scolded Queen Sychorax, and even though these words came from a woman hanging from a mine cart that was flying through the air in an undignified way, they still had the power to sting.

More than anything in the world, Wish wanted to please her mother, so her heart shriveled in sadness to hear the cold disapproval in her mother's golden pear-drop of a voice.

You must be careful what you say to children.

For children will listen.

"Stop this nonsense, and come back home to iron Warrior fort!" ordered Queen Sychorax. You have to admire her, *still* telling her daughter off and bossing her around, even though she was swinging by her fingertips from the back of an airborne mine cart.

"Father, did you tell Looter that you thought I was a disgrace?" cried Xar, bashing on his father's fingers to try and make him let go, for the combined weight of Sychorax and Encanzo was dragging the mine carts, down, down, and making it hard for Wish to steer.

"Of course I did, Xar! You ARE a disgrace!" shouted Encanzo.

"I am not! I am not!" cried Xar, red in the face, pounding even harder on his father's hand. Bodkin was helping him. Bodkin was nearly as cross with Encanzo as Xar was.

Xar can be annoying, but he means well, and what kind of a father calls his son "a disgrace"? thought Bodkin.

"Your plan is just WISH FULFILLMENT!"

roared Encanzo. "There's no such thing as a spell to get rid of Witches!"

Encanzo and Sychorax used their combined weight to tip the carts wildly to the left.

The sudden swerve made Wish lose her concentration for a second, and the swinging carts veered into a running Lumpenogre. The whole train of mine carts came tumbling down, out of the air and onto the cavern floor.

Sychorax and Encanzo leaped to their feet, triumphantly intending to reclaim their rebellious children.

But Wish wriggled her nose, and the iron chains holding Looter's wrists together unhinged themselves as smoothly as if a knot were unraveling itself. The chains flew through the air, and very neatly and precisely clamped Encanzo's right arm to Sychorax's left. And at the same time, the Witchsmeller and Brutal the Heartless grabbed the Wizard king and the Warrior queen by the shoulders.

How quickly jubilation can turn to despair.

One minute the all-conquering parents were rejoicing in the recovery of their children and the success of their quest. The next they were under capture themselves.

"I ARREST YOU IN THE NAME OF THE EMPEROR!" roared Brutal the Heartless.

The Witchsmeller rubbed his gloved hands together in glee. "Ooh, the emperor is going to be so pleased!"

Wish took advantage of this fortunate turn of events by launching the train of upended carts up into the air again. "Bother, we can't leave them to be arrested, though…" she worried, looking down from above at the two parents, shackled together.

Wish need not have concerned herself.

ROOOOOOOOOAAWWWWWWWWWWW!

Through the entrance of the mine leaped a gigantic brown bear. It was unimaginably enormous, at least three times the size of a normal bear. Its ragged fur, upraised either in fury or in fright, made it seem even bigger than it actually was.

The bear was accompanied by two creatures so unusual that even Encanzo had rarely had dealings with them. A couple of gargantuan wild horses, their shapes shifting, sometimes appearing skeleton thin, other times gleaming with powerful muscles, but eyes ever steady, burning like saucers of fire, jaws wide with screaming neighs, foaming at the mouth as they charged forward, storming mad and out of control.

"Rage-foals!" said Encanzo in astonishment.

9. Perdita and the Rage-foals

The Witchsmeller and Brutal the Heartless stared at the screaming Rage-foals charging toward them in absolute astonishment.

Brutal the Heartless just had time to say "What *on earth* is going on?" before realizing the Rage-foals were stampeding right AT them with the speed and bulk of a couple of runaway boulders. Brutal and the Witchsmeller would be stomped dead and flat under those gigantic murderous hooves if they stayed where they were. So they turned around and ran as fast as they could in the opposite direction.

They didn't get far. The Rage-foals caught up with them and attacked immediately, tearing and ripping at their clothes, raking their furs to ribbons, stamping on Brutal's medals till they were twisted and flat, and their vicious onslaught was only stopped by the arrival of the great bear, who roared ascendancy over the Rage-foals.

The dreadful horses-out-of-nightmares reluctantly abandoned their savage attack, aiming a few last vicious kicks at the Witchsmeller and Brutal, and galloped off to guard Encanzo and Sychorax.

The two monarchs were also attempting to run away, but they were hampered by the fact that they were now handcuffed together and trying to run in opposite directions. The steaming, foaming Rage-foals circled them, screaming, snorting, stamping, and the giant bear slammed the Witchsmeller and Brutal onto the mine entrance floor, with one, two of its great paws.

The bear ROOOOOOOOOARRRED right in their faces, with such bear-y horror that it blew back their hair. It powered onto its hind feet and beat its great chest with its huge hairy paws. The Witchsmeller and Brutal the Heartless did not wait to find out the bear's intentions. They joined the screaming, panicking crowd flooding out of the mine, crying pitifully, their clothes raked to ribbons, and they did not look back.

The bear slammed down onto its front paws again.

It gave a satisfied snort...

...and transformed.

Transformation is one of the Wizards' most impressive magical skills.

One minute the bear was a great, magnificent, bearlike beast. The next, the outline of the bear shriveled and became smaller, smaller...until it turned into a very untidy-looking woman of goodness-knows-what-age, rather eccentrically dressed, but with very smiley eyes.

"Madam Perdita!" said Wish, looking down from the mine carts in joyful relief.

"Sister!" cried Caliburn in delight, for Perdita was a

very powerful Wizard, who also just so happened to be Caliburn's twin sister.*

"Oh thank goodness," said Wish, "Perdita will make everything all right..."

"I knew she wouldn't desert us!" said Xar, and Wish made the mining carts fly lower, intending to land...but her way was barred by a small, stern-looking little owl, flying directly in front of them.

This was Hoola, who was Perdita's constant companion.

"And where do you think *you're* going?" said Hoola crossly. "We did not come here for yooooooouuuuu... *You* have a quest to fulfill...off you go, to the Lake of the Lost, to save Xar and Squeezjoos, SHHOOOOO!"

"But I thought you'd come to help us!" said Wish in disappointment.

---

* Long story, told in *Knock Three Times*.

"You're doing perfectly well on your own," sniffed Hoola. "Besides, Perdita will have her hands full getting this lot to safety...we'll have to search for the nearest Wizard encampment who will take them all in..." She pointed a wing at all the young Wizards and Magic creatures running away.

"And then we're going to have to take them all back to their parents," grumbled Hoola. "It's going to be a huge organizational nightmare..." Hoola was moaning, but she was more pleased than she sounded, because she was a pretty bossy little owl and she secretly rather enjoyed sorting out a huge organizational nightmare.

"Can't *I*, at least, get off?" said Looter. "I'm too big for this cart and I don't want to be stuck with these lunatics and oddballs. I'm way too important…"

"No time for making any landings," said Hoola. "And better to be with the lunatics and oddballs than imprisoned in a mine, don't you think, Looter, dear? Count your blessings…shooo, shooo, off with you…your snowcats are waiting…off to find the Kingwitch, now, and rescue Squeezjoos…Perdita will deal with everything here…SHHOOOOOOOO…"

Wish looked longingly over the side of the flying mine carts at Perdita, scarves flying, her living spectacles crawling all over her like large insects, and Perdita gave her a merry wave. Somehow the sight of Perdita calmly beaming in the middle of all this chaos was very heartening to Wish. She looked reassuringly like she was overseeing a slightly out-of-control cooking class back at Pook's Hill, rather than in the center of a stampeding exodus, at the liberation of the appalling Mine of Happiness.

"You're doing really *well*!" Perdita shouted up encouragingly. "Off you go, now!"

Reluctantly, Wish steered the flying mine carts out of

the door of the Mine of Happiness and off to the part of the forest where Crusher and the werewolf and the bear and the wolves and snowcats were waiting for them.

Down below, Queen Sychorax's pretty little foot was tapping, *tap, tap, tap,* and her nose was in the air. She was absolutely frog-freezingly furious. When her servants and subjects saw that expression on her face back in iron Warrior fort, they ducked behind handy pieces of furniture for they knew that it was a sure sign that pieces of crockery could get hurled around the room any moment.

But Queen Sychorax's anger was not helped by the fact that she could not have picked up a handily chuck-able piece of crockery even if there had been one within arm's reach.

Because her throwing arm was currently handcuffed to the wrist of an enemy king with whom she was not only NOT, repeat NOT, in love, but she was supposed to be in outright *war* with him, for mistletoe's sake.

Things had gotten completely out of control and Queen Sychorax absolutely hated it when that happened.

So Sychorax concentrated all her viper-strong anger into the next bitterly sarcastic comment to Madam

Perdita. "They're doing *well*? What do you mean they're doing WELL? How dare you ENCOURAGE them, you deranged, badly dressed tea cozy?"

"Well, people said it was impossible to close down the Mine of Happiness, didn't they?" said Madam Perdita. "And lo! They made that impossible thing happen. And a very good thing too," she added more grimly. "For a more dreadful, miserable place it would be hard to imagine."

"See what cruelty all Warriors are capable of?" taunted Encanzo. "It's an example of how corrupt your so-called civilization is..."

Sychorax's face was flaming red. She *knew* he was going to bring that up. "I make no excuses for the emperor," she sniffed. "But ALL Warriors are not like that..."

"However, by giving your allegiance to the emperor," said Madam Perdita, "are you not saying that places like this are all right?"

This was so unanswerable that Sychorax was momentarily lost for words, and that did not happen very often.

"You are," said Encanzo brutally. "And you know it, Sychorax."

"Oh for mistletoe's sake!" said Sychorax irritably. "I take your point. I am glad this mine has been shut down, and perhaps I should reconsider whether the emperor is the sort of person I and my Warriors should be following."

Curiouser and curiouser! Now *that* was so rare it might only happen on a blue moon. Queen Sychorax admitting she might be wrong! Queen Sychorax reconsidering! Is this the sort of thing that can only really happen in fairy tales?

Madam Perdita gave a satisfied little nod. Sometimes people had to see things with their own eyes, experience things with their own senses, to change the direction of a long-held opinion.

"An independent Queen Sychorax?" sneered Encanzo, spoiling the mood. "No longer kissing her pretty little lips to the hand of the appalling Warrior emperor? I'll believe it when I see it—"

"Oh, do shut up!" snapped Queen Sychorax. "Madam Perdita, what are you doing here anyway? You're not supposed to be interfering with our methods of child-rearing!"

"But *you* called *me*!" said Perdita in surprise. "I said, if you needed help with your children, you should just knock three times? So, you knocked, and I came. I was delighted to help."

"Need *your* help!" gasped Queen Sychorax. "We certainly don't need your help!"

"And *we* didn't knock..." said Encanzo. "It was the

children who knocked. They were knocking to pretend to be Knockers...you know, the little creatures who haunt mines like this one, warning when it is about to collapse? That was what made the Warriors close down the mine."

"Oh, how clever of them!" said Perdita approvingly. "You have very smart children. I noticed that when they were in my learning place. You should be very proud of them, as I am sure you are."

Ah...the two parents shuffled their feet rather thoughtfully at that.

Had they been all that appreciative of their children's cleverness up to now? Not really, but being a parent was so stupendously difficult...and it's hard when your child is breaking all the rules of the tribe and the wildwoods, to admire how jolly clever they are.

"Well," Perdita carried on, "since this has all been a bit of a misunderstanding, and you didn't knock for me after all, you clearly don't need my help, so I should be on my way."

There was a short, significant pause.

As it happened, it occurred to Sychorax and Encanzo simultaneously that they *did* rather need Madam Perdita's help.

"Um, Madam Perdita," said Encanzo casually. "Before you go on your way, could you do us this one very small favor, and undo this handcuff? My Magic will not work on it, and we appear to be a little tied up..." He held up his arm, attached to Queen Sychorax's.

"So you are," admired Madam Perdita. She gave a happy little laugh. "Unfortunate. For that handcuff has been locked by Magic-that-works-on-iron, and the only person who can unlock it for you is Wish. The children will now be on their way to the Lake of the Lost, to face the dreadful horror of the Kingwitch with the spell to get rid of Witches."

"We HAVE to stop them!" cried Encanzo. "If Wish lets the Kingwitch out of the iron that binds him, the entire world that we have known until now will be blasted into total devastation by the Witches. Everything we love will be destroyed..."

"You will have to hurry, if you want to catch up with them," warned Perdita. "But I may be able to offer you the help of one of these Rage-foals."

She turned to the Rage-foals and had a conversation with them in horse language, which sounds rather humorous, lots of neighing and tossing of the head for emphasis.

"They don't normally let people ride them, but as a special favor, the Rage-foals have very kindly agreed that one of them will stay with me, and one of them will carry you to the Droods' stronghold," said Perdita.

Perdita stood at the horse's head and made soothing noises to try and calm the beast down. It was brave of the two monarchs to climb aboard the trembling, furious Rage-foal, for it was not an inviting prospect.

Sychorax insisted on riding sidesaddle, for Warrior queens always ride sidesaddle if they can. It creates a dignified impression.

"You'll fall off," warned Encanzo.

"I...will...NOT..." said Queen Sychorax, as the Rage-foal reared and bucked and screamed and pranced before shooting off madly, hoofbeats ringing out as quick and fast as if the horse were already being pursued by Witches and was shaking her tail at them with contempt.

The Rage-foal's gleaming back was slippery and shifting as mercury—but Sychorax stuck to the horse with the glue of her fierce determination.

Perdita watched them go, shaking her head in amusement. *Whatever you might think of Queen Sychorax, you had to admire her GRIT.*

"Hoo!" Hoola flew down. "Perdita! We need to find and organize those Wizard children and Magic creatures."

"Very good, very good," said Perdita. "I'll leave you to do that...you're very good at organizing...but I have a quest to go on. I've kept the swiftest Rage-foal for myself..."

Hoola landed on Perdita's shoulder and looked her in the eye, very sternly.

"Perdita," said Hoola. "You're not thinking of joining those crazy children on their quest to the Lake of the Lost, are you? *We* are supposed to be retiring. Wizards are made to wander…go a-vagabonding…the wind in our hair…the old trusty walking boots taking us wherever they may…remember? And *you* are not supposed to be interfering."

"I will not be interfering," promised Perdita. "The adventure belongs to the children. *They* will be in charge. But they will need my help."

Perdita's face was very grim.

"Encanzo and Sychorax are foolish and misguided," said Perdita. "But they are right about one thing. If Wish lets the Kingwitch out of the iron, and is defeated by him such horror will be unleashed that—"

Perdita stopped talking, because she could see that Hoola was looking frightened. She stroked the little owl's feathers soothingly. "Trust me, Hoola, I have to follow them and help if I can. You can join us all later on."

So Hoola flew off to assist the children released from the mine in rejoining their parents. And Perdita climbed onto the second Rage-foal to follow Wish and Xar.

Meanwhile, Wish crash-landed the mine carts in the part of the forest where they had left their friends and companions behind.

Padding through the forest, the three beautiful snowcats greeted them with as much enthusiasm as if they had been three gigantic kittens, bowling them over as they climbed out of the mining carts, and covering their faces with licks.

"Kingcat! Forestheart! Nighteye!" cried Wish, burying her face in the deep powder snow of their fur. "Oh! How we've missed you..."

And then she embraced Crusher the Longstepper High-Walker giant around the ankle. "You too, Crusher."

"We were worried about you," said the great giant. "You were gone a very long time..."

"We did it!" crowed Xar, pumping the air with his fist. "We closed down the mine! We rescued Looter and everyone else! I knew we would! *I am the boy of destiny, FEEL MY POWER!*"

Caliburn sighed. At least Xar was saying "*we* did it." Six months ago, he would have been claiming that he did the whole thing all on his own, so he had been making *some* progress.

"And now we can get the Cup of Second Chances

Kingcat! Forestheart! Nighteye!
Oh, how we've missed you!

Perdita
(Caliburn's sister)

from Looter, and we can finally make the spell that gets rid of Witches," said Xar.

"HA!" Bodkin pointed out. "*You* didn't want us to go on that quest in the first place, Xar, so don't go pretending it was all your idea all along."

There was a sudden crashing in the undergrowth.

"What's that?" said Caliburn anxiously.

Were they being followed by Warriors, Witches, or Wizards? Was that the sound of the hairy feet of Lumpenogres, chasing them already?

But to Caliburn's delight, blundering into the clearing, came...

...a gigantic brown bear.

"Sister!" cried Caliburn in jubilation.

"Perdita!" cried Wish and Bodkin and Xar in excitement as the brown bear transformed into messy, cuddly Perdita. Suddenly the whole adventure seemed less terrifying.

Perdita was joined by the pixies.

"Pixies..." hissed Ariel and Tiffinstorm and Bumbleboozle, eyes spitting with annoyance, because sprites cannot stand pixies.

Pixies are a bit like hairy fairies who have never grown up, small and fuzzy, and a lot of them ride on the backs of wasps, which they keep as pets. They are chameleons, and they comb their hair with special thorny twigs into elaborate hairstyles. (The sprites think they do this to show off.)

The pixies swarmed up, in great buzzing hordes. They were a little less cheerful than they normally were, but they were trying their hardest to be jolly under their present difficult circumstances, and they gave their traditional greeting:

"HELLO! HELLOWe'reherewe'rehere!

"Hello! Boy-who-looks-like-a-turnip-in-a-tin-can...lopsidedweirdowiththeeyepatch... boywiththehandthatwillbetrayeveryonetotheWitches... we'rejoining you on your...absolutelycrazy... madlysuicidal...luniotic...breffdiotic...RIDICULOUS new quest!"

Perdita embraced them all fondly, exclaiming, "Xar, Wish, Bodkin, oh, how I've missed you all!"

"Ohandhello,largeverypleasedwithhimselfboy whoisn'tasimportantashethinksheis and oncewasturnedintoaGraxerturgleburkin..." sang the pixies, spotting Looter, sulking in the shadows, still not as grateful as he ought to have been for being rescued from the Mine of Happiness, and extremely annoyed to have all the attention on Xar and Wish and not on his most important self.

Perdita frowned at him. "Oh yes, the older brother. At last I see the point of him—he has the Cup of Second Chances, doesn't he? Quick, quick, hand it over, boy!"

Looter reddened in astonishment and fury. "What do you mean, you've only just seen the point of me? *I* am a king-in-waiting, and I have been told by many people that I have a Magic potential that is truly extraordinary. And I'm not going to give you the Cup of Second Chances, my father gave it to ME."

Perdita gave him a very stern look indeed, and she made a tiny little wink that you would not have noticed if you did not know that like Wish, Perdita was one of the few people who are born with a Magic eye.

When Perdita made that tiny wink, the knapsack on Looter's back began to shake, as if something within it was alive, and the Cup of Second Chances rocketed out with such violence that it gave Looter a nasty rap on the head as it shot toward Perdita's waiting open hand.

"OW!" yelled Looter.

"Sorry, dear," said Perdita cozily, as she caught the cup. "But you should have given me the cup when you were asked, shouldn't you?"

Perdita read out the inscription Encanzo had engraved on the side of the cup in curly sprite-writing:

"'To Looter, my dearest and FAVORITE and most brilliant son on the occasion of his Magic coming in.' Hmmm..." said Perdita thoughtfully. "I have to say, Encanzo's parenting-skills need a little work. It doesn't take very much imagination to understand why Xar and Looter don't like each other very much."

"Give that cup back!" roared Looter, rubbing the bump on his head. "And I insist that I should be taken to some place of safety at the earliest possible moment. It doesn't matter what happens to *Xar*, but *I* am important. In the event of my father's death, I am the last hope of my tribe."

"Yes, yes, I'm sure you're terribly significant, Looter," said Perdita soothingly, "but we don't have time to drop you off at the moment, so you'll just have to tag along and try to not get in the way. Now, what are we doing waiting around here? We need to get as far away from that Mine of Happiness as we possibly can before nightfall."

"I thought you were supposed to be letting Xar and Wish and Bodkin do this adventure on their own?" said Caliburn, unable to conceal his delight in having her company.

"They knocked for me," said Perdita simply. "And you should always answer when children knock for you. It means they need your help."

10. Suddenly It Looked Like Everything Might Be Going Well

On the run again, with their little band of companions.

They went as far as they could before Perdita decided it was safe to set up camp, in a hiding place under a great overhanging boulder in the heart of the wildwoods

And that very first evening Perdita helped them make the spell to get rid of Witches.

"Unfortunately I'm traveling light, so I don't have a cauldron with me." Perdita frowned. "Cauldrons are essential for really good spellwork but they *are* a little bulky. Crusher, dear, can you help us?"

Madam Perdita shouted up to Crusher. Giants are BIG, and so they tend to have BIG thoughts, and Crusher was a Longstepper High-Walker giant, and they are among the deepest thinkers of all. It can be hard to get the attention of a Longstepper High-Walker giant when they are thinking these deep thoughts.

As Crusher dreamily picked off a few leaves from the highest treetops and chewed on them slowly like a ruminating cow he was thinking:

The problem is that these leaves are green, but how do I know that the green

that I *see is the same green that someone* else *sees?*

Crusher was so excited by this problem that he chewed a little faster. Not very fast in human terms, for giants move very sl-o-o-wly, but exceedingly fast for a Longstepper High-Walker giant.

And why do we cry when we are happy? Are they the same tears as when we are sad?

The return of his little friends had made Crusher so happy that his giant brain was going into overdrive, forming question after interesting question, preventing him from seeing that the little friends down below were going crazy, jumping up and down and trying to get him to see them.

If you love your enemy, do they become your friend? thought Crusher,

Does expecting the unexpected make the unexpected expected? What if two mind readers are reading minds . . . who is reading whom? And what is the answer to the question: "I am lying—true or false?"

"Crusher!!!!" yelled Crusher's little friends from down below, and eventually he gave a great start and bent over, putting his kind moon face down to see them.

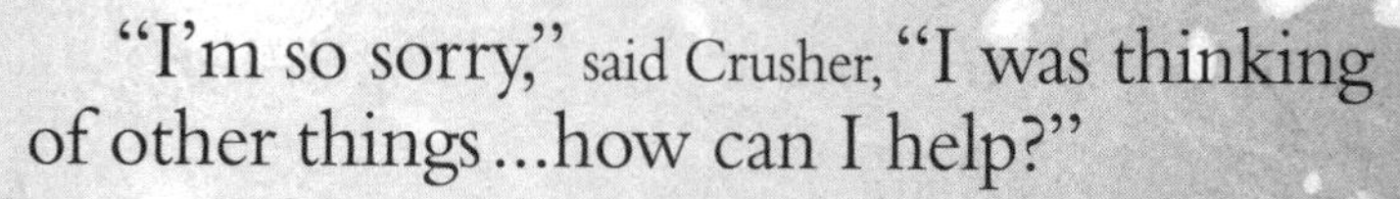

"I'm so sorry," said Crusher, "I was thinking of other things...how can I help?"

When they asked their question, Crusher was a little disappointed, because he rather hoped they might be asking something important like "Is the universe really expanding and what happens when it stops?" but he good-naturedly turned his great mind on to the rather more prosaic problem of whether he had a cauldron on his person.

He didn't.

But he offered them his metal tinderbox instead, which was the size of a matchbox to a giant but cauldron-sized to human beings.

Perdita lit the wood under the tinderbox-cauldron with the special fire Tiffinstorm had been keeping for her, a single flame taken from fires drawn from all over the archipelago.

Then she got the Once-sprite to get out the ingredients of the spell, and she sprinkled them into the cauldron, one at a time, singing in each element, as if the ingredients were friends meeting at a feast, and she was introducing them to each other. "It's so they mix well together," she explained to Wish.

"One! Giant's last breath from Castle Death (forgiveness).

"Two! feathers from a Witch (desire).

"Three! tears from a frozen queen (tenderness).

"Four! scales of the Nuckalavee (courage).

"Five! tears of the Drood from the Lake of the Lost (endurance)...

"A double dose of tears goes in," said Perdita, shaking her head in a worried way. "I have no idea why there are so many tears in this recipe. It does trouble me somewhat that it might be a bad omen..."

Looter had his arms folded furiously. "Which is why we should not be going on the quest at all. It is far too dangerous, particularly for someone like me who has such brilliant spell-making potential. I would be too great a loss to the world."

PA-A-A-A-A-ARRRPPPPP! said Xar's trumpet triumphantly. The trumpet used to get *fairly* excitable in response to *Xar*, but now that *Looter* was around, it was outdoing itself, doubling the loudness and the rudeness of its sound. It had gotten to the stage that whenever Looter opened his mouth, the trumpet would perk up, stiffening to attention, making a low humming noise in readiness to go into full blast mode.

Looter's face darkened. He blamed Xar for this, just like everything else. "Can't you keep your trumpet under control, Xar?" snapped Looter.

The spell frothed and foamed, turning different colors, until eventually it was bubbling up so wildly that one particularly large bubble burst all over Madam Perdita's face and she tasted it with interest. "Perfect! And, may I say, also absolutely truly scrumptious, which will help the efficacy of the Magic. The more toothsome and flavorful the spell, the more likely it is to work. BRING ME THE CUP OF SECOND CHANCES!"

Bodkin brought the cup to Perdita, and she poured the spell into the cup.

"The spell to get rid of Witches must be stirred by a living spoon," said Perdita. "So, Enchanted Spoon! This is your big moment...I bid you to whisk this spell, with all your might and main!"

Delighted to have such a vital role to play, the spoon jumped into the cup and mixed the last little drops of the spell to get rid of Witches with such energy and excitement that they frothed up even farther, and the spell doubled, then tripled in size, still changing color, and making little squeaking noises, as if the ingredients in the spell were talking to one another.

"Excellent," said Perdita with satisfaction. "You can stop now, little spoon."

The spell smelled delectable. Mellow clouds of honey-sweet yumminess made their way up Wish's nose, making her taste buds perk up excitably, and her mouth water in delightful anticipation.

"Ohhhhhh..." sighed Wish, "can we just have one *tiny taste* of it, Perdita? Just so we can check the recipe is right?"

The others were sniffing too, for that smell was so giddyingly, head-spinningly alluring that it made you lose your senses entirely, and want to grab the cup out of Perdita's hands and gulp the whole thing down in one go. Xar's hand with the Witch-stain on it itched forward, but Perdita whisked the cup out of reach.

"We can't taste the spell now," explained Perdita, pouring the spell into a bottle, firmly putting the stopper in, and giving it to the Once-sprite for safe-keeping. "We need it to fight the Kingwitch later on. Every single drop must count."

Wish gave a sigh of relief, because now the spell was safely in the bottle, it was no longer tempting them with its confusing and

tantalizing aroma, and they could all cheer wholeheartedly as Perdita lifted the spell-in-the-bottle in the air, triumphantly crying, "Well done, everyone! Through your extraordinary endeavors, your courage and fortitude, your patience and your determination, you have already achieved the impossible. For the first time in human history, you have created A SPELL TO GET RID OF WITCHES!"

Wish and Xar and Bodkin whooped in excitement, the snowcats capered, Lonesome and the wolves howled, the sprites whizzed around bashing celebration spells around the clearing like little fireworks, and the enchanted objects rushed around in excitable circles.

Only Looter was grumpy, even after Perdita returned the Cup of Second Chances to him. But the grumbling of Looter did not spoil everyone else's evening.

They were all buoyed up with satisfaction at an impossible job well done and also hopeful anticipation of how their greater quest might meet with similar triumph. They talked and laughed by the fire, long, long into the night, feasting on one of Perdita's mouthwatering stews, which she had made in the tinderbox-cauldron after she had made the spell, so it tasted particularly heavenly.

The spoon, the fork, the key, and the pins were thrilled to be back in the company of so many other enchanted objects, for like Wish, Perdita was surrounded by normally inanimate objects that came to life in her presence. After the meal, no one had to clean up, for the bowls and the cups rolled themselves off to a nearby stream to wash themselves, and the knives and forks hopped afterward.

One of the larger knives smashed the ice in the frozen stream, and then they all had a very

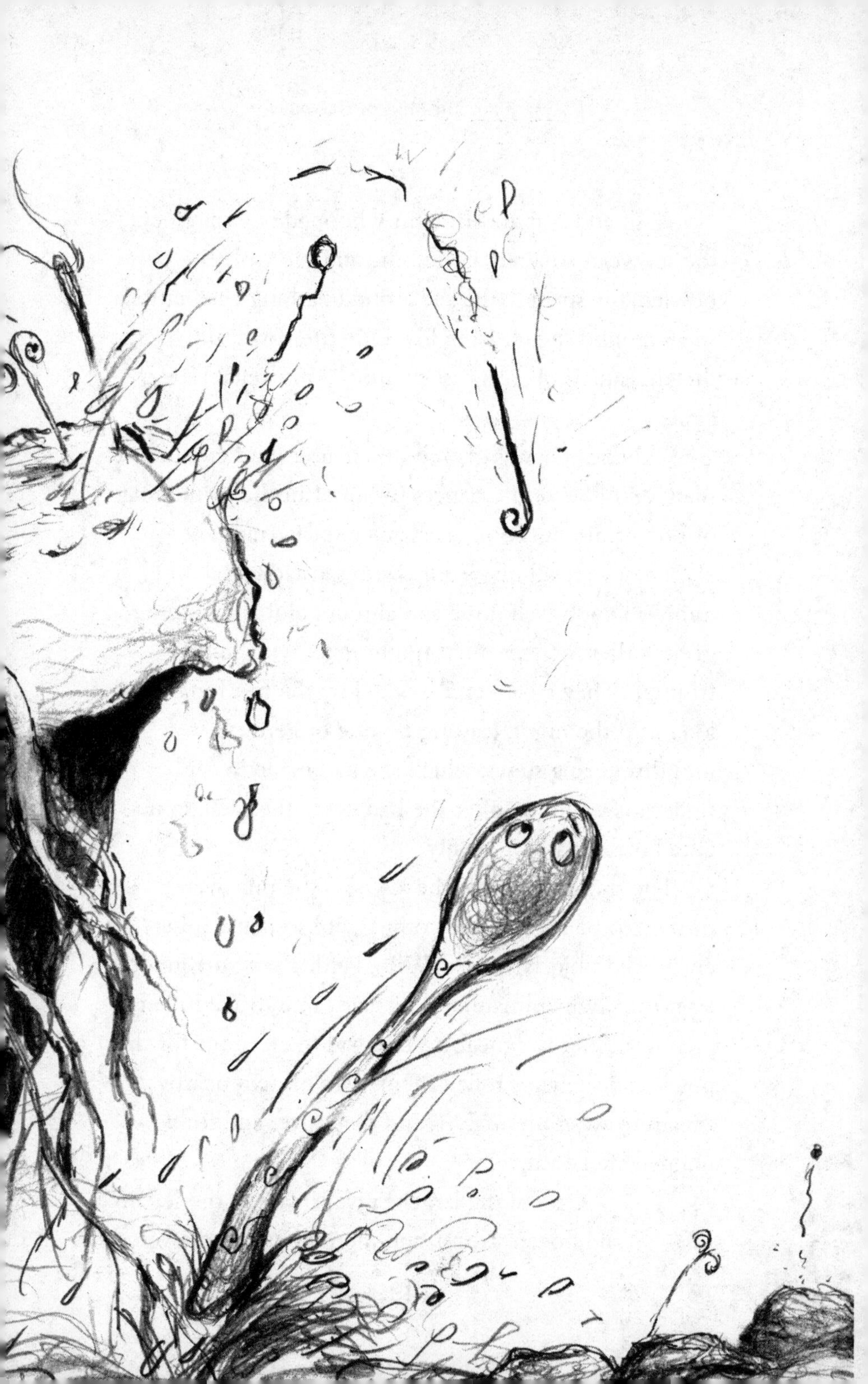

whe-e-e-e!!

merry midnight bathing party. The fork made a spectacle of itself, trying to impress the key, because it was an excellent swimmer. It high-dived off a snowbank, doing several backflips before it entered the water, and glided through the creek, showing off its nifty and fast front crawl, its languid backstroke, its double-handed butterfly, all using its prongs instead of arms, moving through the water like a teeny-weeny little squid.

However, to the fork's fury, the Enchanted Key was more impressed by the spoon's thoughtful behavior than by the fork's splendid freestyle skills. A lot of the smaller pins couldn't really swim yet, but they didn't want to be left out. So following the fork's lead, they threw themselves enthusiastically off the snowbank, wriggling with excitement (and if they could have spoken they would have been squeaking, "Wheeeeeee!")...

My hero!

...and of course, the *moment* they plunged in, they sank to the bottom of the stream, and so the spoon had to rescue them, catching them in his bowl as they fell through the water or digging them out of the mud at the bottom.

The little pins didn't seem any worse for the experience, for as soon as the noble Enchanted Spoon had rescued them and put them safely on the side, they hopped up the snowbank and threw themselves off again, just as enthusiastically and joyfully and recklessly as ever.

The key stood in the shallows, shouting, "There's another pin going down, over there! Oh, spoon, you are MY HERO!" and you can imagine how irritating that was for the Enchanted Fork, who had just demonstrated a swimming stroke that it had made up *itself*, something very flashy indeed that involved a lot of dazzling splashing that the fork had named the Double-Pronged-In-and-Out-Back-to-Front-Stroke. (Please note, you can only do this swimming stroke if you are a fork, so don't try this at home—unless you ARE a fork, of course.)

When the cutlery had swum, and they were all getting sleepy, Perdita made invisible spells of air as bouncy and comfortable as feather beds so that they didn't have to sleep on the hard ground. The pixies made themselves little cocoons where they slept, Perdita and her knitting needles helping them whip them up.

Wish snuggled herself into the thick, comforting coat of Nighteye, feeling the joyful warmth around her as she went to sleep.

Kingcat tenderly licked Xar's arm with the Witch-stain on it, trying to soothe the burning agony of it, so that Xar could drop off too. *Don't worry, Squeezjoos,* was Xar's last thought before he fell asleep, *we have the spell to get rid of witches now, and I kept my promise, we're coming to save you…*

So that was the end of a gorgeous evening, full of triumph and hope.

And perhaps it was lucky that nobody saw the Moonrakers, watching them from above.

Moonrakers are terrible gossips.

Their so-called secret mission was not going to be a secret much longer.

By the end of the night, every sprite in the wildwoods would know that Perdita and her odd little outcasts had made this incredibly powerful new spell to get rid of Witches, and how they were on their way to the Lake of the Lost to get rid of the Kingwitch.

And it would not be long before that news reached the ears of the Kingwitch himself…

11. What Happened to Poor Little Squeezjoos?

Meanwhile, even though it was way past his bedtime, Squeezjoos was still plodding all alone through the snow, plagued by infesta-pests, every frozen little hairy foot aching so hard he could barely lift it, desperate *not* to head to the Lake of the Lost but unable to help himself from going toward it nonetheless.

He was such a very small creature that he was making slow progress, and he still hadn't gotten far enough away from the quantities of iron in the Mine of Happiness to be able to fly yet.

He had seen Wish and Xar and Looter and everyone sailing over his head in the flying mine carts. The old Squeezjoos had returned for a second, and he had a brief moment of joy. *They's got out! They hasss escaped! Xar will come and save me!*

He tried to call out to them, but he was so small, and they were so far up, that however hard he shouted, they could not hear. And then the Witch Magic took over his brain again, the infesta-pests hummed and bit, and he thought savagely, *They don't care abouts ME...they'd rather save the big-lumping-brute-of-a-Looter because he isss a HUMAN BEING...*

And then later still, the Rage-foal carrying Sychorax and Encanzo thundered past him. In fact it didn't just pass him, it very nearly SQUASHED him. He was within an absolute whisker of being an *ex*–hairy fairy. There was a terrible sound of drumming, shaking hoofbeats, and the great dreadful hoof of the Rage-foal stomped down on top of Squeezjoos so close that it removed a part of one of his tentacles and he fell into the impression of the hoofprint in the snow. By the time he had climbed up to the top of the hoofprint, shaking with the shock of it, Encanzo and Sychorax had pulled the steaming, quivering Rage-foal to a halt just a few feet away from him.

They were arguing.

"YOU'RE supposed to be map-reading!" howled Encanzo. Sychorax had indeed gotten out the map, which was a sort of pullout one from inside Encanzo's Spelling Book, but the Rage-foal had been running at such a rate that it was impossible for her to read the beastly thing, it was plastered so closely to her pretty little nose by the blizzard of the flurrying snowflakes.

"Oh for mistletoe's sake, I'd forgotten how you ALWAYS know best," snapped Queen Sychorax, getting

the map under control and saying, "SEE! What did I say? We're going *the wrong way*! You should have let *me* steer the Rage-foal...How are we going to break into the Lake of the Lost anyway, without the Droods killing us? We're kind of conspicuous, handcuffed together like this."

"It's the centaurs' annual migration south," said Encanzo. "The Droods let them cross their bogs to do that, and the Rage-foal can mingle in with the centaur herds..."

"Good plan," approved Queen Sychorax. "This way!" And off the Rage-foal galloped, slipping like steaming quicksilver through the trees and the whirling snow.

"King Encanzo and Queen Ssssychorax..." whispered Squeezjoos to himself.

Squeezjoos hadn't even *tried* to shout out to THEM. He was absolutely petrified of Queen Sychorax, even when she wasn't on top of a great big Rage-foal that had very nearly trodden on him.

"I can tells my masster the Chiwgink that'ss they are coming...I cans warn him of theirs dissssguise and then he will be pleasssed with me..." said Squeezjoos to himself, as the Rage-foal thundered away. And then his thoughts cleared for a second, and he remembered that the Kingwitch was supposed to be his enemy. "*O how hass I ended up on the wrong sssside???*" wept poor Squeezjoos, to himself, in an agony of confusion. "I LOVESSS my *real* Masster Xar more than life itself. Pleasse, great green gods that look after the wildwoods, do not let ME be the one who betrays him..."

But it appeared that in the wild and whirling roar of the ever-worsening snowfall, the great green gods were not really listening to the tiny plea of one wretched hairy fairy.

That had been an hour earlier. An hour of weary plodding through the tempest of snow, eyes burning, tentacles stiff and frozen, heart failing, in the direction that he knew was the wrong one.

"Maybe my masster the Chiwgink isssn't going to be SO ANGRY," the poor little hairy fairy kept repeating to himself. "Wassn't Squeezjoos's fault..."

Way up above Squeezjoos's head there was an unearthly, ghastly scream. Nighttime was the Witching-time, and three gigantic Witches were circling up above. Even through the howling blizzard of snowflakes, they had smelled the smell of the infesta-pests and the reek of one of their own. They had spotted the little struggling sprite and now all three of them dived toward him with vengeful, ghastly shrieks.

Squeezjoos gave a howl of horror and tried to dig himself into the snow.

The Witches dug him up and tossed him in the air, one to another.

"Where ... isss ... the girl with the Magic-that-workss-on-iron????" hissed the largest of the Witches.

Poor, shivering, broken Squeezjoos tried not to look into the well of mercury that was the Witch's soulless eyes.

"They wouldn'ts come with me ... wasn't Squeezjoos's fault ... *please* don't be angry ..." begged Squeezjoos.

For answer, the three Witches made not a sound.

They just destroyed the entire clearing.

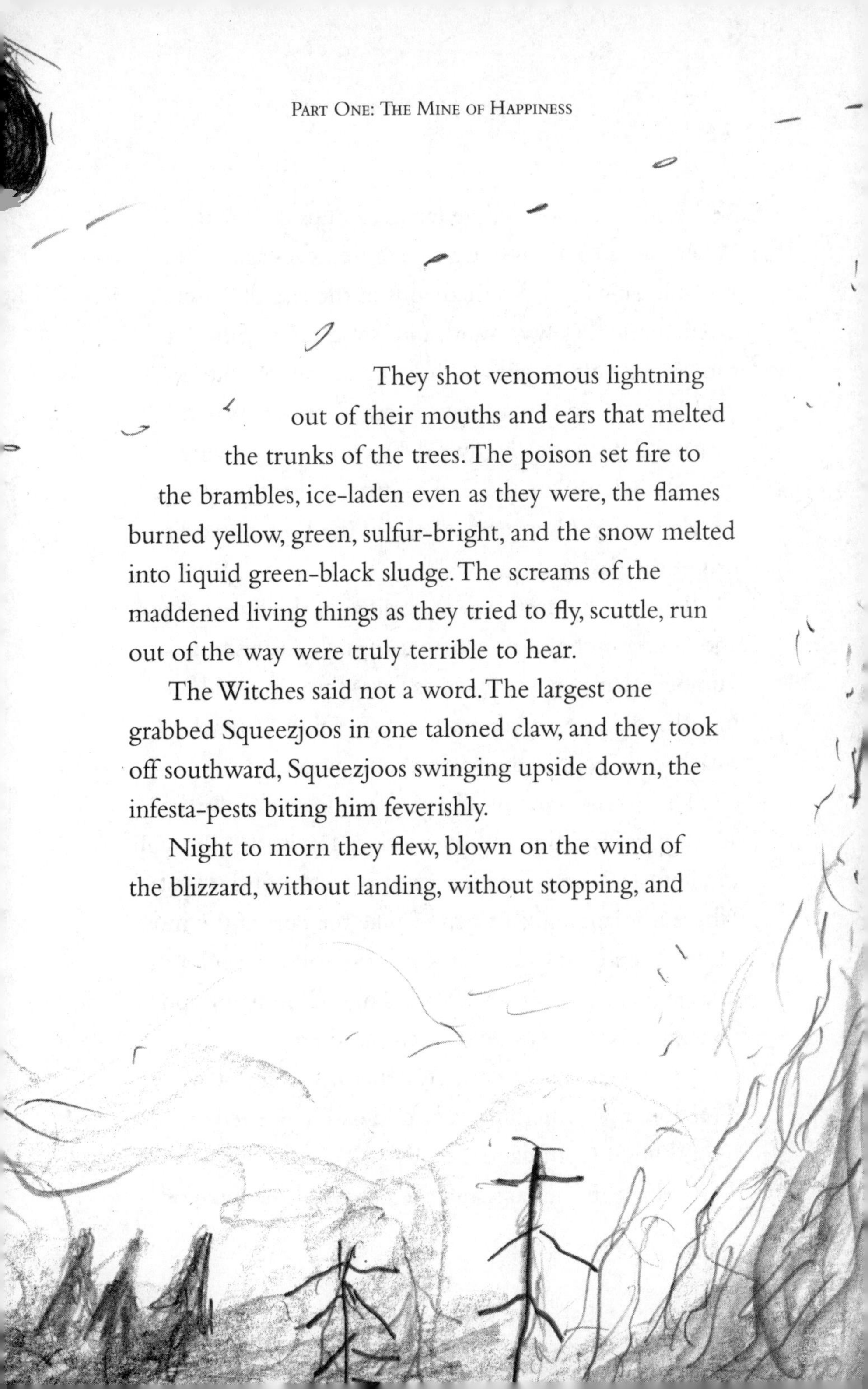

They shot venomous lightning out of their mouths and ears that melted the trunks of the trees. The poison set fire to the brambles, ice-laden even as they were, the flames burned yellow, green, sulfur-bright, and the snow melted into liquid green-black sludge. The screams of the maddened living things as they tried to fly, scuttle, run out of the way were truly terrible to hear.

The Witches said not a word. The largest one grabbed Squeezjoos in one taloned claw, and they took off southward, Squeezjoos swinging upside down, the infesta-pests biting him feverishly.

Night to morn they flew, blown on the wind of the blizzard, without landing, without stopping, and

Squeezjoos was so tired he fell asleep upside down. When he opened his exhausted, bitten eyes again, he was still dangling from the talons of the largest Witch, moving relentlessly onward, and it was light again. The sun was shining bright and high up above in a bitterly cold blue sky, so it must have been afternoon. When he craned his neck downward, he could see, moving queasily below him, the shifting mazy mists that always crawled sluggishly over the Lake of the Lost, however bright the day.

Beneath the mists was the bridge of the Sweet Track, and herds and herds of centaurs, in such astonishing numbers that they stretched as far as the eye could see in every direction, making their way south across the treacherous bogs in their winter migration.

The Sweet Track meanders down from the north, across miles and miles of the Slodger Territories, through the Forever Forests, and it ends at the Lake of the Lost, where it forms a gigantic spiral, like the curl of the most beautiful and enormous fern, and right in the center of that perfect gyration was Drood High Command, and that was where the Witches were heading.

They were not the only Witches heading in that direction. For something very odd had happened at Drood High Command.

Lurking in the bogs and the grasses of the Lake of

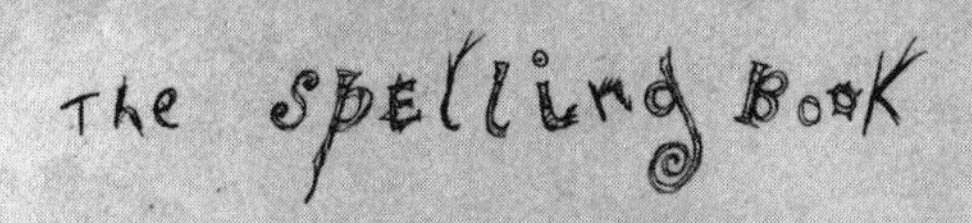

Centaurs

Centaurs are noble animals, with great magical powers and abilities. During winter, herds of centaurs migrate south to warmer climates in huge numbers.

the Lost were the gathering of the Witches. Witches' eyes were peeking out of the frosted cattails, watching the migrating centaurs, long dribbles of black saliva dropping from their lips, waiting for the moment they would be given the command to attack. Witches were roosting, on one leg, in the depths of the marshes. Witches were steadily flying, thick and fast from their hidden perches in the Witch Mountains and they were swarming toward the Lake of the Lost as if they were drawn there.

I do not know how to explain it. For Witches are age-old enemies of the Droods, but…

The Droods' patrols were stopping and talking to the Witches as if they were old friends and allies.

It was almost as if the Witches had been invited.

Impossible! Inconceivable! Unimaginable.

But this was what was happening.

They iss taking me to the Chiwgink, said Squeezjoos determinedly to himself. *But I's do not have to do what he assssks… I do nots have to ssay anything that might betray Xar… I iss small but I can be strong…*

Drood High Command was built on the great grassy battlements of an island that looked out over the most open and vast bit of the frozen lake.

The island was an enormous dug-out inverted bowl, with descending levels. There were rings of trees and rings of stones and places where only the most worthy of Droods could enter. And right at the bottom of this inverted bowl was the sacred amphitheater. It was here where the spellingfights took place. It was here where the poor Wizards and Warriors captured in war were made to battle for the right not to be the next human sacrifice.

But the Witches flew right into that sacred space. The Droods guarding the top of the amphitheater waved them in, as honored guests.

And the Witches carrying Squeezjoos landed right in the center, tossing the little sprite onto the ground in front of them, as if he were a piece of litter.

Squeezjoos passed out for a second, for he had landed on his head, and when he opened his dazed eyes, a great big lump on his forehead, the infesta-pests were going mad with excitement.

Through the maddening clouds of buzzing, swarming fleas, Squeezjoos could see...

...THE KINGWITCH.

Squeezjoos's little stomach melted in terror. The Witch was encased in a great lump of iron that Wish's Magic had melted all around him in a horribly misshapen mass of spears and arrows and shields. The ghastly, malformed mess gave off a dreadful reek of evil, and Squeezjoos whined and shrank back, as the Kingwitch opened up his eye right inside the center of that ominous ball. The captured Kingwitch had a tiny piece of Wish caught in there with him in the form of a miniscule particle of blue dust, and he had been using this to rub away at the inside of the ball of iron, so that bits of it were now transparent, and the beam of light from his open eye revealed the dreadful sight of him lurking in there, folded in on himself like a gigantic grasshopper.

The Kingwitch was ANGRY.

Squeezjoos could see the electric currents of his fury sparking inside the iron like bolts of furious lightning. When the Kingwitch spoke, it was with a boiled-down apothecary-poison of hatred that sent the hairs on Squeezjoos's neck prickling and freezing upward in little icicles of fear.

"*Where... is... she??????*" spat the Kingwitch. "Why have you not brought her?"

Be strong, Squeezjoos, said little Squeezjoos to himself.

So Squeezjoos said nothing, he just stood there, his eight little legs quivering with terror.

And then the infesta-pests *really* attacked. Biting him everywhere, and the Witch Magic flooded over him so that he could not think for himself anymore.

"Theys wouldn't come with me..." wept Squeezjoos, when he was able to speak. "Theys went into the Mine of Happiness to get the Cup of Second Chances..."

"You FAILED..." raged the furious Kingwitch. "Greenbreath! Hemlock! Go to the clearing where this sprite was born, where he first was an egg, and ANNIHILATE it!"

Two of the Witches crouching in front of the Kingwitch bowed their beaks to the ground with pleasure and rose up into the air, Squeezjoos crying, "*No, please no!*"

"Where are they now?" said the Kingwitch.

The infesta-pests attacked again, and Squeezjoos had no chance of resisting. "I dids BITES him, the wicked Xar," said Squeezjoos when he could speak again, hoping to ingratiate himself and say what the Kingwitch wanted to hear. Do not blame poor Squeezjoos, dear reader. He was a very small creature facing an unfathomably great evil.

"Tell me EVERYTHING," said the Kingwitch. So Squeezjoos told him everything.

"Theys are coming this way...they wills be on the flying mine carts...they has the Cup of Second Chances...Sychorax and Encanzo is comings too...they is on a Rage-foal and they iss going to pretend to be part of the centaur herdsss to break in..." gabbled Squeezjoos.

his eight little legs quivering with terror.

"Viperion!" ordered the Kingwitch. "Go and tell the Droods and the Witches to look out for a Rage-foal among the herds of centaurs..."

The last great Witch bowed low before the Kingwitch.

"If the girl is stupid enough to let me out of this iron prison that binds me, you know that this pathetic little spell of theirs they are putting all their trust in *will not work*, don't you, Squeezjoos?" mocked the Kingwitch.

"No, no!" said poor Squeezjoos, putting his eight legs over his ears.

"And when I defeat the girl and take all her Magic," sneered the Kingwitch, "and I *will*...I will have NO MERCY.

"I will turn on these Droods who have been so stupid as to ally with me...I will kill them ALL...I will lay waste to these wildwoods until everything as far as the eye can see is poisoned, smoking rubble," swore the Kingwitch.

Staring into the ball of iron, Squeezjoos could see the full extent of the contained, boiling anger of the captured Kingwitch, and he knew that this was true.

"I need you to stay alive until they come," explained the Kingwitch. "For you are *bait*. But you will never get away again, Squeezjoos, do you hear me? Put your hands on this ball of iron, and know that you will never get away."

So
mesmerized,
bitten Squeezjoos
put his hands on
the ball of iron,
even though he knew
he would never be able
to take them off, unless his
master willed it so.
And there he stayed. And every
now and then when he came to
himself again he would think, *Don't
save me. I take it back. Don't come here, stay
away . . .*

12. On the Way to the Lake of the Lost

Meanwhile, still some way farther north, Xar and Wish and Bodkin and Perdita were making their way as fast as they could toward the Lake of the Lost, unaware of poor Squeezjoos's plight. But even without hearing the appalling speech that the Kingwitch had just made to Squeezjoos, they all knew how high the stakes were, and how close the world was to dreadful disaster.

The forest was full of noises: the shriek of sword against talon, the screams of frightened people and creatures as they fled the army of advancing Witches. Whole swathes of the wildwoods had already been burned to the ground. Great trees were torn up by the roots, half buried in the steadily falling snow. Many times the oaks seemed to have been deliberately defaced by Witch talons, their branches torn off and deep gouges scratched into their bark, and every time she saw this, little Bumbleboozle burst into tears, for she dearly loved the trees, and it was awful to see them targeted like this. What has a tree ever done to hurt anyone? A more innocent giant than a tree you could not possibly imagine. And Crusher looked very grave as he put his hands on each suffering tree trunk to heal it.

They were now deep in Drood Territory, and the

forest was thick with Witches. Bodkin's heart beat very quick as he saw them, and he could feel his palms sweating when he looked up to see them roosting in the treetops or flying in vast numbers in the skies up above.

Luckily, Perdita was a very powerful Enchanter, so she was able to conceal them all by making the trees thicken and become impenetrable jungle if they passed too close to a Drood hunting party or a Witch raid.

Perdita wouldn't let them fly on the back of the flying door, because she said that used up too much of Wish's magical energy, and Wish was going to need every single drop of that Magic in the battle to come. Which was a worrying reason, in a way, but it was such a relief not to have to fly it—Wish had been giving herself headaches with the effort of keeping it up in the air.

Perdita got Wish to disassemble the door and carry it in her bag. The door subsided in there with what sounded like a sigh of relief. "Now it just looks like a bundle of little wood chippings," worried Wish.

"Don't worry," Perdita assured Wish. "It won't forget its door shape when you need it. This will just give both of you a much-needed rest."

They were all cold, because of the extraordinarily freezing weather, so Perdita set her knitting needles going on their own, to knit them all sweaters. Therefore Perdita was followed by the *click-click-click* of the needles

knitting busily in the air as she tramped along. And as the day wore on, the weather grew colder and colder, and they were exceptionally grateful for the extra magical warmth that those sweaters gave them.

There *was* the slight problem that the knitting needles kept on knitting bits of other stuff into the sweaters, so not just wool, but bits of leaf, bits of twig and scarf and a part of her knapsack, and some of Wish's hair, so the sweaters could end up being a bit eccentric. Bits of wool. Hair of werewolf. Wish loved *hers* because it smelled of snowcat. Looter had a sweater that was rather smelly, because it seemed to have picked up some bog-boar fur in it. But he was so cold he wore it anyway.

At lunch, Perdita seemed to be able to create a delicious meal out of virtually nothing, even though she got a lot of it in her hair and muddled up the recipes.

They traveled on the backs of the snowcats and wolves, and as they went, Perdita ran through the rules of spellfights. She taught Wish how to transform into many things other than fluffbuttles, so that that wouldn't become Wish's default position. She had them spending

whole hours being a bear, a falcon, a wolf, concentrating on the fiercer animals, hoping that experiencing life as these creatures might give Wish a more combative attitude.

All of them had their favorite animals to turn into. Perdita turned Bodkin into a wolf, because he was not naturally a ferocious character and it gave him license to growl and snarl. While Wish appreciated life as a bear,

because being a very small, skinny, twiglike little person, she really felt the cold, so it was a delight to have a couple of hours wrapped up in the cozy warmth of her own fur coat.

What Xar particularly enjoyed was being a falcon, because of the extraordinary freedom it gave him. Flying on the back of doors or mining carts is wonderful, of course, but you do not know liberty until you have flown on your own wings. The lack of restraint was intoxicating—with wings, Xar could move anywhere, up as far as the cloud tops, swooping down gloriously to the sea of green that was the wildwoods.

By the evening, they knew they were getting very close to their destination, for they came across the herds of migrating centaurs, who had Drood permission to travel across the Lake of the Lost while the ice was thick.

"Oh, how beautiful they are!" breathed Wish, as the centaurs galloped past them all, long hair flying behind them, the snow deep on their backs, for these creatures had been traveling many a weary mile and many a weary day from the north in constant snowfall.

They could hear, in the distance, the sound of thousands and thousands of centaur hooves beating against the ice as they crossed the Lake of the Lost. The centaurs took no notice of Xar and Wish and their party, for they were completely concentrating on their migration south before deepest winter began.

"Not much longer to the lake, now," hooted Hoola. Hoola had completed her mission to make sure all the children released from the Mine of Happiness were safely on their way back to their parents, so she had rejoined the little party.

But even though they were very nearly there, Xar kept on nagging Perdita to do some weather spells to make the last hour or so easier for them all, for he was fed up of the constant battle with the wind and the snow.

"Interfering with the weather is one of those things you should only do in an emergency, Xar," explained

Perdita, all through the day. "It has unforeseen effects. There are some forces so large and so complicated that you have to respect them and not tamper with them unless you are absolutely forced to. We're nearly there, anyway."

But Xar's own natural disobedience and the will of the Witch-stain hand drove him to try and do some weather spelling of his own.

The results were, predictably, disastrous.

When they all stopped for the next rest, Xar stole one of Perdita's Magic staffs and loitered at the back of the group where he hoped he would not be noticed, searching the Spelling Book for spells for calming the weather. He found what he thought was a really good one.

But he had no sooner pointed Perdita's staff upward, unfortunately using both of his hands, and chanted the words of the weather spell than there was the most almighty crack of thunder as if the whole snowy heavens were opening.

Wish had never seen anything like it. She didn't even know it was *possible* for there to be thunderstorms at the same time as snowing blizzards and drenching rain—it was truly extraordinary.

They didn't even try and travel through this appalling tempest. They just set up camp where they were and tried not to expire with the cold of it. They shivered in the snow, and they fretted about the battle they would face in the morning. Xar was thinking, *Will I be good enough?* Bodkin was worrying, *Will I be brave enough?* and Wish was wondering, *Will I be strong enough?*

Until eventually, the blizzard blew so madly that all three of them crept under Perdita's great thick cloak, as she stood, defiant, in the tempest. They stood on her warm furry feet, so that the cold could not creep into their bodies. And they slept fitfully, standing up, while the wild winds screamed around them, drawing strength from the bear-wizard's intransigence and her obstinate refusal to bow before the storm.

The snow-wind-thunderstorm lasted for another twenty-four hours.

When the weather finally got back to normal again, they could see that all the time they had been camping just a few hundred yards away from the very outermost edges of the actual Lake of the Lost. Now that the fog and the wind and the snow had cleared, they could see that the atmosphere in the wildwoods around them had turned very grim indeed.

It was the silence that was so awful.

A truly ghastly silence.

Where had all the centaurs gone?

Nothing could normally dissuade the centaurs from the focus of their migration quest. But there was not a single centaur in sight, not a solitary sound of a hoofbeat on the pin-sharp cold air.

And laid over that silence came a sound that turned Perdita absolutely white.

Drumming.

Drum drum drum.

Drum drum drum.

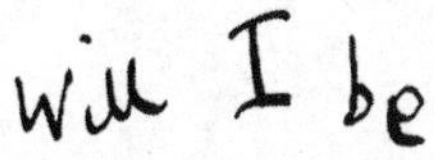

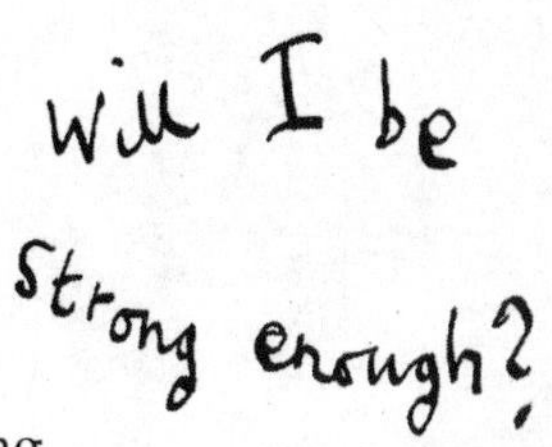

"What…is…that?" breathed Bodkin, taking out his lance in one shaking hand.

"That is the sound of the Droods," said Perdita grimly, "…about to put some poor soul to death."

You will be good enough. You will be brave enough. You will be strong enough.

Part Two

The Lake of the Lost

Drood High Command a

t the Lake of the Lost

13. The Trial of Love

I am afraid to tell you, but I must, that those drums were sounding for Encanzo and Queen Sychorax.

The two monarchs had arrived at Drood High Command a whole twenty-four hours before their children.

Wish and Xar and their party were held back by the snow-wind-thunderstorm. But Sychorax and Encanzo arrived at the edge of the Lake of the Lost before that extraordinary event happened.

The Rage-foal ran like wildfires were chasing it through the forest, threading through the trees like a needle through silk, Encanzo and Sychorax arguing with each other all the way, until they joined the herds of centaurs galloping toward the icy shores of the Lake of the Lost.

The Lake of the Lost is not really a lake at all.

It is a gigantic and confusing mosaic of marshes and islands and water and reeds, out of which the Droods can appear as if from nowhere and ambush any intruders. In summertime, the Droods stalk through their watery home on stilts, like gigantic waterbirds, their cloaks billowing out behind them, enticing attackers to follow and then leading them into quick-bogs that swallow them up.

Whole regiments of Warriors and Wizards have disappeared under those muds. The dark sludge closes over them with a revolting belch, and they are sucked under forever, a nasty, murky, sticky end. The only reminder that they were ever there is that the Droods like to fish their helmets out of the swallowing mud and stick them on the ends of poles as a pious warning to others.

But in winter, the entire area freezes over, and the ice was already three feet thick, and the hooves of the centaurs rang out as they crossed it.

Sychorax and Encanzo joined in the centaur migration, ceasing their argument and bending low over the Rage-foal's back, concealing themselves under Encanzo's cloak.

Under normal circumstances, they would have escaped detection.

But Squeezjoos had been unable to be quite as strong as he longed to be, and he had told the Kingwitch exactly how Encanzo and Sychorax were going to be attempting to break into Drood Territory. So the Kingwitch had told his Witches and his Drood allies to be on the lookout for a Rage-foal hidden in the throng of migrating centaurs.

The Droods do not travel on stilts in the winter. They travel on skates. So the first sound that told

Sychorax and Encanzo they might be being followed was the cruel

swish!

swish!

swish!

of skates on ice.

The Rage-foal gave a whine of terror. He could not turn back, even if he wanted to, for there were centaurs crowding around, galloping, relentless, behind, to the right, in front, to the left.

The mists came and shifted, bewildering, treacherous.

The call of will-o'-the-wisps was hauntingly scary, even to adults like Sychorax and Encanzo. "Come with u-sssss…stay here with ussss…"

And then forms flittered through the mist lightly, fleetly.

Swish! Swish! Swish!

There was only one magical being that was capable of moving across the ice in that silvery fashion.

"Oh for Thor's sake," said Encanzo. If he had had a heart, it would have skipped a beat. "*Droods.* We're being followed by Droods. How did they know we were here?"

They heard the curses first, whispered like the whispers of a will-o'-the-wisp, but way more horrible.

And then suddenly, swiftly, out of the mist, the

Droods surrounded them, shooting magical bolts that halted the Rage-foal.

The Chief Drood, Incorruptor, was leading the hunting party.

He peered down through his hood at the trembling Rage-foal and its riders.

"A Wizard. A Warrior..." Now he put his hood back as if unable to believe his eyes. "Bound together with *iron,*" he ended thoughtfully.

"Now what in the name of the great green gods could be going on here? No wonder the Witches were concerned. Thank goodness they warned us."

Sychorax and Encanzo were pulled from the Rage-foal's back and dragged across the ice after the skating Droods, like two sacks of cabbage. Not very dignified for these reigning monarchs.

And the drums Perdita and Wish and Xar were hearing, were drumming for Encanzo and Sychorax, who were being tried in the amphitheater at Drood High Command, and who were now in the most dreadful danger.

For nobody leaves a trial such as this alive.

For the Droods were severe where justice was concerned. "If people were not guilty, why would they be being tried in the first place?" was the Drood way of thinking.

Beside the ranks and ranks of Droods sitting on the ascending steps of the amphitheater, lurked the folded wings of Witch after Witch.

And right at the top, one truly enormous Witch was cradling in his talons the longest Wizard staff ever seen, the Great Staff of Power that had been guarded by the Nuckalavee for so many years.*

Confirming this point was the still, dreadful presence of the Kingwitch himself, locked in a great ball of iron, right behind Incorruptor, the leader of the entire Drood world.

In front of Incorruptor stood Sychorax and Encanzo, chained together at the wrists, standing tall and straight and defiant.

"May your vengeance be sharp, gods!" cried Incorruptor, holding up his arms and addressing the heavens. "For this is no ordinary trial and no ordinary crime. If the two defendants here, a Wizard king and a Warrior queen are found guilty they shall be put to death"—he turned to the watching audience with a snarl of contempt—"for they are accused of the most appalling transgression of all...

"...they are in *LOVE*," sneered Incorruptor with such distaste that it was as if the word were a slug in his mouth.

---

* This was the explanation for this new alliance between Droods and Witches. The Droods had lost control over their most precious magical objects, and they had fallen into the claws of the Witches. Therefore the Droods, ever practical, had sought to collaborate with the enemy rather than fight them.

There was a horrified intake of breath from the watching audience. "LOVE????? But it's not possible! Surely not? How can this be?" "A *Wizard king* love a *Warrior queen?* No wonder the gods are angered," the Droods whispered to one another.

"How plead you, Sychorax and Encanzo?" barked Incorruptor.

Sychorax sniffed contemptuously. "I plead not guilty. I would not love this worm of a Wizard if he were the last man alive in the wildwoods."

"HA!" snorted Encanzo. "I would rather be licked to death by vermy-sprites than be in love with this werefox of a woman!"

And they both jolly well seemed to mean it.

"Why, then, are you chained together in this indecent manner?" said Incorruptor in outrage.

"You think we handcuffed ourselves together *on purpose*?" said Sychorax sarcastically. "I was taking King Encanzo as my prisoner to the Mine of Happiness to work there as my slave, and we were ambushed by enemy Warriors who handcuffed us together..."

"Lies!" roared Encanzo. "*I* was taking Queen Sychorax as *my* prisoner to the great prison of Gormincrag, and *that* is where we were ambushed by these so-called enemy Warriors..."

"You could never take me prisoner! I am way too tough!" yelled Queen Sychorax, completely losing her temper. "I bet you are better at *knitting* than you are at sword fighting!"

"Typical!" sneered Encanzo. "You Warriors have this *obsession* with physical violence... Can't you see that knitting is a more positive and practical skill than chopping people's heads off or are you too busy burning down forests to think straight?"

"IT WAS YOU WHO THOUGHT IT WAS SUCH A GREAT IDEA TO SNEAK IN AMONG THE HERDS OF CENTAURS!" bellowed Queen Sychorax at the top of her lungs, so cross that her golden pear-drop of a voice had turned into a foghorn. "HOW IS THAT IDEA LOOKING *NOW*, BIRDBRAIN?"

Incorruptor was a little baffled. The prisoners were

The Drood Incorruptor
You are accused
of being
IN LOVE!

doing a very good job of looking like they weren't in love at all.

But it was his job to make sure they were found guilty, so he was going to make sure that happened, come what may.

"I call my first witness!" cried Incorruptor.

"This is all your fault!" hissed Queen Sychorax to Encanzo, as the crowd chattered together in excitement. "I TOLD you we should have turned left at the Forests of Forever! But *oh no*, you thought you knew best..."

"For the hundredth time, I was *steering the Rage-foal*!" spat King Encanzo. "*You* told me to turn left with no time to make the turning; I mean, it's very difficult to steer and listen to the directions at the same time, you should try it some time—"

"Will the guilty parties on trial COME TO ORDER?" said Incorruptor in astonishment.

People on trial in front of Drood High Command were normally in tears and on their knees begging for mercy at this point, not squabbling furiously between themselves.

"The first witness is Swivelli of Crookstree!" cried one of the Drood Guards.

Encanzo's old enemy Swivelli came sliming forward. Swivelli had wanted to be king of the Wizards for many, many years, and now he could see he had his chance.

"Your Droodly Highness," said Swivelli, bowing low to Incorruptor, and Incorruptor *loved* that. "I have been suspicious of Encanzo's softness and weakness toward the Warriors for years…and now we know Encanzo's weakness stems from his love for this woman, the forest-burner, Queen Sychorax."

"You should be ashamed of yourself, Swivelli. My so-called weakness toward the Warriors stems from the fact that *I* have not forgotten what we Wizards stand for," retorted King Encanzo proudly. "The Wizard way of life is about *creation*, not war and destruction. So how is it that you and the Drood Wizards are making friends with the *Witches*?"

"We have made a *temporary* alliance with the Witches because the real enemy are the *Warriors*," snapped Incorruptor, white with anger at this insolence. "In times of war, sometimes it is necessary to do morally bad things."

"Ah yes," said Encanzo, thoughtfully, "I've heard that one before. The ends justify the means. A fine outcome excuses a bad method..."

"...and it's all in pursuit of a higher good," finished Sychorax.

Sychorax and Encanzo were both thinking the same thing. *How far have we strayed from the place where we ought to be?*

The pursuit of their children had led them to places they had closed their eyes to. The Warrior extreme of the Mine of Happiness.

The Wizard extreme of the Droods at the Lake of the Lost.

A strange new thought was entering the parents' heads at the exact same time.

Maybe our children have been right all along.

Maybe Wizard and Warrior should be joining TOGETHER to fight the Witches, not each other...

"But it's not possible..." whispered Sychorax.

"It's against tradition," whispered Encanzo, as the two monarchs looked sideways at each other out of the corners of their eyes.

"I CALL MY SECOND WITNESS!" cried Incorruptor. "The Kingwitch himself!"

Incorruptor swept his arm theatrically backward, to the menacing metal ball that contained the Kingwitch.

He had been standing there so silently that they had almost forgotten he was there.

But when the Kingwitch opened his eyes and revealed himself in his full, imprisoned, raging horror, it was so petrifying that they all stepped back involuntarily.

Something rustled in front of the Kingwitch, something small and insignificant that was collapsed like a dropped rag in front of the ball of iron. But now the Kingwitch let this unimportant something release its eight hands from being stuck to the ball of iron so that it could play its part in the drama. It rustled and scuttled into life, and launched itself into the air, hissing and moaning, crawling with hopping little pests that were humming and biting around its twitching, screeching little flying body.

"I...speaksss...for...the...Chiwgink..." whispered the poor, tortured, little thing, eyes glowing that ghastly, nauseous neon yellow.

"What...is...*that?*" whispered Sychorax in horrified revulsion.

Encanzo's voice had rarely been grimmer. "I am very much afraid," said Encanzo, "that it is my son's sprite Squeezjoos who has been turned to the dark side by these evil Witches."

"May the gods preserve us!" exclaimed Incorruptor, drawing his spelling staff. "Come no closer, spawn of evil!"

The Little-Creature-That-Was-Once-Squeezjoos hovered midair and narrowed his crafty little eyes. "You isss right. I...*bite*!"

Incorruptor kept his staff steady, and the Creature-That-Wasn't-Squeezjoos laughed a nasty little laugh and said, "I knowsss the story...I heards it myself, from the dying giant who belonged to the Wizard Pentaglion...they wasss in LOVE..." The not-Squeezjoos sneered and made little vomiting noises.

"WHO were in love? Point them out so that we can be sure of their guilt..." said Incorruptor.

"*They* wasss..." hissed not-Squeezjoos, pointing his wing at Encanzo and Sychorax. Incorruptor and the crowd gave a sigh of satisfaction.

"And they is *foolsssss*..." said not-Squeezjoos savagely, and now his eyes suddenly turned back into being his own desperate self again and tears ran down his little face, "becausssse...

"Because...

"Because..." gulped the little sprite, and the utter desolation in his voice was pitiful to listen to, "*love doess not exist*...

"There is no such thing as love. Wisssh and Xar left me...they dids not love me...they dids not come back to save me..."

"And who," said Incorruptor, "are Wish and Xar?"

Squeezjoos's eyes clouded over as he became not-Squeezjoos again. A deep growling began in his little furry chest, he drew back his lips in a snarl, and he spat out each word as if it were poison. "Wissh and Xar are my enemiesssss...and they are the punishment the gods sent Encanzo and Sychorax for their crime. The boy is cursssed with a Witch-stain...

"And the girl..."

The crowd leaned in to hear what Squeezjoos would say next.

But the Kingwitch spoke first.

In a voice that creaked with evil, but so loud and full of greedy longing it made them all jump.

"And the child that was born to Sychorax has *Magic-that-works-on-iron*!!!!!"

14. Guilty of the Crime of Love

Uproar in Drood High Command.

Incorruptor's eyes were alight with greed. "If we get hold of Magic-that-works-on-iron, we can finally fight back against the Warriors!" he said with excitement.

"And better than that," croaked the soaked-in-evil voice of the Kingwitch, "with the Great Staff of Power in our hands, I—I mean *we, of course, WE*—" (he corrected himself hurriedly) "will be invincible..."

Up above on the Steps of Judgment, the Witch holding the Great Staff of Power shook it in his right talon.

Great cheers shook Drood High Command, as the hooded Droods stamped their feet in appreciation of this plan.

Incorruptor turned to Sychorax.

"Bring us your child and we will pardon you freely," said Incorruptor. "A life for a life, her life for yours. You will have my Drood's Dreadful Promise on it, and a Drood's Dreadful Promise is as solemn and as binding as a Drood's Death Curse. I'll spit on it with my green tongue and the phlegm shall make it true."

"EWWW," said Squeezjoos, momentarily himself once more. "Yucky."

"Yes," agreed Queen Sychorax, with distaste. "How thoroughly barbaric."

Now.

The trial of love had taken a slightly different turn.

It was no longer just a trial of Sychorax's love for Encanzo.

This was a trial of her love for *Wish.*

Queen Sychorax had shown herself to be a little lacking in the mother-love department so far what with one thing and another. She hadn't meant to be; it was just that Wish was a disappointment and a bit weird, and what with the whole embarrassing Cursed Magic and everything it was hard for her to feel as loving as she ought.

But when it came down to it, when she was put to the absolute test of it here on the heights of Drood High Command and being offered a life for a life and so on, it seemed...

...that Sychorax did love Wish after all.

"Never," said Queen Sychorax. "Never will I bring you my child."

Oh, Queen Sychorax.

Maybe heartless Queen Sychorax had a heart after all.

And it took a situation as bad as this one, to bring that heart out of her.

"Have it your own way." Incorruptor shrugged.

"In which case, we will see whether the child loves the mother as much as the mother loves the child.

"SILENCE for my judgment!" cried Incorruptor.

He held up his great spelling staff to the heavens, and as he spoke, the staff turned dark in his Drood Wizard hands.

Three times the Drood Incorruptor struck the blackened staff on the stone in front of him.

"Let it be proclaimed far and wide in these dominions..." cried the Drood Incorruptor. "Queen Sychorax and King Encanzo are proclaimed GUILTY of the crime of being a Wizard and a Warrior falling in love...they are sentenced to be put to death at two o'clock in the afternoon tomorrow!"

A great greedy sigh went around that amphitheater. The Droods stamped their feet and their staffs on the ground, chanting joyfully.

"UNLESS..." said Incorruptor, holding up a finger to quiet the crowd, "Queen Sychorax's daughter arrives to come and save them.

"SOUND THE DRUMS OF DEATH!!!" yelled Incorruptor.

"Wish and Xar will be close enough to hear those drums," said Encanzo, as the drums began their direful drumming.

"And Wish will come to save us if she knows we are

to be put to death," said Sychorax. "I brought her up all wrong. She has too much love in her, and as we both know, love is weakness."

"It is indeed," said Encanzo. "If Wish comes, the power of Magic-mixed-with-iron will fall into the talons of the Witches."

Queen Sychorax looked at King Encanzo. "Are you thinking what I'm thinking?"

"I believe I am. We could escape by jumping into the lake," said Encanzo. "But that would be impossible," he added.

"We've done impossible things before," said Sychorax. "Remember when we believed in impossible things? We can be young again, why not?"

"But we are no longer young, Sychorax," said Encanzo, very tired. "And we are both wearing an iron handcuff. Our Magic will not work. The iron will carry us down to the bed of the lake and that would be our grave," said Encanzo.

"We have hearts too strong for drowning," said Sychorax. "Tell you what, *I'll* save you, if *you* save me. We'll beat the waves, I know it..." And then she shot him a slightly teasing, affectionate look. "What, are you afraid?"

"Never!" cried Encanzo.

"And forever!" cried Sychorax.

And the two monarchs turned around and hand in hand they ran, stride for stride, to the edge of the grassy cliff at the limit of Drood High Command, with Incorruptor crying to his guards, "Noooo!! CATCH THEM!"

Too late.

Hand in hand, Sychorax and Encanzo threw themselves off the grassy cliff, crying at the tops of their voices:

"NEVER AND FOREVER!!!"

15. Never and Forever!

"NEVER AND FOREVER!" cried Sychorax and Encanzo, as they plummeted downward.

Bold and strong, they fell, absolutely sure that they would survive the drop and that they were too brave a force for the iron to drag them down.

And I do not know if I was *quite* as sure as they were.

Even in the summer, the plunge itself might be enough to kill them, for that grassy cliff they had leaped from was fifty foot tall. And they had forgotten that winter had come early and that the lake had frosted over, so the water below them was hard as bone.

But they had been monarchs all their lives, commanding, surviving, transcending all obstacles by their cunning and their Magic.

So I cannot tell you how joyous they were, how positive in their invulnerability to the laws of physics, crying, "NEVER AND FOREVER!" as they fell.

We will never know whether they were right in their belief that they were not born to drown.

Because as they dropped, *something* came skimming very low over the ice and snow of the Lake of the Lost, faster than it had ever moved before. The broken door of the Punishment Cupboard, with Wish and Xar and Bodkin on the back of it, screaming to the rescue.

A bolt of light from Wish's eye shot the handcuff apart as Sychorax and Encanzo fell. And Sychorax's and Encanzo's joy turned to fear as the door skimmed above them and on up to Drood High Command, for though they had been saved, they did not know they needed rescuing in the first place, and they were more worried about their children getting to their destination than they were about their own imminent deaths.

The door carried on, over their heads and up, up, up, traveling toward its inevitable confrontation with the Kingwitch.

"Sorry, Mother!" cried Wish as they passed.

Sychorax and Encanzo reached out their hands as if to try to clutch the door and catch it as they fell.

Which was never going to work.

Sychorax and Encanzo turn into diving gannets.

And it was as if that failure *finally* woke the two great monarchs up to the fact they were not entirely invulnerable.

Not only that, but also they were plunging toward the Lake of the Lost with such brutal speed it would be like slamming into a plate of metal.

"TRANSFORM!" yelled Queen Sychorax.

Without the iron around their wrists, both sovereigns could perform Magic.

In the blink of an eye, and in the needle-nick of time, they transformed.

Both into diving birds, and both, coincidentally, into gannets.

(Maybe it's not that much of a coincidence. What with one thing and another, I can't see either Sychorax or Encanzo as a *duck*.)

Down below, Crusher was

tramping through the Lake of the Lost, making great footprints in the ice. He was carrying the other companions, the snowcats, Perdita, the wolves, and Looter and his cronies in his pockets, because the door wasn't strong enough to carry everyone.

Sychorax and Encanzo just had time to fold back their brown-tipped wings, point their beaks, close the special membranes that protect a gannet's eyes when it dives, and enter the lake at a point where it had been broken with one of Crusher's footprints, like two white torpedoes.

"They're fine," said Wish in relief, watching the two little splashes down below that showed their parents diving into the water.

"*They're* fine," said Bodkin, "but what about us?" as the flying door screeched up to the top of the grassy cliff, and Wish paused it for a second. The door trembled in the air as the three heroes peered over the other side at the full horror of the amphitheater down below, the hooded Droods, the Witches, the circle of fire, the Kingwitch in his ball of iron right in the center of it like the pupil of an eye.

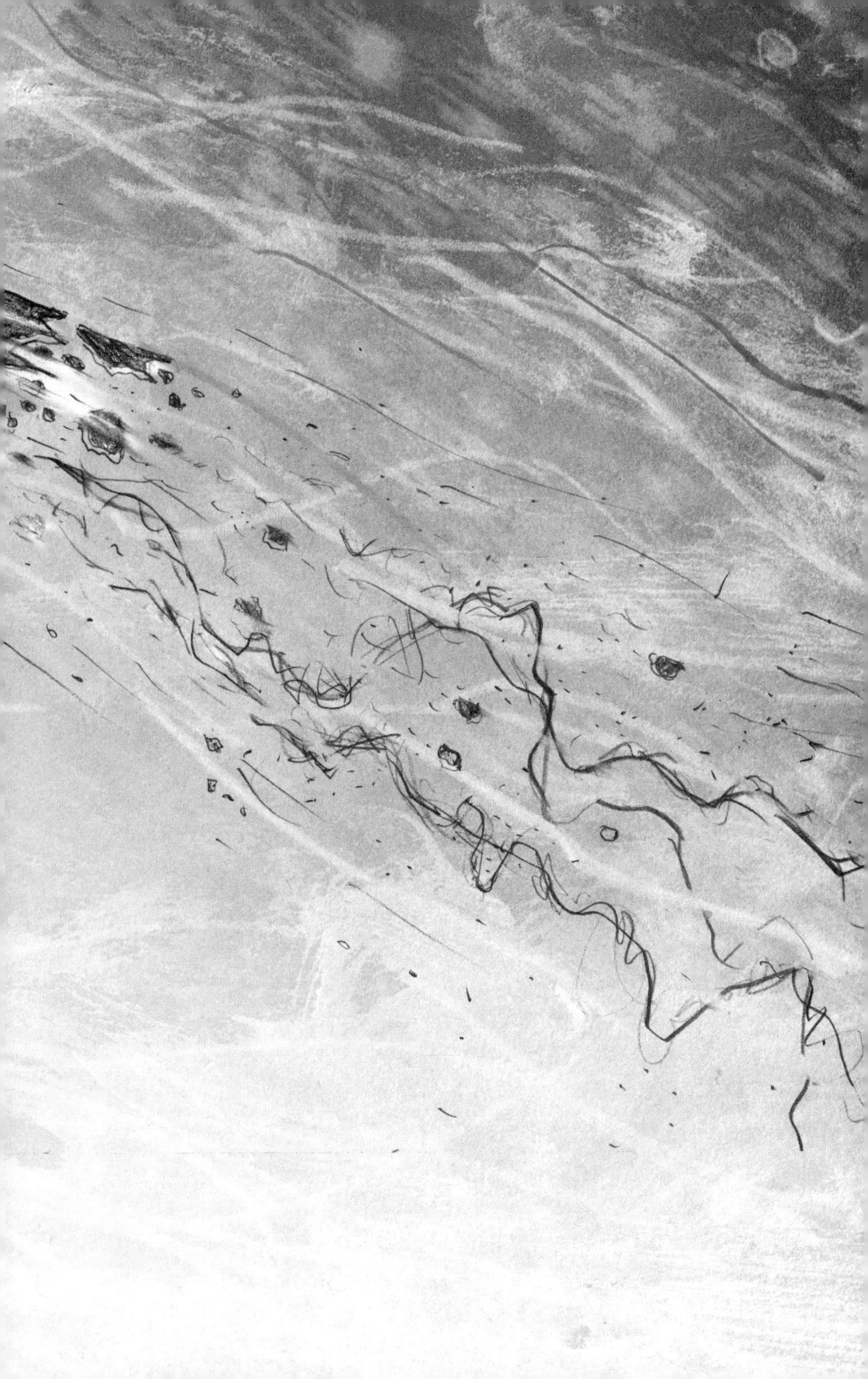

"*We*..." whispered Bumbleboozle, "izz in big trouble..."

"We're going in!" said Xar, eyes alight, and his hand with the Witch-stain on it grabbed the key from Wish's hand and steered it down in the keyhole so the door shot downward at crazy breakneck speed, followed by Caliburn losing feathers and the sprites streaming anxious Magic like the tails of fireworks.

"Be careful, young man!" warned the key, furious at being pushed so violently.

"Stop!!!" yelled Bodkin.

"I can't!" replied Xar, looking confused and scared for a second, for the arm with the Witch-stain really did feel out of his control now, and the door rocketed downward, scattering Droods in all directions as the Droods shouted and pointed upward.

And we have to follow them, as they shoot down to their—

I was going to say "DOOM" but that sounds a little negative.

Let's say "FATE," instead.

16. Is It Too Late For Squeezjoos?

The door hit the floor of the amphitheater with such force that it broke up on impact, its pieces scattering so that they could soften the blow and bits of it could land underneath all three children, who were catapulted off the back of it, somersaulting into the center of the circle of fire.

It didn't seem a very good omen for the final confrontation.

Xar and Wish and Bodkin could see the terrible eye of the Kingwitch glowing and blazing through that part of the ball that the Kingwitch had rubbed thin with a single tiny piece of blue dust that contained Magic-that-works-on-iron. It would take him many centuries to break out of his iron prison using only that single piece of blue dust. It would be like trying to drain the Lake of the Lost with a teaspoon.

No, the Kingwitch needed the rest of Wish.

And now he thought he had her.

"She's come..." whispered the Kingwitch, and there was no mistaking the triumph in the creaking, croaking, evil whisper-hiss of his voice. "Shee'sss *come*, at last, and now I can *finally* seize my inheritance after so many years of waiting curled up in the darkness..."

"Oh adder's fork and blindworm's sting," cried

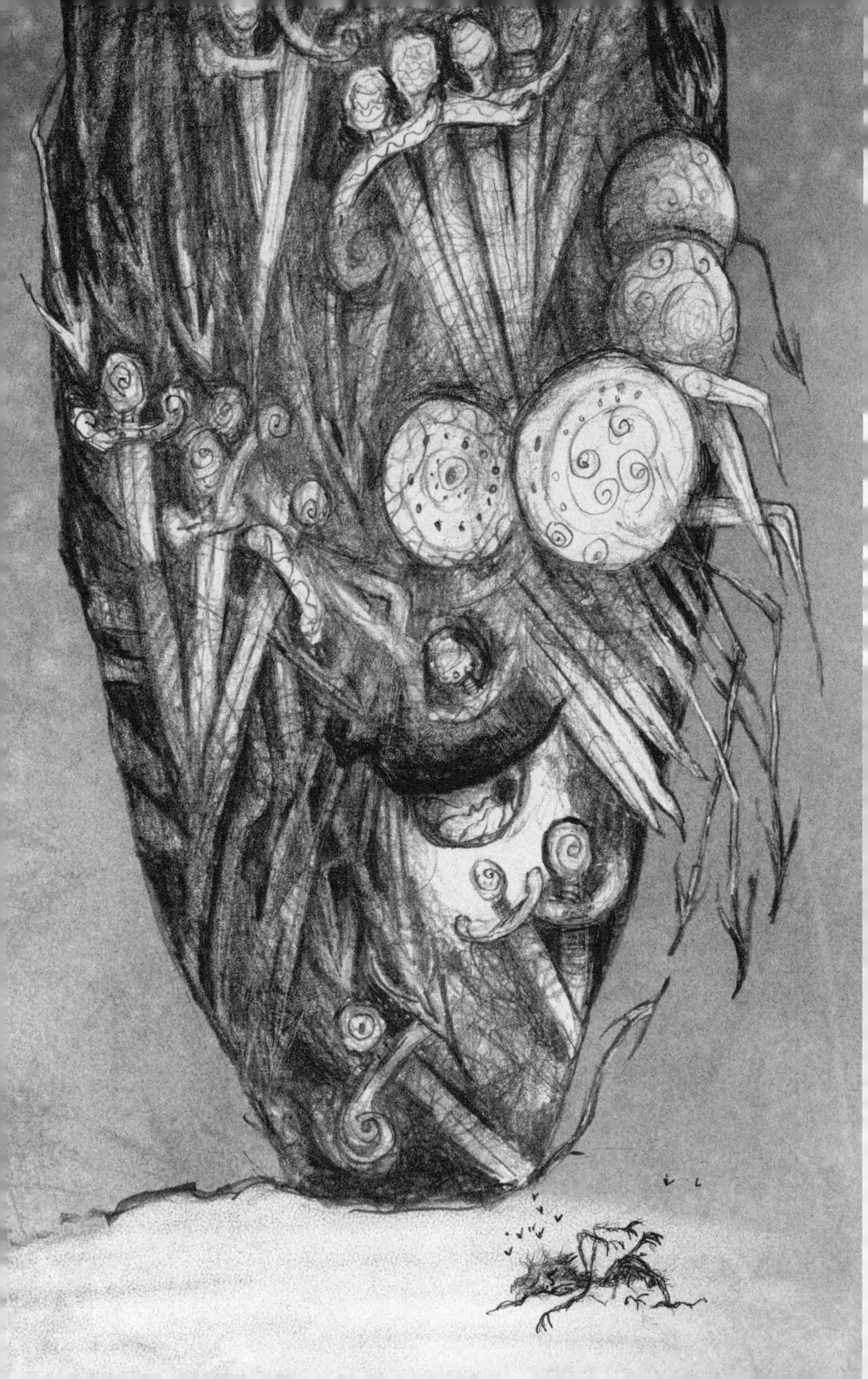

Caliburn. "Lizard's leg and flipping owlet's wing! They are waiting for us. We are expected."

A gigantic chalk circle was drawn in the center of the stage, and all around it a circle of fire. And right in the middle, quiet, menacing, was the ball of iron containing the Kingwitch. Beside him, arms crossed, was Incorruptor. Circles of stone seats, all filled with Droods, sitting there, hoods up, stock-still, ramrod straight. They had been waiting for the death of Sychorax and Encanzo. But now they had a better death in mind.

"But…but…but this can't be her!" spluttered Incorruptor, his eyes boggling. "This is an *unimport* of a child! A *scraggle* of a person…a *batsqueak* of a human being…*she* can't possibly be the person of destiny!…*The first Wizard ever known to have Magic-that-works-on-iron?* To be this child? Impossible!"

"But nonethelesssss," whispered the Kingwitch gloatingly. "She issss."

And hopping out of Wish's hair came the spoon, the key, the fork, the pins, and Incorruptor gave an exclamation of amazement, as he saw that these enchanted objects were, indeed, made out of iron.

Wish stepped forward. It was like having to step off the top of a cliff, her knees were trembling so much, but she made them do it, one after the other. "So, Kingwitch, I have come to take up your bargain," said Wish. "If you take away the Witch Magic that is poisoning Squeezjoos and Xar, I will meet you in a spellfight, single combat, you and me."

It was very, very quiet in the amphitheater, for everyone realized the importance of this moment.

Apart from the satisfied hissing of the Witches.

Hissssss...they hissed from all around, like a nest of waking serpents...*Hissssssssss*...and from inside the iron ball the Kingwitch hissed too, a hiss of affirmation that the time of the Witches had come at last.

"I take your bargain," hissed the Kingwitch, and there was no mistaking the satisfaction in his voice.

"Squeezjoos first," said Xar. "Where have you hidden my sprite, you evil-great-iron-covered-locust-hearted *weasel* of a Witch?"

"What is left of your miserable little sprite is here," croaked the Kingwitch.

Something in front of the Kingwitch that Wish and Xar had just thought was a bit of old crumpled leaf covered in flies, began to move.

It was Squeezjoos, so weak he could barely drag himself forward, and so far gone he did not even recognize them. "Enemiessss..." he whispered. "Enemiesssssssss..."

Xar gave a start when he realized this pathetic tangled mess of a creature crawling toward him was once his own beloved sprite Squeezjoos. White as a sheet, he exclaimed, "Squeezjoos! It is too late...oh please, please let it not be too late..."

Squeezjoos staggered forward a little more, before collapsing, face in the mud, infesta-pests buzzing madly, viciously biting his motionless form.

Wish's enchanted objects had given starts of horror when they saw Squeezjoos, and hidden in Wish's hair and her clothes, but Wish ran forward eagerly, saying, "No, no, it is not too late, do not say that, Xar!" and ignoring the danger, Wish picked him up. The little sprite was so out of it that he barely woke up as Wish held him. His shriveled voice could barely form the words "I iss with the Chiwgink..." He tried to bite Wish's finger, but his poor tiny fangs barely even had the strength to do that, just scraping the skin a little.

Too late to help, Crusher arrived, climbing over the edge of the clifftop, and he set Perdita and the others down, and she came running toward them, very harassed, trailing scarves.

"Can I just say that I am not WITH these people!" said Looter furiously, pointing at Xar and Wish and Perdita. "They kidnapped me, and they are traitors to the Wizard-and-Drood world!"

Everyone ignored him.

Tears were running down Xar's and Wish's cheeks as, frantically, Xar brushed off the infesta-pests, and Wish stroked Squeezjoos's fuzzy little head.

"Don't worry, Squeezjoos, we're here now, we're here," said Xar, in great distress. "I promised you we'd come, didn't I? This is all my fault…you followed me…you got the Witch-stain trying to protect me…you begged us to come earlier…"

It was now that Squeezjoos had his true hero moment.

Focusing all of the last remains of his energy, he lifted his little head up to Wish and Xar and whispered, feebly but with all the urgency that he could:

"No! Do not sssave me! The Kingwitch…he ssaid the spell would not work…he ssaid…if he got out of the iron…he would destroy the WHOLE WORLD...I's not worth the risk..." blurted Squeezjoos.

He tried to warn them.

How wonderful that something so small as the tiniest of hairy fairies—who had borne the dreadful stain of the Witch-stain for so terribly long and had been kneeling, eight hands stuck to the iron ball for nearly two days now—could yet withstand the force of the evil that was the Kingwitch!

But...

Squeezjoos was the world to Xar.

"*Take your horrible stinking Magic out of my wonderful sprite, you cowardly, repellent-viper-of-a-Witch-hiding-in-your-great-tin-can!*" yelled Xar fiercely. "But be gentle with him. If you do *anything* that hurts him permanently...if you have already hurt him so much that it really *is* too late...I will not let Wish fight you, I promise you that, for I don't care what happens to *me,* if Squeezjoos is lost."

"Ass you wissssh..." purred the Kingwitch.

So, with shaking hands, Wish held up Squeezjoos, and Xar picked up Squeezjoos's little barely there foot, and placed it gently on the great lump of iron that held the Kingwitch.

Please, please, let him live, wished Wish with all her heart. *Please.*

Please, please, please, please, PLEASE.

But as the whole world seemed to be holding its breath, and Wish and Xar and Bodkin muttered prayers to all the green gods to let him live…

…nothing happened.

Xar held the little foot steady, but Squeezjoos's rigid form remained hard as emerald, and the infesta-pests hummed and buzzed louder and more tauntingly.

Another minute passed, and it felt like a lifetime.

And as Wish wished and Bodkin prayed and Xar muttered, *Save him, save him, save him*…longing with all their hearts for this to work…

…Squeezjoos's tiny chest began ve-ry gently to beat up, down…

Up, down…

Up, down…

The dreadful green receded…His eyelids flickered and opened, and the infesta-pests fell off him, falling like scabs, dead to the ground, as if they needed the Witch Magic to feed on.

Oh, the relief of it.

"He's alive!" cried Xar joyfully. "Oh thank mistletoe and ivy, he's ALIVE!"

"Have you taken away every last DROP of Witch Magic, as you promised, Kingwitch?" said Wish fiercely. "NOT ONE PARTICLE remains, this time? Do you promise?"

"I swear, by the Witches' Code, that not one morsel, not one driblet, of my precious hemlock-velvet Magic is left in the sprite," said the Kingwitch. "What Magic he has left is his own."

Squeezjoos got himself onto his eight feet unsteadily on Wish's hand, like a baby calf getting to his feet for the very first time, staggering in an unsteady circle around Wish's palm. He looked up adoringly into Xar's eyes.

"My masster sssssaved me!" whispered Squeezjoos (which was unfair if you like, for this had been what is known as a

team effort, but now that he was back to his old self again, Squeezjoos was never going to give up hero-worshipping Xar). "I knewss he would...whats did I say...

"Xar isss the...

"best...

"master...

"in...

"the...

"world!"

On the word "world," Squeezjoos sprang into the air, and Xar said gleefully, "And he can still fly!"

The Kingwitch had been as good as his word, and very precise about removing absolutely all the Witch Magic that belonged to him, but leaving the little sprite's own Magic untouched.

They had reached him just in time. An hour later, maybe even half an hour, and the little sprite would have been dead. The dark Magic is too much for the smaller things of this world—they cannot take that level of hatred.

"I iss no longer with the Kingwitch!" crowed Squeezjoos. "I cannss thinks for myself!"

"Oh, Squeezjoos, that's wonderful!" cried Wish.

Squeezjoos landed on Xar's ear, and leaned his little head against Xar's and gave a deep, satisfied, blissful little sigh.

"I iss HOME," said Squeezjoos.

Sometimes home, you see, is not a place.

It is being with the person that you love.

Where *they* are, is home.

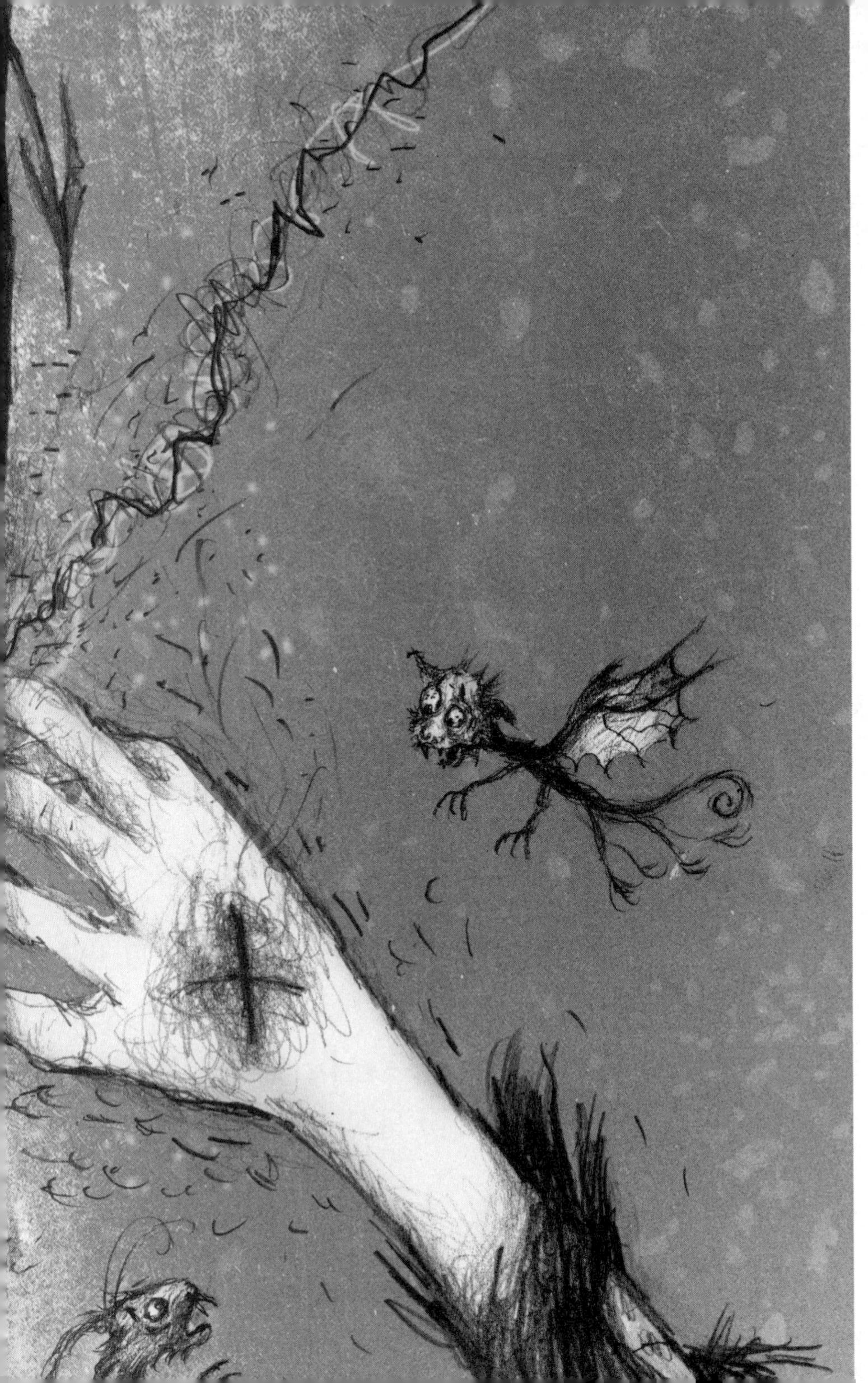

17. And Now... Is It Too Late for Xar?

"The sprite lives," said the Kingwitch. "But I should warn you, not everyone survives the little operation of having all their Magic removed...Step forward, boy with the stain on your hand, if you are willing to take the risk, and I will drain the Magic dry, if that is your will."

Xar gave a great sigh, for some bit of him did not want to get rid of the Witch Magic, even after all the trouble it had caused. Without the Magic, he would be just an ordinary Wizard boy with no Magic at all...the son of a great King Enchanter, who had no Magic of his own.

But he knew he had to do this now.

A year ago, Xar had put his hand on the Stone-That-Takes-Away-Magic, and he had taken it away too quickly, so the Witch Magic had stayed with him. He had to be sure not to do that again.

Xar put his hand on the ball of iron.

The Witch Magic had been building in Xar at such a rate, entwining around his nerve endings, curling into his blood vessels, soaking into the very marrow of his bones, that extracting it was agonizing. Xar let out yell after yell, soaked in sweat, boiling as if he were on fire, panicking, trying to get away, as the Magic was torn out of him, with Bodkin and Wish shouting, "Stop! Stop!" very distressed to see their friend in such pain.

Until eventually, the last little drop was pulled out, and there was a huge BANG! And Xar was catapulted backward off the ball of iron, across the grass on his back, like a rag doll, with Bodkin and Wish running after him.

"Is he all right? Is he all right?" begged Wish, in a frenzy of anxiety, for Xar was lying horribly still, arms thrown wide in a star shape, and Tiffinstorm, kneeling by his nostrils, could feel no breath of life coming out of him.

There were a dreadful couple of seconds with Xar unmoving...

...but like Squeezjoos, Xar was made of tough stuff, used as he was to a hard life out in the open air and resisting capture. His defiant nature meant that he had held on to his own self and life even with the Kingwitch probing into him and digging out the Witch Magic.

"He's fine," said Bodkin in relief, as Xar unsteadily got into a sitting position, and Bodkin held up Xar's arm, "and look, no Witch-stain!"

Sure enough, the ugly green mark that had been crawling up Xar's wrist, elbow, and had nearly reached his shoulder, was now entirely vanished. Even his hand was stain-free. The only whisper of a reminder that

any of this had ever happened was a very faint white scar of an X right in the center of his palm, already magically healed, as if it was only a memory of something that had happened a long time ago.

Xar came around, and the first thing he did, to his embarrassment, was burst into tears. It was very unlike Xar, but it was the shock of what had happened. He sobbed as if his heart would break, and then rubbed his nose defiantly with the sleeve of his left hand. (He couldn't move his right arm yet. It was completely numb, still, as if he had lost it entirely.)

He staggered to his feet. He had been living with the pain for such a lengthy time, it was a revelation to be rid of it. Not only was the torture of his arm, twitching, nagging him in the wrong direction, taken away, it was as if he could think clearly for the first time in so, so long, without the Witch-stain interfering and muddling him. He felt fragile, but peaceful.

Wish turned to the Kingwitch-in-iron. "Have you taken everything? Every last crumb of your horrible evil Witch Magic?"

"Of course," said the Witch. "Did I not swear on the Witches' Code?"

"Thank mistletoe and ivy and all things green." Xar grinned, punching the air. "Finally, I'm free!"

Bodkin and Wish hugged Xar, Perdita patted him on the back, Caliburn nibbled him on the ear in an affectionate and congratulatory way, and Squeezjoos did a couple of somersaults in the air.

Even *Looter* was secretly rather impressed with how brave Xar had been, and a niggly naggly doubt popped into his mind as to whether he himself would be able to give up such power if he owned it—but he had many a score still to settle with Xar, so he stifled that thought, by sneering, "How does it feel to be back to being what you always were, baby brother, a lunatic of a loser who HAS NO MAGIC...your little escapade hasn't really been worth it, has it? You're right where you were at the beginning!"

Xar's face fell.

"Oh, shut up, Looter!" snapped Bodkin.

"Now it is *your* turn to risk your life, girl with the Magic-that-works-on-iron," purred the Kingwitch. "I have kept *my* part of the bargain. It is time to keep *yours*. Release me from this ball of iron in which you so wickedly imprisoned me!"

A cold, cold feeling got hold of Bodkin's heart. You

see, Bodkin was not only Wish's bodyguard, he was also secretly in love. And he had a very nasty feeling about this.

"Xar and Squeezjoos are saved; maybe you don't have to do this," whispered Bodkin in a panic, into Wish's ear. "You heard what Squeezjoos said earlier...the WHOLE WORLD is at risk if the Kingwitch gets out of the ball of iron!"

"But I promised," said Wish, white as snow. "I cannot break a promise as large as that one. This whole disaster *started* with a broken promise. My mother broke her promise to Xar's father. You cannot *end* it by breaking another promise. And you can't run from Witches forever, Bodkin. Sometimes you have to face them."

"LET...ME...OUT!!!!" croaked the Kingwitch.

"Be careful," warned Caliburn, flapping down onto Wish's shoulder.

"Be UNBELIEVABLY careful," cautioned Perdita, creeping up next to the raven. She had turned herself into a mouse. "Oh dear oh dear oh dear...What you are about to do is exceptionally dangerous," she whispered, in a high, squeaky, mouselike voice. "Once the Magic is flowing between you and the Kingwitch, he will try and take all of it."

"No mice or ravens on the shoulder," spat the Kingwitch. "That was not part of the bargain. No help from powerful Enchantresses hidden inside the bodies of rodents..."

Caliburn flapped off, and the little mouse-that-was-Perdita scurried down Wish's arm.

Wish was alone...but she did have the spoon, the fork, the key, her pins, clustering protectively around her.

Wish put up her eyepatch.

She was going to need her Magic eye, full-strength for this.

Trembling, Wish knelt down beside the ball of iron. Just looking at it made her feel sick. She looked into the bitter depths of that great eye in the part of the ball of iron where her own blue-dust magic had worn it thin as a membrane, and could feel her heart running fast and quick like it was a panicking rabbit, because the Witch was so close now, it was almost as if she could touch him. She forced herself to put her shaking hands on that thin membrane between them.

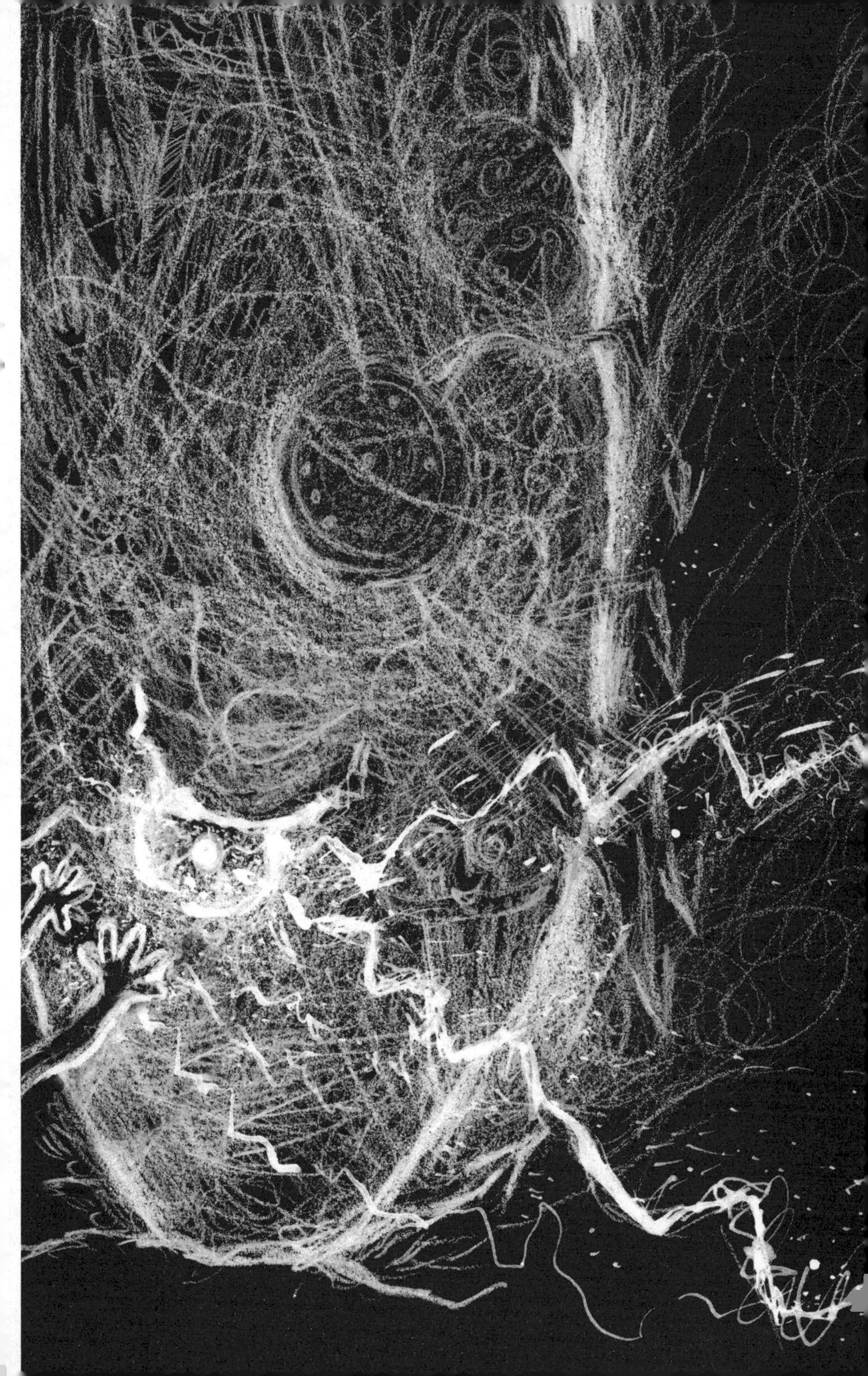

The effect was immediate.

Her hands were stuck to the membrane of the ball of iron and she could not pull them off.

The Kingwitch inside gave a greedy hiss of joy.

Wish's hair sprang up like an electrified hedge. There was the familiar sickening sucking sensation as her Magic was dragged out of her, even more strongly and violently than last time, because this time she was *letting* it happen.

So violent was the pull, the spoon and the pins and the fork and the key were slammed up against the membrane themselves as if by the force of a magnet, and they stuck there, wriggling, poor things.

"GIVEMEYOURMAGIC, GIVEMEYOURMAGIC, GIVEMEYOURMAGIC!" roared the terrible scream of the Kingwitch, roaring now in Wish's head.

Everyone watching gasped with astonishment and put their hands over their eyes.

For the ball of iron lit up like a burning star, the dark iron now entirely see-through, with the roads of bright Magic, a color that no one has ever seen before, so it is undescribable, unbearably brilliant, crossing from Wish to the Kingwitch like fizzing, miraculous, wandering paths through a dark green forest.

Wish could feel the numbing effect of the Witch's thoughts scrambling with her own and the dreadful struggle to retain her own independent judgment. For what the Kingwitch was offering was a great temptation.

Only she could hear the offer, coming to her not through her ears but her stuck hands.

"We would be all-powerful…stay with me…Together we would rule forever…All would bow down before us…"

DON'T GIVE HIM TOO MUCH…thought Wish. *BY THE GREEN GODS…Give him only enough Magic to break out of the iron…wait for the right moment…*

The ball of iron was rocking, beginning to crack like a great illuminated egg.

Steady…okay…the right moment is…

"NOW!" shouted Wish.

"FIGHT IT!" cried Caliburn.

"REJECT IT!" growled Perdita, who had turned back into a bear, to be more of a powerful background presence.

"GET ANGRY!" shouted Xar.

Think of Xar, defying his father, thought Wish. *Think of myself, of how I have learned to defy my mother. Think of Perdita, how strong she is. Think how strong I am, and own it.*

"EVERYONE DUCK!" roared Perdita.

The Droods dived onto the steps, and everyone flattened themselves on the grass.

Wish thought of Xar, defying his father. She thought of Perdita, as a bear.

And she turned her eye on the ball of iron to cut herself free.

BANNNNNNNGGGG!

The ball of iron exploded, sending spears and arrows and shields as screaming missiles in all directions. The Kingwitch did not care where they landed...

...but Wish did.

And such was her new-found control of her power that Wish had the presence of mind to control the explosion, making sure that each spear, each arrow, each molten fragment carried over the heads of the humans and the Witches, on and out of the amphitheater, and then fell into the Lake of the Lost, like dark rain.

Leaving the Kingwitch...

...FREE.

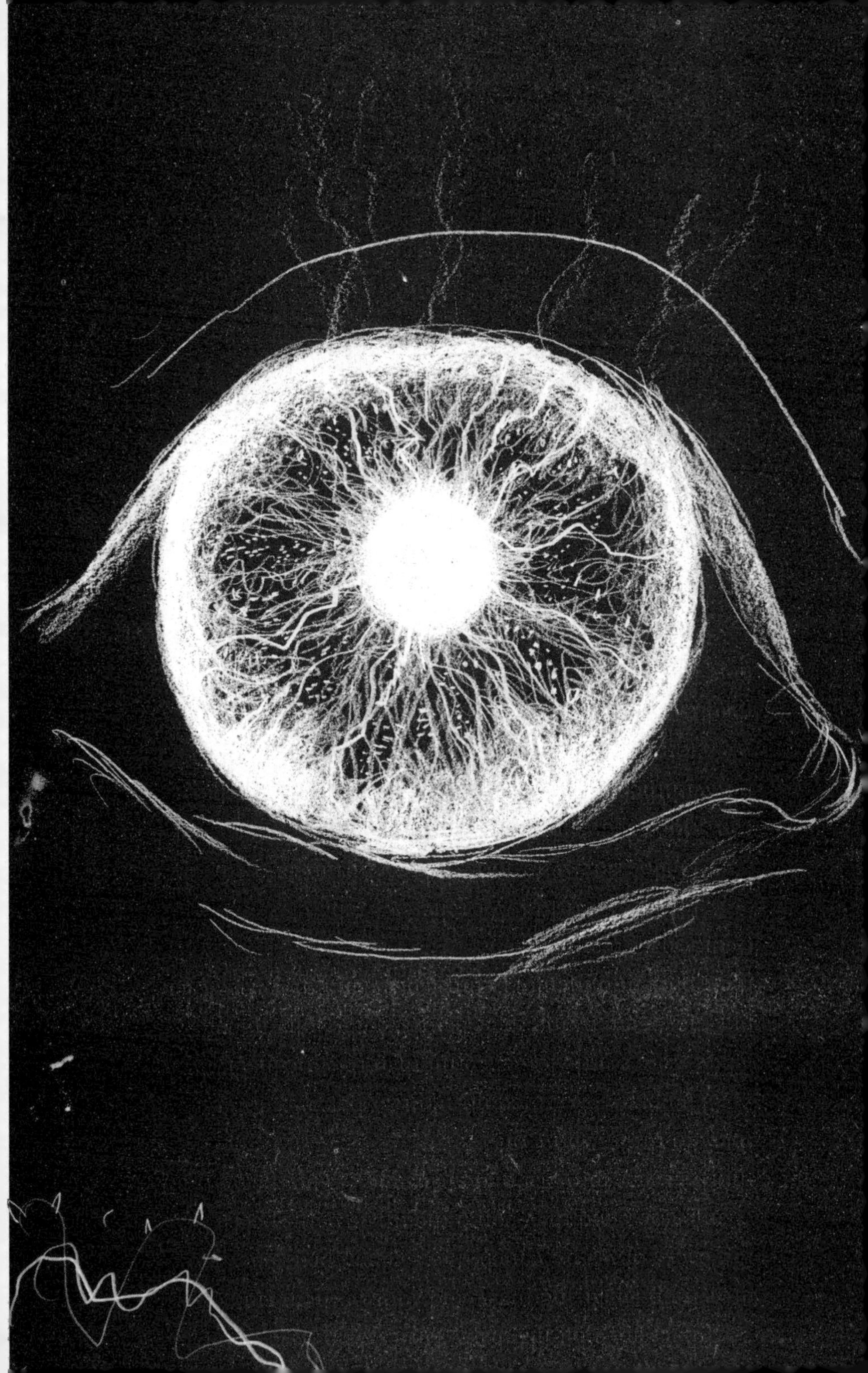

18. The Spellfight to End All Spellfights

"Murmuring mistletoe and frittering ivy and eye of newt and toe of frog," cursed the Drood Incorruptor. *"What have we done?"*

Unfortunately, only now when it was too late did the Drood leader realize exactly what a dreadful evil they had allowed into the Drood heartland. For the Drood Incorruptor had been given the same bargain that the Kingwitch had just offered Wish. And he had accepted it.

But a Kingwitch contained within the iron prison of a ball of iron is a very different proposition than a Kingwitch freed.

Power reeked from that feathered thing, as the Kingwitch opened his great dark wings to their full, dreadful extent, slowly unveiling them. Great black smoking drips fell from his hungry fangs. He threw back his terrible head and let out a dreadful scream to the heavens, a scream of no mercy and evil triumph, more dreadful than the screech of foxes torturing some poor animal, the death screech.

The Witches, sitting beside the Droods, hissed like kettles in satisfaction.

Then the Kingwitch turned his eyes, two wells of hate, gleaming with the sick glint of mercury in the bottom of them, on to Wish.

What have
we done?

"I swore on the Witches' Code, girl-who-has-Magic-that-works-on-iron, that we would fight each other in single combat," said the Kingwitch. "Just you and I. The winner takes on the loser's Magic," he said greedily, and his hate-eyes lit with the thought of it. "And then... *watch me torch the world to carbon*!

"Prepare the battle ring!"

Incorruptor came cringing forward, to draw the chalk circle. The Greencoats, a sprite species that worked for the Droods, gathered and spat out a little vomit, which turned into the fires of a spellfight circle.

There was no turning back now.

Sychorax and Encanzo finally arrived back on the scene.

The two monarchs had plunged to the bottom of the Lake of the Lost, so far and so fast that they hit the reeds at the bottom, and it took them a little while to shoot up out of the lake, reborn in the water. Up, up, they flew, their gannet heads with the splash of yellow on them shining as if they were crowns, as fast as they could, to try and help save the children they had put into this mess in the first place.

But Wish was already in the circle of fire.

Sychorax and Encanzo flew down, down, on their wide gannet wings, transforming back into humans as they landed next to Xar and Bodkin, and Looter.

"I TRIED to stop them from coming here, Father,"

said Looter piously. "I told them and I told them, but they would not listen to ME..."

For the first time in his pampered life, Encanzo snapped at his spoiled elder son.

"Oh, *will* you shut up, Looter? For once, this is not about *you*, and your brother and his friend are doing their *best*!"

Looter was amazed not to be the center of attention in his father's eyes.

But all eyes were fixed on the girl and the Witch standing in the gently falling snow.

One small girl.

One gigantic, terrifying Kingwitch with no boundaries, no mercy.

The parents were helpless now. Perdita, Caliburn, Xar, Bodkin, no one could help Wish. She was on her own.

"Name your weapon," hissed the Kingwitch.

Wish drew the Enchanted Sword. It made a satisfying, comforting *swish* as she drew it, and even the act of drawing it brought back a memory of when Xar had illegally drawn the sword in his battle against Looter.

"I name the Enchanted Sword as my weapon," said Wish. The sunlight glittered on the part of the blade where the writing now blazed bright and clear, *Once there were Wishes*...and on the other side...*but I killed them*.

"Don't worry, Father and Queen Sychorax,"

whispered Xar confidently to Encanzo and Sychorax. "That sword is dipped in the spell to get rid of Witches. The Kingwitch hasn't got a chance."

"Very good," purred the Kingwitch. "I choose as *my* weapon...the Great Staff of Power!"

Up on one of the highest steps of the grassy amphitheater, the Witch who had been cradling the Great Staff of Power rose to his feet. The Drood who wielded that staff would traditionally have been wearing stilts so that he or she was tall enough to use it.

But the Kingwitch was three times as big as a normal human being. He could handle the staff without any need for stilts. The Kingwitch put one taloned hand in the air, and the two Witches threw the staff at him, and when he caught it, the staff fitted his hand as if it had been made for him.

"And now," said the Kingwitch, pointing his beak at Wish, "for me to get the rest of your Magic. With this staff and your power, we Witches will be INVINCIBLE..."

The watching Witches cried out dreadful screams of glee.

"Oh dear, oh dear, oh dear," worried Bodkin, "I hope that spell to get rid of Witches works, because if it doesn't, I get a very bad feeling about this spellfight..."

"Is Wish any good at these things?" asked Encanzo.

"She's *terrible* at spellfighting," said Bodkin anxiously.

"Now, that's not quite fair," said Perdita, turned back into her human form, the rose-colored glasses jamming themselves rather desperately onto her nose. "She's not so bad; I have taught her everything I know."

At that, the horn on Xar's back made a very rude raspberry noise. PARRPPP!

"All right, not quite everything," admitted Perdita. "But she's still ready, I think."

The horn on Xar's back disagreed even more strongly with that PARRPPP!

"I am *trying* to look on the bright side," said Perdita in exasperation.

There was a short, sharp humming noise and a force field of Magic leaped over Wish and the Kingwitch, in a thin, see-through dome, hissing with power.

The small girl holding the sword and the great Witch holding the Great Staff of Power circled each other warily.

Wish's Magic eye was burning bright.

Human eyes do not change color. They are not the pure unnatural distillation of green one minute, as bright as a yellow star the next. They are fixed, bound by the laws of nature.

A Magic eye is an entirely different proposition. It changes color like the sea before a storm…and—this is weirder still—it can even turn into a color that does not exist in the human world.

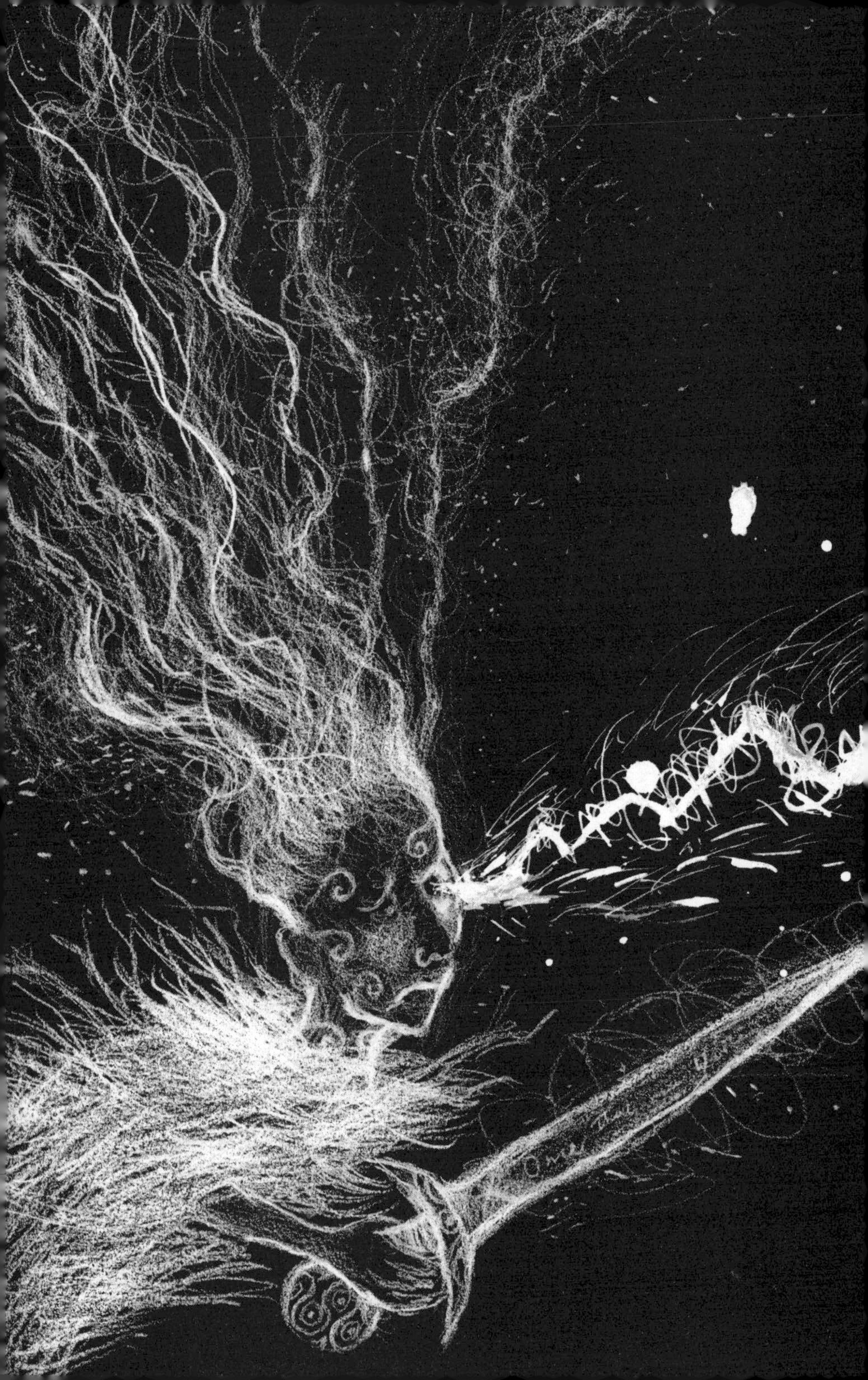

All around the eye was a strange purple bruise, a violet shadow, as if the human flesh surrounding it found the eye a burden to carry.

"Start the battle!" cried Swivelli, bringing down his white-cloaked arm.

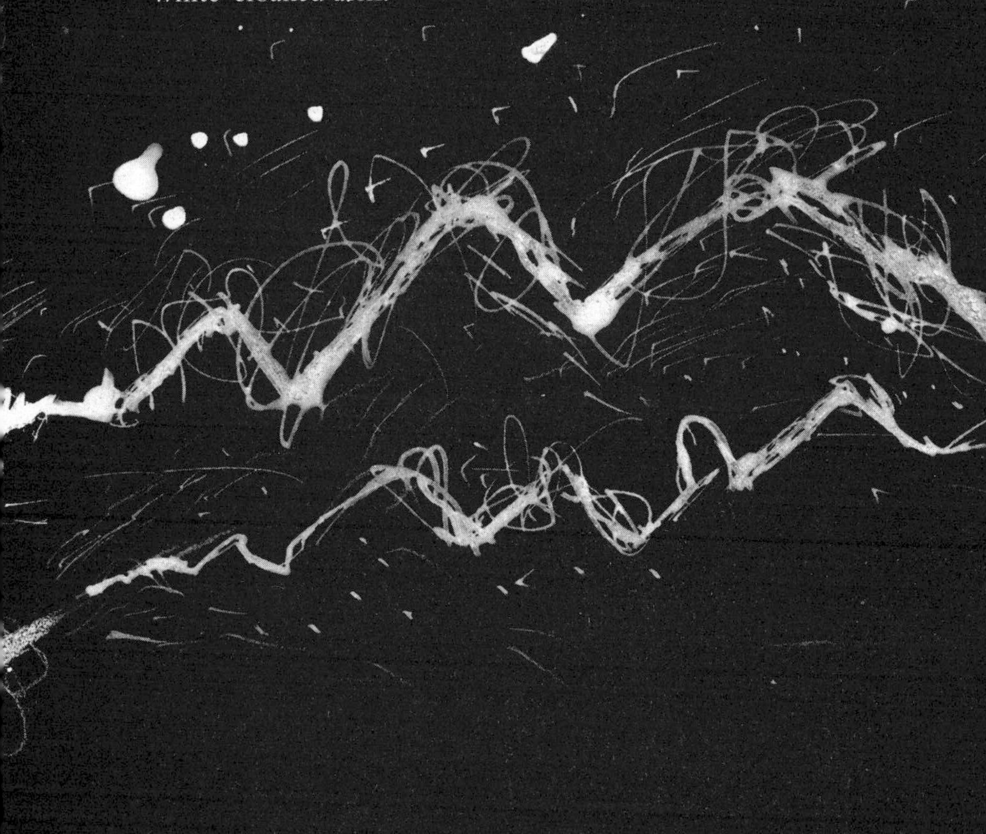

He had barely finished the word before the dome containing the Witch and Wish exploded with noise, and such brilliant jagged fire bolts of Magic that it was punctured this way, that way, like a star, as Wish used the Enchanted Sword to deflect bolt after bolt of Magic that the Kingwitch sent screeching toward her.

"All those sword-fighting lessons did come in useful," said Sychorax with satisfaction. Which was only partly true, for the sword came to life like a freshly caught salmon in Wish's hand, seeming to have a life of its own, anticipating where the next Magic fire bolt might come from and dragging Wish with it.

The point came that Wish had been waiting for.

The Kingwitch mistimed his thrust. For one millisecond his chest was exposed toward her.

This was the moment.

They had been planning this for months. Bodkin had been teaching her with his best bodyguard training.

Wish tried to remember that she was a Warrior, descended from generation after generation of Witch-killers.

She focused her eye and her hand together, and the sword exploded out of her fingers like it had been shot from a bow, and straight at the Kingwitch's heart.

"ONCE THERE WERE WITCHES!" shouted Wish, as fiercely as she could. *"BUT I KILLED THEM!"*

The Kingwitch looked down, almost comically, in surprise, at the sword sticking out of his chest.

Bodkin had his eyes shut.

"Please…let the spell work…" whispered Bodkin to himself and up to the sky. "Please, good universe…let the spell work. Please, stars in the sky…let the spell work. Let the good in the world defeat the bad…

"just…

"this…

"ONCE."

But it appeared that this time, the universe was not listening.

And the stars in the sky were deaf to Bodkin's plea.

The Kingwitch looked down at his chest, and whispered, "A Kingwitch has TWO hearts, girl with Magic-that-works-on iron…"

The Kingwitch reached down and took the sword out of his chest, and when he took it out, the wound automatically closed about itself, and the Kingwitch's chest was just as whole and unbroken as it had been a minute before. "Two hearts, and many lives. This merest scratch has healed itself already—see how my heart missed a beat, but is pumping again." The Kingwitch's two hearts lit up helpfully within his chest to show Wish how vigorous they were.

The Kingwitch turned the ancient sword around in his hand.

"A ytterp elttil yot..." he whispered, "but Magic-that-works-on-iron no longer has any fear for me. The sword has not only lost its Witch-killing power, but I have enough of your special Magic now even to use the sword for myself..." and quick as a weasel the Kingwitch threw the sword with all his might toward Wish.

Witches are phenomenally strong, and for a minute, the Enchanted Sword did not seem to care anymore that Wish was supposed to be its owner. The sword sliced through the air at head-height, and it looked like it might even have gone for Wish if she had not automatically ducked. (Wish had six older stepsisters so she was used to ducking.)

The Enchanted Sword carried on traveling over her head, before Wish regained control of it, and the sword remembered who it was, and who was its real owner, and returned to its rightful place in her hand.

Wish gulped as she straightened. She had turned white as the few remaining white bits on her shirt. Caliburn lost twenty-five feathers on the spot. They dripped from him like black rain, poor bird.

Things were not going according to plan.

"You think I did not see your plan?" jeered the Kingwitch. "The eyes of the Kingwitch are everywhere. You have dipped that sword in five ingredients," he sneered. "Tenderness, desire, courage, endurance, forgiveness: This is a LOVE SPELL."

Now he threw back his head and laughed, and it was almost as unpleasant a sound as his death screech, because there was so much triumph in it.

"There is no such thing as a spell to get rid of Witches," sneered the Kingwitch. "That is just *wishing*... and all the wishing in the world will not get rid of us. The spell you have just hit me with is the Spell to Undo Love Denied...

"What use is THAT? It's a love spell. You didn't even know what you were doing...the spell was written in the raven's feather because he wanted to repair the past, he knew he should never have intervened in the love between your parents. Wish fulfillment on his part. And YOU wrote it, girl whose Magic-works-on-iron, because you thought you could make your parents love again, you little fool..." said the Kingwitch. "Wish fulfillment on your part.

"How AMUSING!" crowed the Kingwitch. "You've braved the Nuckalavee...you've brought down the wrath of the Droods...and you've come up with the WRONG SPELL..."

"I said so," said Sychorax sadly.

"And I," said Encanzo.

"You should have listened to your parents," hissed

the Kingwitch gleefully. "At least they are worthy opponents of mine. Children are so foolish, believing in impossible things all the time.

"A poxy little *love spell* will not work on ME, weird little girl, especially if it has my own Witch feathers in it," scoffed the Kingwitch. "How can *I* love again? I have never loved ONCE, let alone TWICE...did nobody ever tell you that *love is weakness*?"

"Yes," said Wish wearily, "yes, I've been told that before."

All the excitement of drawing the sword had gone. She was feeling very, very sick, her stomach heaving as if she was standing on a deck above a greasily undulating sea. The world had turned underneath her, and she knew she had taken too large a risk. All that bold talk about not breaking promises...oh, why had this beastly curse of power been given to HER? She did not want it...she had never wanted it. The responsibility of it was too much.

"Eye of newt and toe of beastly frittering frog!" cursed Caliburn. "Destiny has led us up the garden path again! It's the wrong kind of star-cross! It's the universe in one of its trickiest moods! It's fate having a VERY BAD DAY INDEED!"

All that they had striven for, so courageously, in getting the ingredients, in finding the cup, in making the spell, all, all for nothing.

They had failed.

And when all that you have done comes to nothing, what do you do?

Do you give up and accept the fate of the story?

Or do you shake back your shoulders, as Wish did now, and look back at the Kingwitch with all your defiance and your obstinacy, and try another way?

Time for Plan B.

She turned around.

Behind her was a great flat stone. I'm afraid it might have been the stone where the Droods made their human sacrifices. I don't know, hopefully not, but it may have been, the Droods were not very nice, what with one thing and another.

Wish made an X in the stone with the point of the sword.

"X marks the spot," said Wish.

And then with all her strength and all the power of Magic that she had, she drove the sword hard into the middle of the stone, so that it was buried there, nearly up to the hilt.

No one would be able to get that sword out again in a hurry, for it had been dipped in a very powerful love spell, not to mention the blood of a Kingwitch, and driven into the stone with all the force of Wish's extraordinary Magic, at the crossing of two sword points. Even Wish *herself* might struggle to draw the sword now.

That surprised the Kingwitch.

His jaw, already unhinged so that he could swallow her whole, now dropped a little farther.

"Why would you do that?" said the Kingwitch. "Now you have no weapon. Just because *you* give up your sword does not mean that *I* will give up the Great Staff of Power. A Witch is not squeamish about an unequal battle."

"You said you had more than one life, Witch!" said

Wish. "Well, *so do I.* Let's see how many lives you have left..."

The Kingwitch shot great blasts of Magic at her, but Wish had disappeared.

"Where is she?" snarled the Kingwitch, whirling around. "You're not allowed invisibility in a spellfight..."

But Wish had transformed...

...into a fluffbuttle.

A fluffbuttle, as its name suggests, was not a particularly scary creature. Slightly smaller than a bunny rabbit, it had so many natural predators that it was in danger of extinction in the wildwoods.

But as it happens, on this particular occasion, a fluffbuttle wasn't a bad choice of something to turn into. The Witch wasn't expecting that, he was looking for something larger and more scary, and as the Kingwitch swirled around, the sheer length of the Great Staff of Power getting in his way but shooting off Magic out of the end of it randomly, Wish-as-a-fluffbuttle hopped silently through his legs, unnoticed, and attacked the Kingwitch from behind.

Strange clouds of power formed in the eye of the fluffbuttle, the eye that was that extraordinary color that you cannot describe. The little creature's hair blew up like a puffball, and the Magic screamed out of the eye of the Wish-fluffbuttle so forcefully you could see the

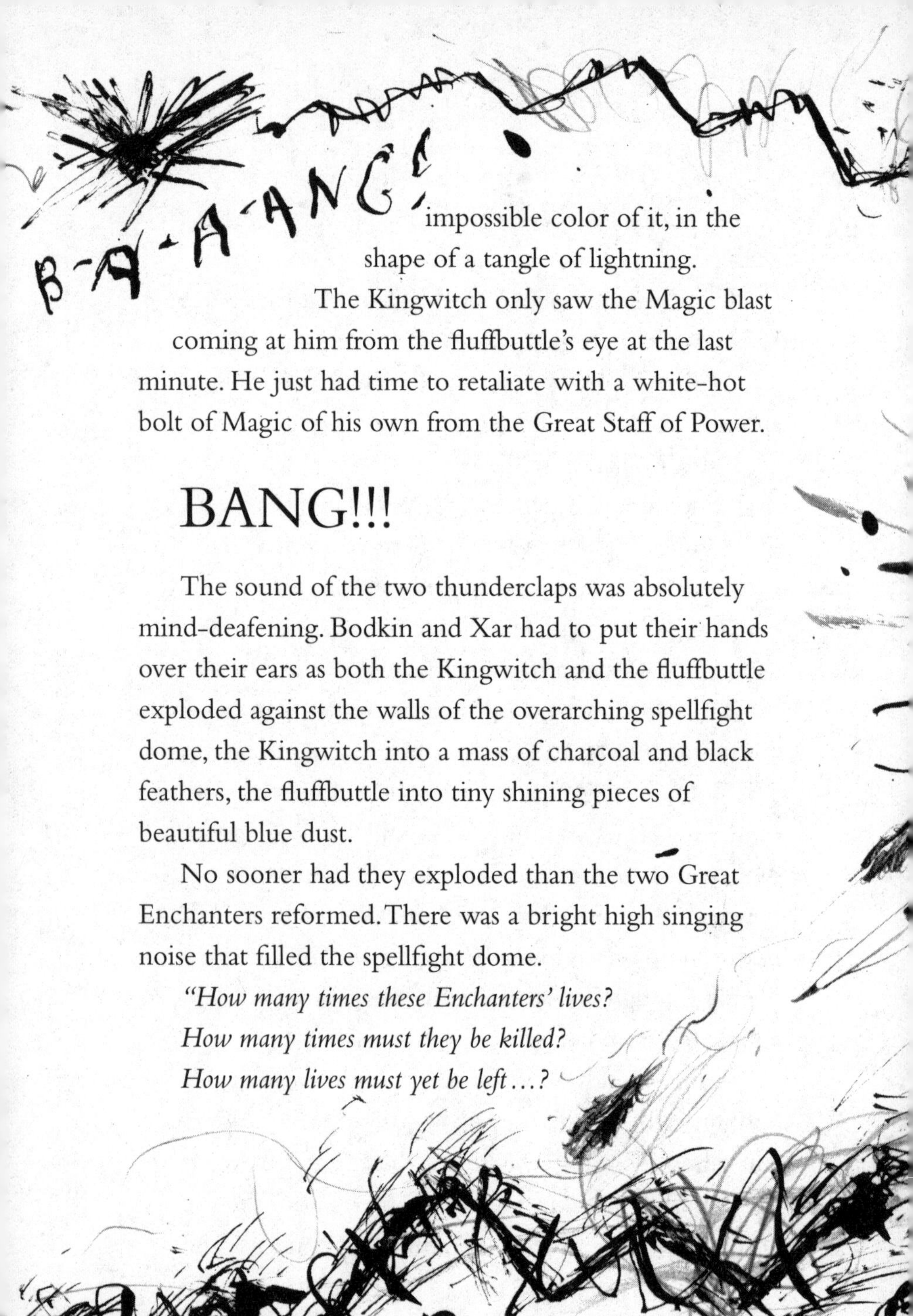

impossible color of it, in the shape of a tangle of lightning.

The Kingwitch only saw the Magic blast coming at him from the fluffbuttle's eye at the last minute. He just had time to retaliate with a white-hot bolt of Magic of his own from the Great Staff of Power.

BANG!!!

The sound of the two thunderclaps was absolutely mind-deafening. Bodkin and Xar had to put their hands over their ears as both the Kingwitch and the fluffbuttle exploded against the walls of the overarching spellfight dome, the Kingwitch into a mass of charcoal and black feathers, the fluffbuttle into tiny shining pieces of beautiful blue dust.

No sooner had they exploded than the two Great Enchanters reformed. There was a bright high singing noise that filled the spellfight dome.

"How many times these Enchanters' lives?
How many times must they be killed?
How many lives must yet be left . . . ?

Risk it all…
Risk it all…
Risk it all…"

The fragments of blue dust and the feathers and the charcoal lifted into the air like tiny little swarms of bees, whizzing and shuffling and reshuffling themselves, as if they had some internal memory of where they ought to be, extracting and disentangling each from the other. There was a moment of chaos, before the little dusty fragments began to build up the jigsaw puzzle of the Kingwitch on the left-hand side, Wish on the right, and they had barely settled into their new forms before

BANG!!!!

The two Enchanters, Kingwitch and Wish, blasted Magic at each other again. The explosion was even louder this time, and so forceful that it sent the fragments punching the spellfight dome into an exploding crystal shape, like a giant snowflake.

"What are they doing?" whispered Bodkin, ears ringing with the noise of it.

"It's an explosion battle to the death," said Perdita grimly and sadly.

"As great Enchanters, both the Kingwitch and Wish have more than one life, but no one knows exactly

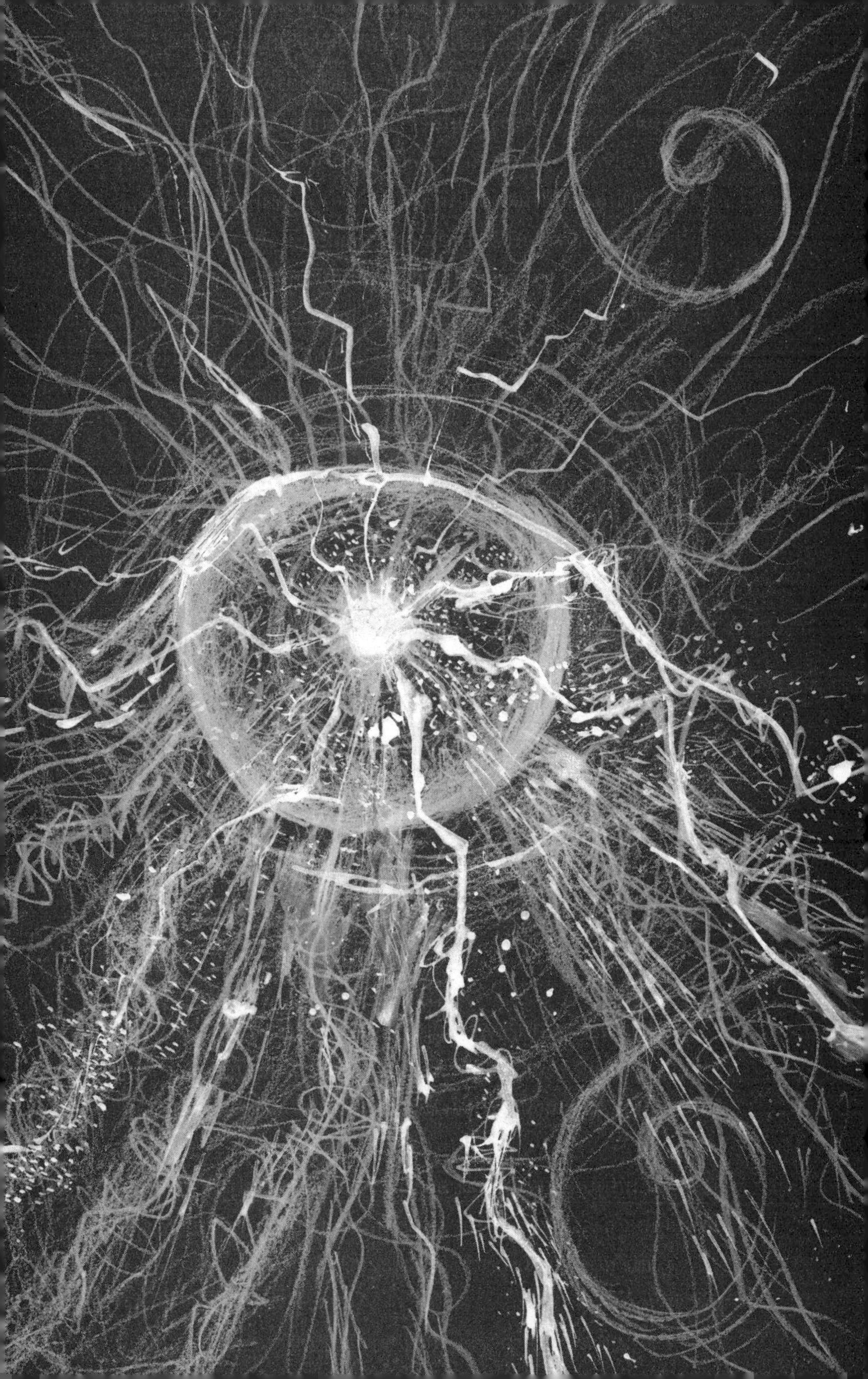

how many, so at any point this could be their last. It's a question of who can outlast the other. It's astonishingly brave, but also ... what a waste."

The Droods, the Witches, Perdita, Caliburn, all, were so mesmerized and focused on the battle in front of them that they had not noticed what was going on outside the center of Drood High Command.

They had not observed the trembling of the ground underneath their feet, shaking as if the earth itself were turning into sea, the waves forming on the Lake of the Lost, like water trembling in a glass. Or if they had, they mistook its cause for being the spellfight in front of them.

Until a warning Drood cry from without alerted them all.

"GIANTS AND WIZARDS ARE ATTACKING FROM THE LEFT-HAND SIDE!!!"

And then a few seconds later, "IRON WARRIORS ARE ATTACKING FROM THE RIGHT!!!"

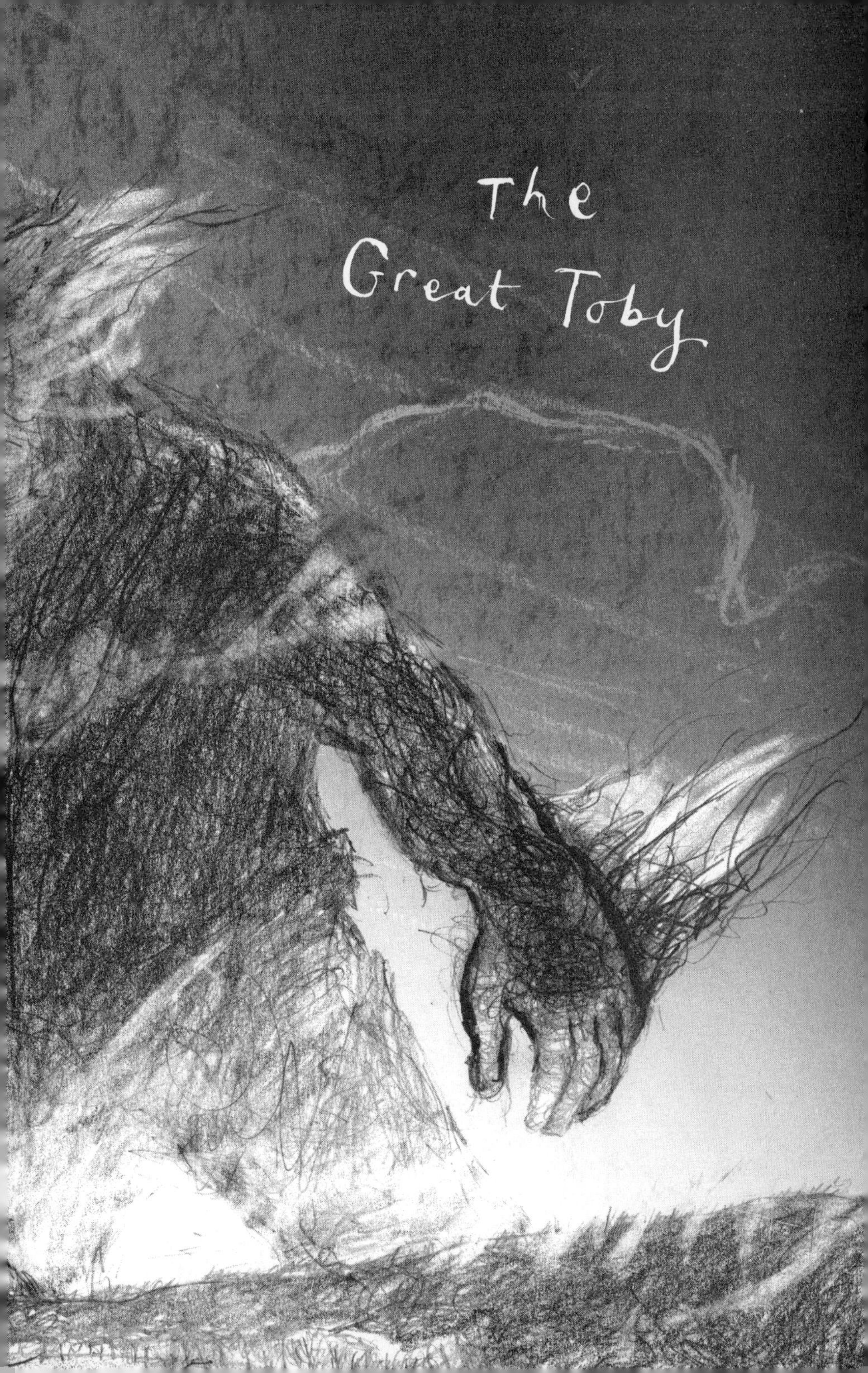
The
Great Toby

The two forces of Queen Sychorax's iron Warriors and King Encanzo's Wizards had taken the unprecedented step of invading the Drood stronghold of the Lake of the Lost, because of their monarchs being held under capture there.

And this would normally have been a suicidal quest, for the Droods had held that stronghold for many thousands of years.

But the Droods were taken by surprise.

And the iron Warriors and the Wizards had been joined by some unexpected allies.

GREATER GIANTS.

"They've joined us," said Perdita in relief. "I hoped they would, I thought I had persuaded them, but you never know with giants."

Perdita's boots had taken her on a quest to the western isles in between this and the last adventure. Out to the Giants' Footsteps, the series of islands that were said to be made once upon a time by the greatest giant of all, Worldshaker himself, many millennia before. The Greater Giants had been

wandering west along the Giants' Footsteps for a while now. And I am not talking, now, of the smaller kind of giant, like Crusher. These were the REALLY BIG guys, the Starcrossers, the Atlasroamers, the Profounders, huge mountains of people, who waded out into the great Atlantic Ocean as if they were crossing a river.

It was hard to tell if they were fleeing the incoming of the Warriors.

Magic as large as that is difficult to beat, even with iron swords, so the Greater Giants should not really have had much to fear from the pinpricks of Warrior weapons. Perhaps they went a-wandering looking for a quieter place to think, for like Longstepper High-Walkers, the Greater Giants thought deep thoughts and needed peace to consider them.

Whatever the reason, they had abandoned the wildwoods when the Magic creatures needed them most. I am not quite sure what Perdita had said to persuade them to set aside their lofty disinterest, their dreaming abstraction, and reenter the fray at this critical moment. It is thought that the Greater Giants had no love for Witches. Maybe it was that.

The Greater Giants, walking that way, treading carefully like elephants trying not to stomp on a mouse, were led by a Thunderstride Tobunder, known simply as "Toby," or "the Great Toby," if you wanted to be more respectful.

So then battle reigned in the stronghold of the Lake of the Lost.

And in the center of the amphitheater, the explosions of the two Great Enchanters got louder and louder, bigger and bigger, more and more frenzied and frantic until the dome that should have kept their battle confined was in imminent danger of being broken.

So, on the outside, there was the lightning of Drood Magic, the ring of iron sword on Drood staff, the scream of attacking Witches, as the Warriors, the Wizards, and the Greater Giants joined forces against the Droods and the Witches.

A personal battle, and a wider one, taking place at the same time.

Queen Sychorax and King Encanzo were fighting against the Witches back to back, as synchronized as if they really were still linked together with some invisible iron handcuff.

She really does still have an extremely pretty nose, thought King Encanzo as Queen Sychorax dispatched a particularly unpleasant Witch with a superb sword thrust.

Lives were lost on both sides.

War is not a pretty thing, or something to enter into lightly.

But Toby was quite a benevolent fighter—you can

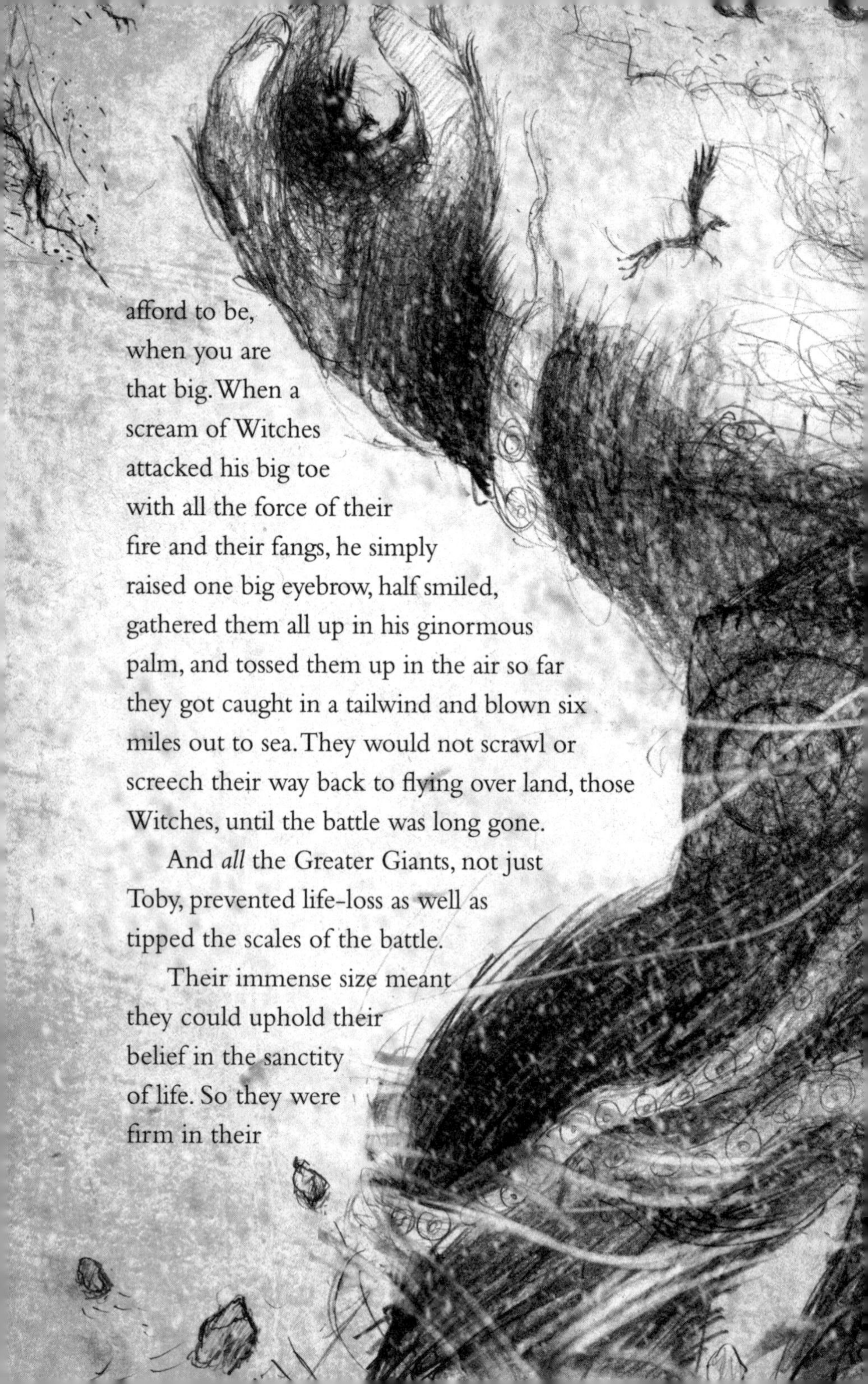

afford to be, when you are that big. When a scream of Witches attacked his big toe with all the force of their fire and their fangs, he simply raised one big eyebrow, half smiled, gathered them all up in his ginormous palm, and tossed them up in the air so far they got caught in a tailwind and blown six miles out to sea. They would not scrawl or screech their way back to flying over land, those Witches, until the battle was long gone.

And *all* the Greater Giants, not just Toby, prevented life-loss as well as tipped the scales of the battle.

Their immense size meant they could uphold their belief in the sanctity of life. So they were firm in their

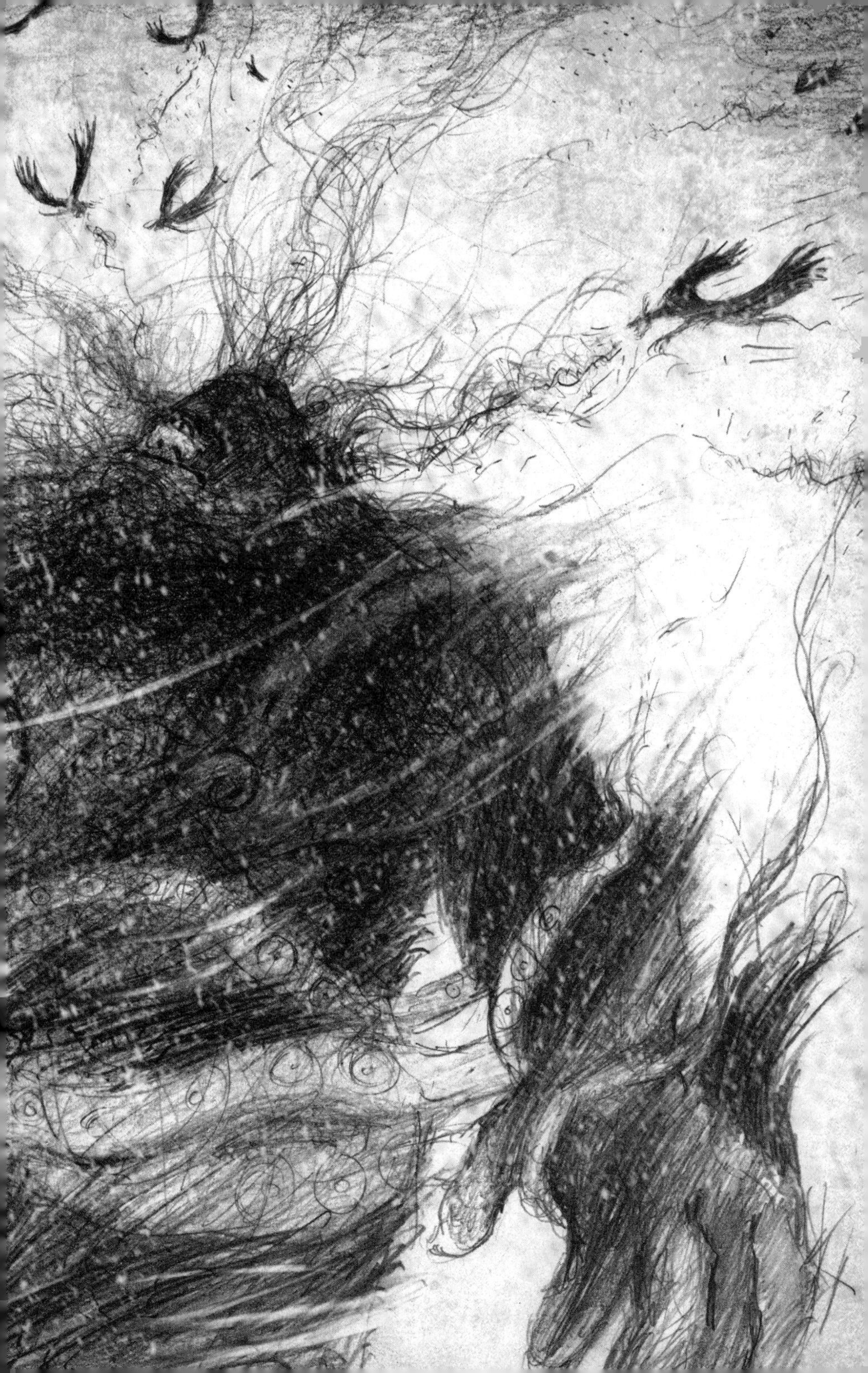

handling of the Witches, gathering them up, and flinging them gently far from the battlefield, confident the Witches' wings would carry them safe. And they were

mild in their treatment of the Droods, picking them up as softly as if they were tiny insects, delicately removing their staffs and their stilts, and putting them in trees.

Bodkin fought a heroic battle. He had lost his sword. And now he picked up a staff from a fallen Drood, and although he could not make the staff do Magic, he had a clever idea of how he could use it instead. Climbing on his snowcat, he charged Drood after Drood with the staff held out in front of him, knocking them over one after the other.*

* Bodkin did not know it, but he had just invented a new weapon called "the lance," which had never been used in battle before.

Looter even played his part. He had traveled all this way, sneering at his brother, furious at the attention Xar was getting, giving them all excellent advice that they had completely ignored. But his father's snapped-out words had shaken him out of his usual sense of satisfaction with himself. He had been expecting praise for trying to stop disaster, and instead he had been told off, and it made him see things differently.

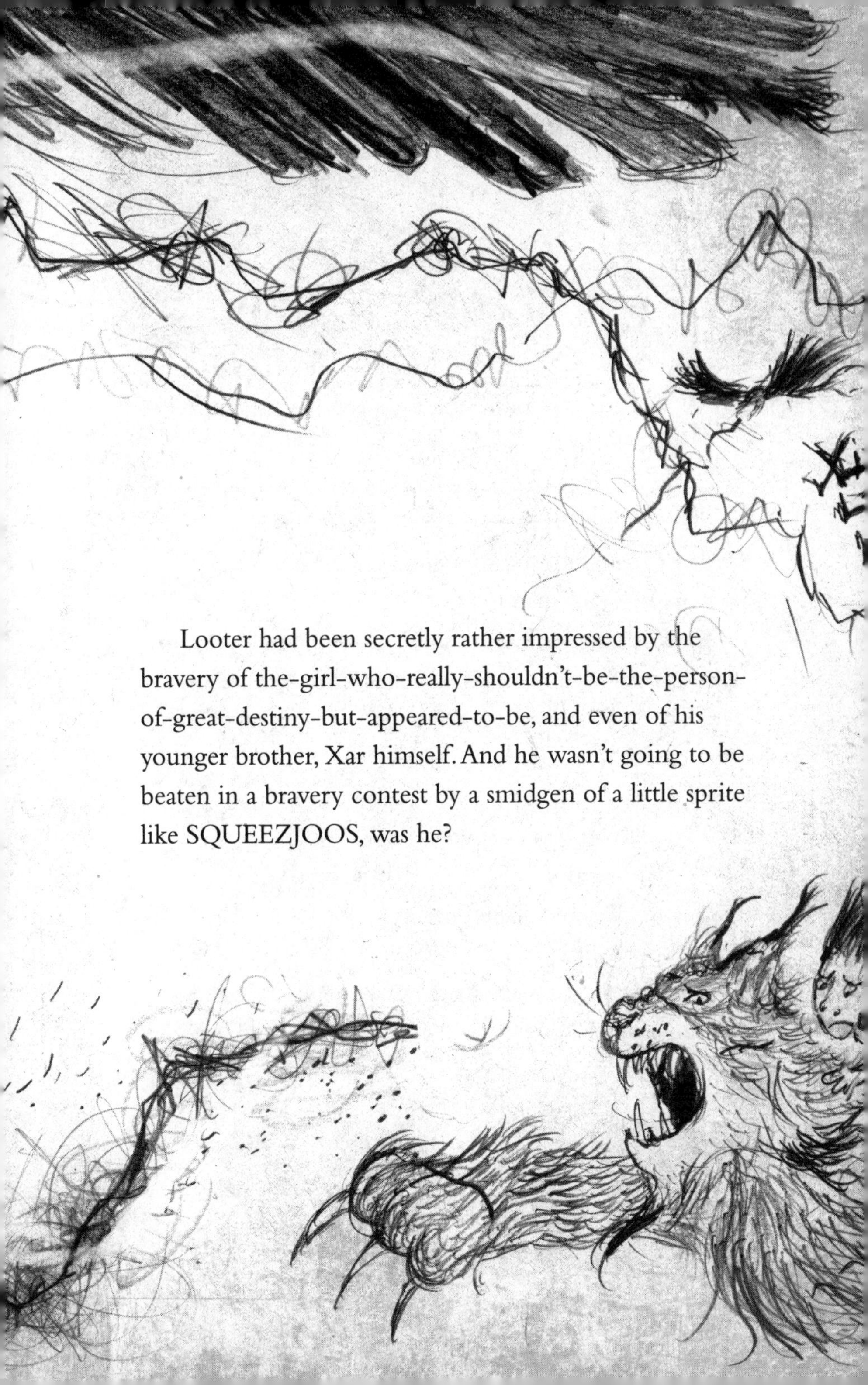

Looter had been secretly rather impressed by the bravery of the-girl-who-really-shouldn't-be-the-person-of-great-destiny-but-appeared-to-be, and even of his younger brother, Xar himself. And he wasn't going to be beaten in a bravery contest by a smidgen of a little sprite like SQUEEZJOOS, was he?

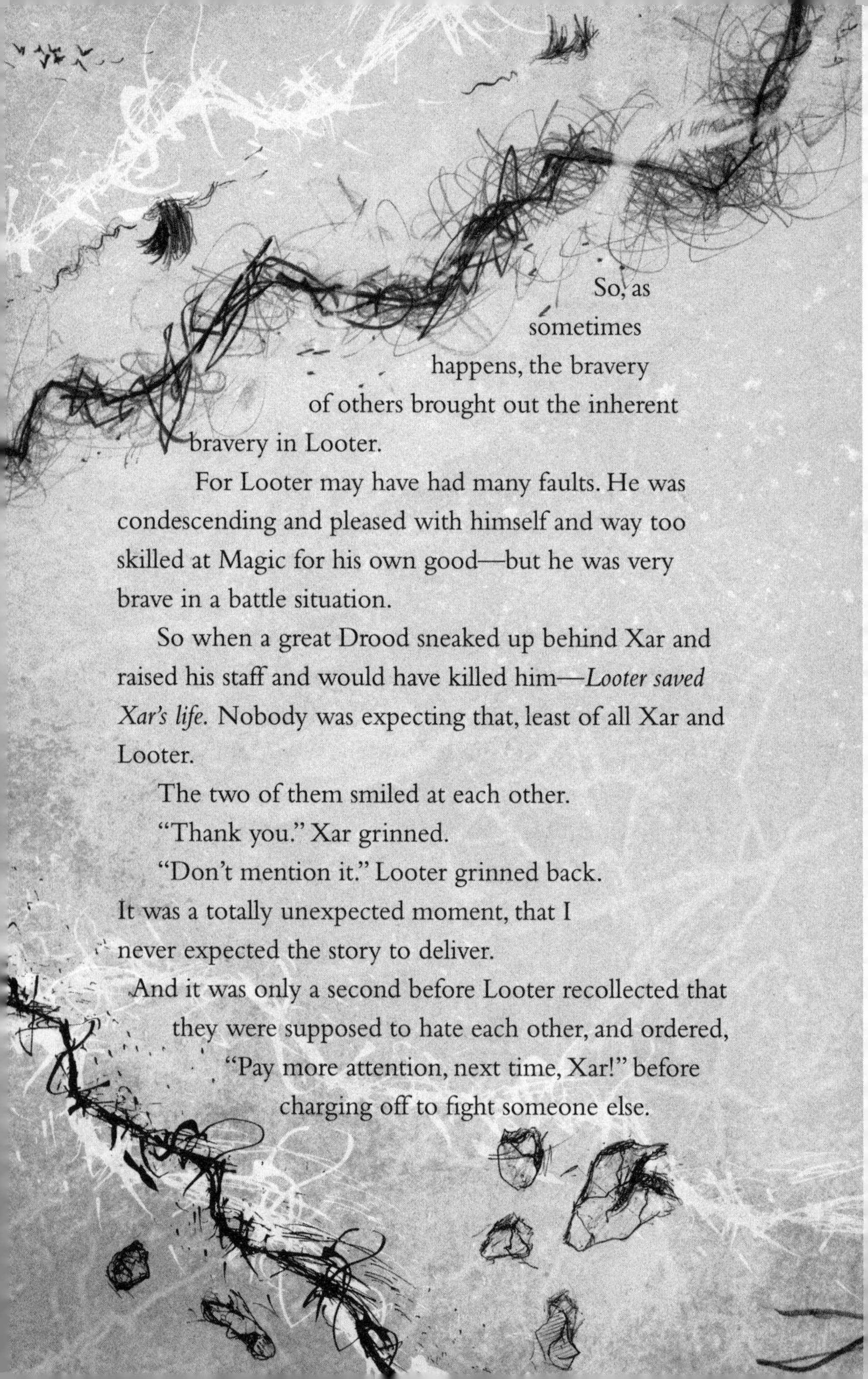

So, as sometimes happens, the bravery of others brought out the inherent bravery in Looter.

For Looter may have had many faults. He was condescending and pleased with himself and way too skilled at Magic for his own good—but he was very brave in a battle situation.

So when a great Drood sneaked up behind Xar and raised his staff and would have killed him—*Looter saved Xar's life.* Nobody was expecting that, least of all Xar and Looter.

The two of them smiled at each other.

"Thank you." Xar grinned.

"Don't mention it." Looter grinned back.

It was a totally unexpected moment, that I never expected the story to deliver.

And it was only a second before Looter recollected that they were supposed to hate each other, and ordered, "Pay more attention, next time, Xar!" before charging off to fight someone else.

In the midst and heat of the battle, Looter and Xar smiled at each other...

Xar hadn't been paying attention because he was concentrating so hard on the spellfight and now he ignored Looter's advice, and the hordes of fighting Droods and giants all around him, to focus on the battle Wish was having with the Kingwitch.

Bodkin was sitting, crouched on the back of the Enchanted Door, Kingcat by his side.

They were ready for Plan B.

The last explosion was so gigantic that the dome containing the battle finally burst, and the feathers and the blue dust were blasted so far away that it seemed like it might be impossible for the Kingwitch and Wish to regather.

"Oh, thousands and trillions of stars in the sky and dirtiest fingernails of the slimiest trolls!" swore Caliburn, looking up into the sky. "They've gone too far...they'll never return..."

"Coulds that happen?" worried Squeezjoos.

"In theory, yes," said Perdita gravely. "Even if a life is left, if the explosion is too huge, the center is lost, and the person is scattered too widely to get back and reform."

"Come back, Wish!" cried Bumbleboozle, as if a hairy fairy as small as she could do anything to help. "Come back!"

For five agonizing minutes, though they stretched their ears and their eyes out as far as they could, there was no sign of Wish or the Kingwitch.

And then slowly, slowly, a few little tiny pieces of blue dust fell out of nowhere...and more and more and more...they thickened, clustered, joined up, forming the jigsaw puzzle of Wish.

"Wish!" welcomed Squeezjoos joyfully.

"Plan B," panted Wish, as her scattered pieces reformed into one whole once more. "I think he'll be weak enough to go for Plan B this time."

Wish was weak herself. She could barely hold herself up, and she was steaming hot with fever. She couldn't think properly, her brain felt scrambled, as if all the cells in there were struggling to reconnect. She was so hot she felt she might be about to go up in flames any minute.

"Don't come any closer!" she warned them.

"Maybe the Kingwitch won't return?" said Squeezjoos hopefully.

"No, he's coming," said Wish feverishly, shivering all over. "I know he's coming."

She pointed her Magic eye, with the last regathering of her strength, sent the Enchanted Door with Bodkin and Kingcat clinging to it up, up into the air. It shot over their heads up, out of the amphitheater, and laid itself on the shimmering, humming surface of the Lake of the Lost, in one of the places where Crusher, or one of the Greater Giants, had planted a great footprint that had broken the ice.

Wish made the door larger, bigger, just as she had once upon a time when she had put the door against Pook's Hill.

"Oh, very clever," said Perdita. "The lake is said to be the entrance to the Otherworld."*

* Back in the Bronze Age, people believed that there were certain places that were doorways into another world.

THE PUNISHMENT CUPBOARD

Magic is BANNED

Knock! Knock! Knock!

Kneeling there, bracing himself, Bodkin lifted his fist and knocked three times.

Knock!

Knock!

Knock!

The door opened with such violence that Bodkin and Kingcat were flipped out into the lake.

Bodkin, who was not a strong swimmer, went under one, two, three times before Kingcat dragged him, coughing and spluttering, to the surface.

"Take the staff, Xar," said Wish.

The Great Staff of Power was lying on the ground where the Kingwitch had dropped it when he last exploded.

Xar could barely lift it, it was so huge. "Lift me up, Crusher," said Xar. The Longstepper High-Walker giant lifted the boy carrying the staff and slowly began to wade out to where the door was lying on the Lake of the Lost.

Meanwhile, the air in front of Wish darkened with one feather drifting in, two, three, four, five, a whirl of feathers, and the very faint whisper of singing, creaky, croaky, disjointed, and even the ears of the listening sprites could barely hear it now.

"How many times these Enchanters' lives?

How many times must they be killed?

How many lives must yet be left . . . ?

Risk it all . . .

Risk it all . . .

Risk it all . . ."

The smell of burned feathers. The panting, stinking, rotten-corpse stench as the jigsaw pieces of the Kingwitch slowly, slowly put themselves together again, the arsenic whiff, the furious, green, hot, spitting clouds as the dreadful form of the exhausted Kingwitch reappeared.

The girl.

And the Witch.

The two great Enchanters looked at each other one last time.

"The spellfight is ended," said Perdita. "You are both alive. The battle is a draw, and neither of you can cast a single spell now, or you break the Witches' Code."

"We are both alive," panted Wish. "We are quits... but look... Kingwitch! My friend has the Great Staff of Power. You will need that now you have lost so many lives."

Wish pointed a shaking finger out at the Lake of the Lost.

There stood the quiet figure of Crusher the Longstepper High-Walker giant.

Holding Xar.

And in Xar's hands was the Great Staff of Power.

The Kingwitch lifted his weary death-crow head.

And screeched.

19. The Door to the Otherworld

It was a still moment for Xar as he and Crusher looked down through the open door of the Lake of the Lost. For there in that rectangle that should be water, the door had opened onto the midnight sky of another world. Staring down into those stars, those possibilities, his hands closed around the Great Staff of Power, Xar could not help but think,

If I hold on to this staff I would have all the Magic I ever dreamed of…

"See!" called Wish. "Xar is throwing the staff into the

Otherworld. If you want it, Witch, you will have to follow!"

That was Xar's cue to throw the staff down through the door.

Everything within Xar wanted to hold on to that staff at all costs.

Many an adult would have struggled to relinquish it, so strong was the pull to hold on to that power.

It was the ultimate test.

Caliburn watched him gravely.

I could be great...thought Xar.

Looter would have to bow down...my FATHER would have to bow down...I could move mountains...train dragons...hunt on the back of Greater Giants...The possibilities shot enticingly through Xar's highly imaginative brain.

But Xar, it seemed, was no longer the same boy of a year ago, who would do anything to get Magic and had set a trap to catch a Witch.

The adventure had changed him.

Wish believed in him and her faith in him made him trust himself. She could have asked Crusher to do this. She could have asked Bodkin.

But she had relied on *him*, Xar, in spite of everything.

Xar threw the staff down through the open door, shouting:

"I'VE MADE AMENDS!"

I AM
good
enough!

Caliburn breathed again, tears in his old bird eyes.

"Oh, Xar," said the raven. "I knew you could do it! I knew it all along."

Back on the spell battleground, the exhausted Kingwitch saw the staff fall. He knew he needed that staff to regain his strength. He no longer knew if he had any lives left.

He screeched again in fury.

Tricked!

Tricked by a whippersnapper of an Enchanter girl and a rude little Wizard boy...hundreds of years of waiting, curled up in the darkness, patiently, nursing his wrath to keep it warm, only to be disappointed at the last, for victory to slip eel-like through his talons at the last.

The Witch-trap had been baited and sprung, and now it had turned and trapped him.

He staggered to his feet, and took clumsily to the air, so weak his ragged wingtips dragged in the water and the ice as he flew over the dark mirror of the surface of the Lake of the Lost. When he reached the Enchanted Door, he hovered over the rectangle of the night sky Otherworld, a defeated terrible scarecrow, boiling with hate. And his last act before he dived through the open door, out of this world, and into the next...

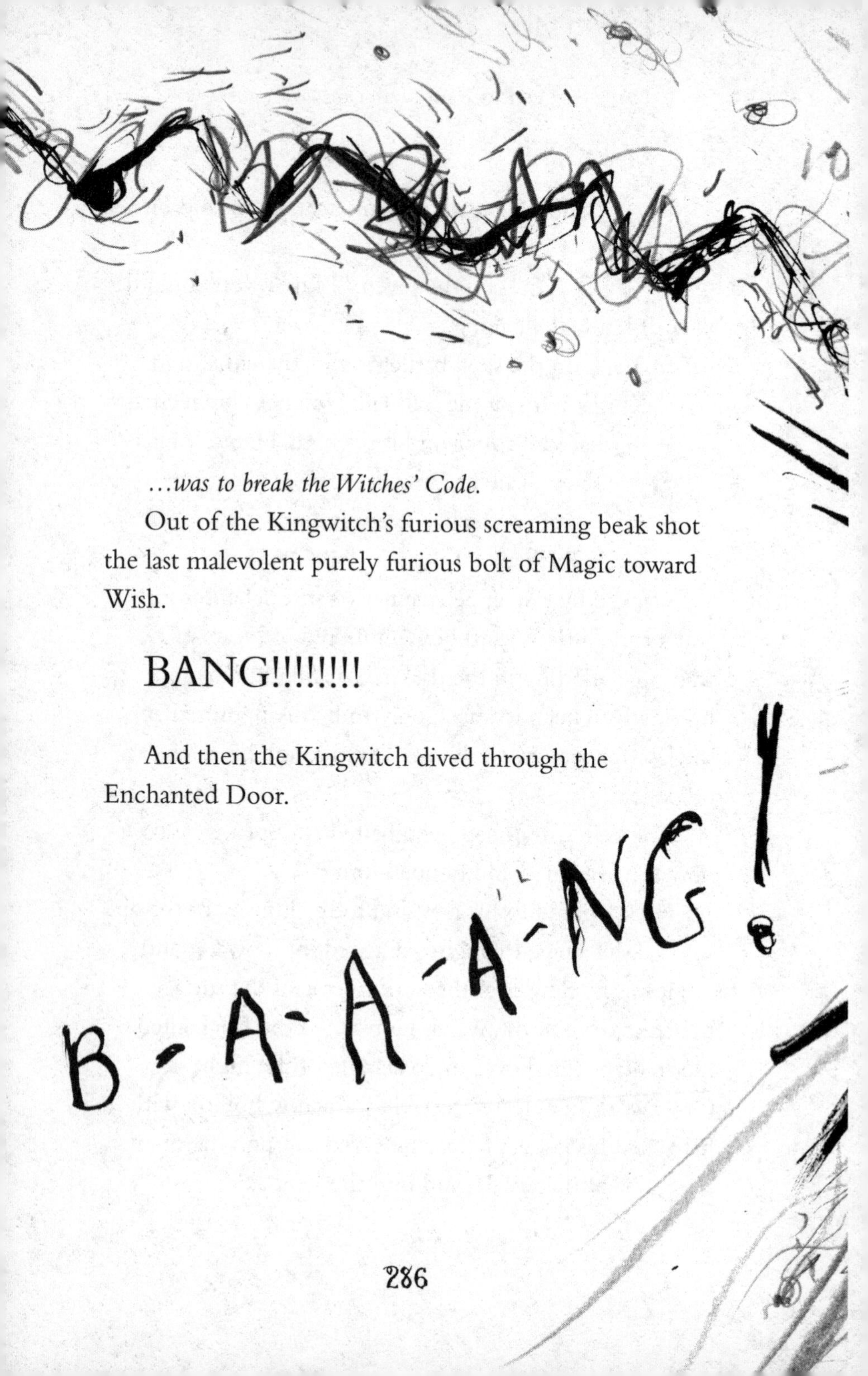

...was to break the Witches' Code.

Out of the Kingwitch's furious screaming beak shot the last malevolent purely furious bolt of Magic toward Wish.

BANG!!!!!!!!

And then the Kingwitch dived through the Enchanted Door.

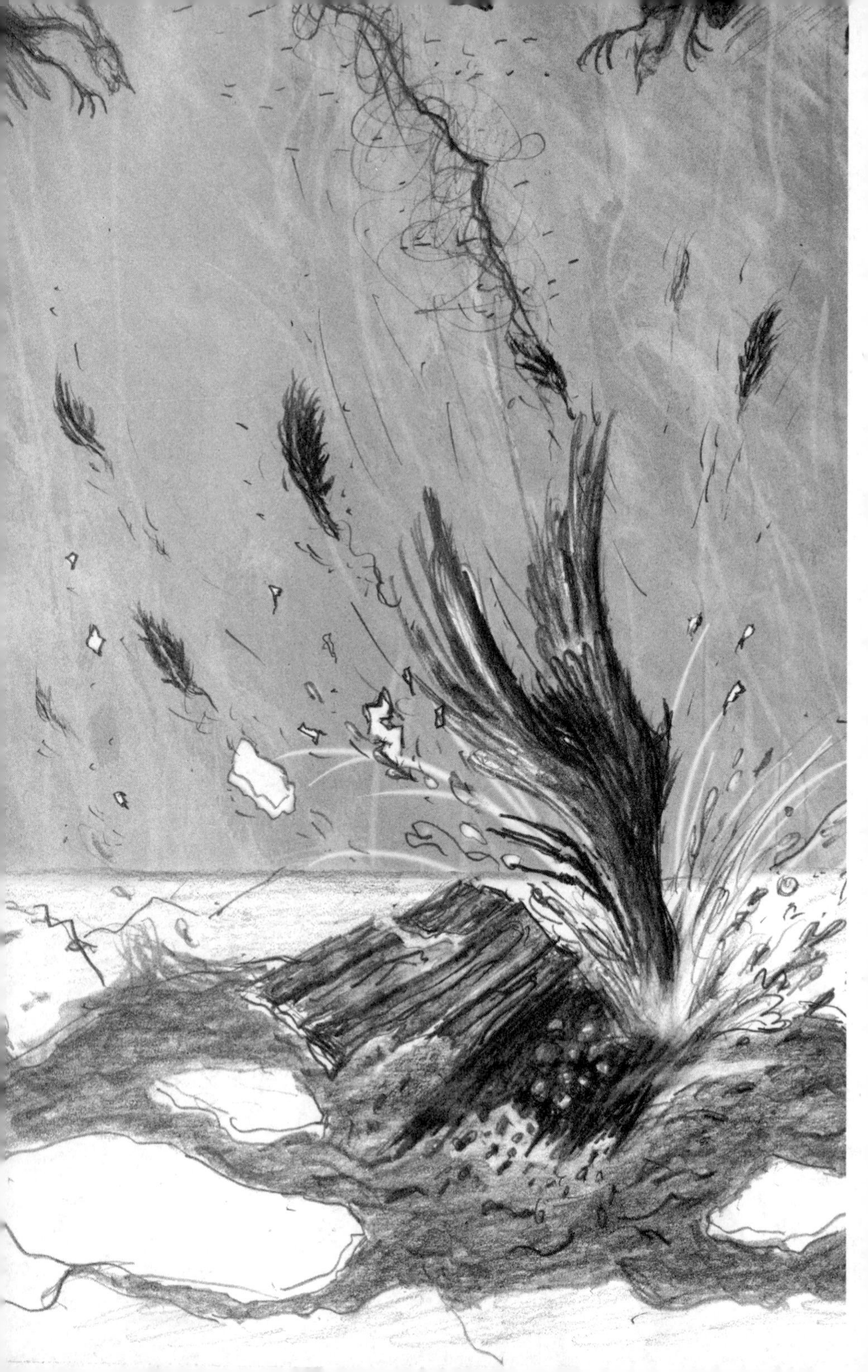

Thick and fast, the Witches followed the Kingwitch in great screeching swarms, like hosts of giant taloned flies, diving into the portal after their leader. Hordes of them, streams of them. And when the last horrible evil pest had flapped through the yawn of the hatchway, Crusher carefully closed it shut.

Gone.

The Witches had gone.

The quest was over.

The world was rid of Witches.

And that was the end of *them*.

20. The Fates Foretold That One of Xar's Company Was Going to Die

As the door rose humming from the surface, and Crusher began to wade out of the broken ice of the lake, a great ragged cheer rose up from the victorious Wizards and Warriors, Greater Giants and magical creatures gathered on the battlements and grasses of the Drood stronghold.

Droods and Witches defeated, Sychorax and Encanzo saved to be monarchs of their respective tribes. It was a triumphant moment.

But Xar and Bodkin, being held safe in Crusher's hands, were urging Crusher to be quick.

"Wish! What's happened to Wish? Did he hit her, that treacherous Kingwitch, with that one last spell bolt?" said Xar anxiously.

The great gentle giant, who normally did everything so slowly, was moving quicker than Xar had ever seen him, so fast that the water and broken ice of the Lake were splashing up about them as he rushed to find out what had happened.

"She'll be all right...the universe will save her..." said Crusher, but he did not sound as confident as Xar and Bodkin might have hoped.

Crusher climbed out of the lake, and up the cliff,

arm over arm, gently pushed aside the cheering crowds and knelt down beside the sword pushed hard into the stone, and placed Xar and Bodkin onto their feet. Perdita and Hoola and Encanzo and Sychorax and the Greater Giants were already there at the top of the cliff where Wish had been standing, staring upward at the sky.

Wish was not there.

Xar's heart dropped.

He *had* hit her.

And she had exploded, one…

final…

…time.

That was why everyone was staring upward, looking to see where Wish had gone…and whether she would come back.

The Enchanted Spoon was lying on the ground, immobile. The pins scattered all about. The fork, the key.

But they had been in this situation, so many times before. That very first adventure, this had happened, and it had all been fine, she had returned.

It would be just like that again, they said to themselves.

"And she must have so many more lives than that Kingwitch," said Xar, to reassure himself that all would be well.

"This is not a question of

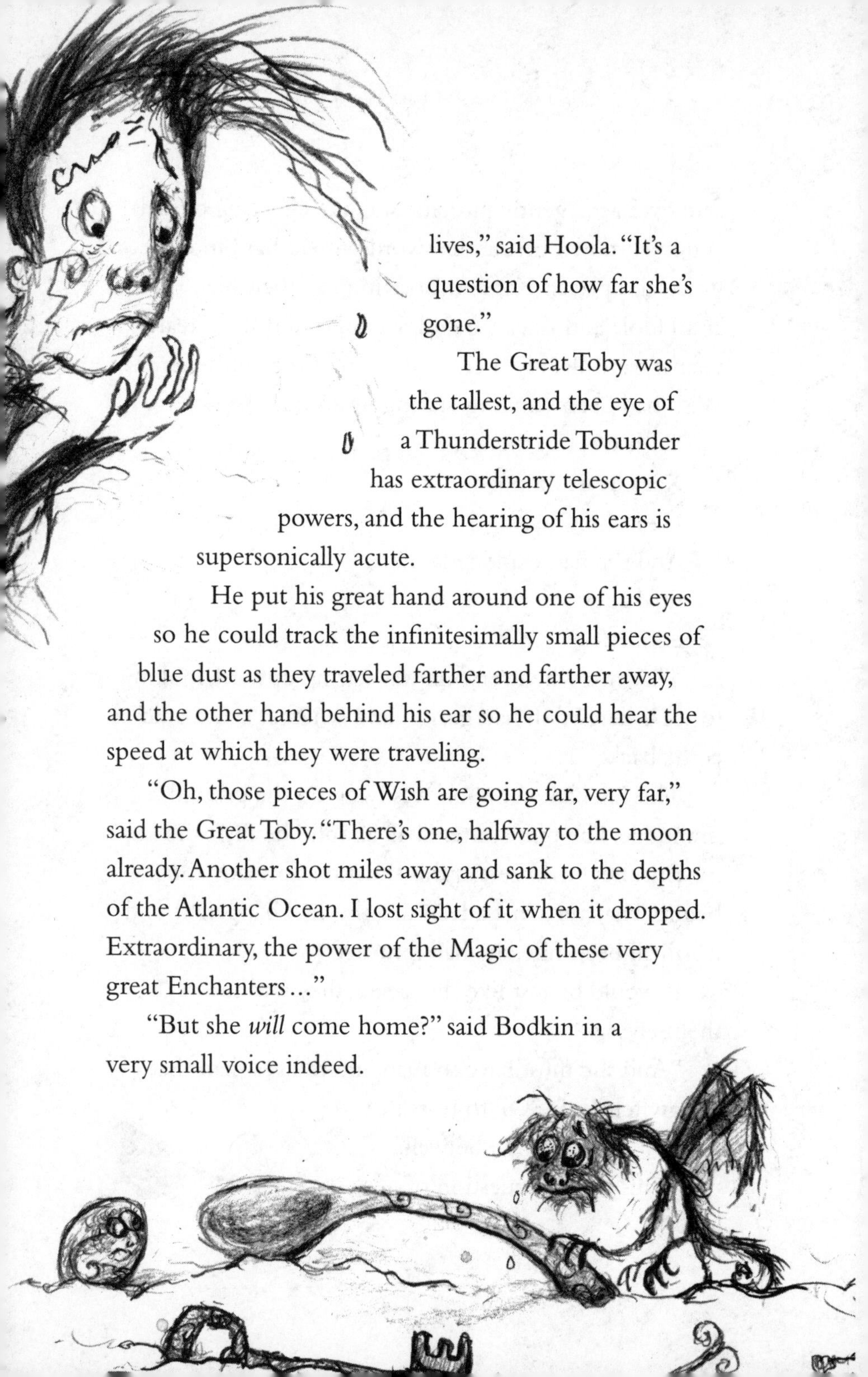

lives," said Hoola. "It's a question of how far she's gone."

The Great Toby was the tallest, and the eye of a Thunderstride Tobunder has extraordinary telescopic powers, and the hearing of his ears is supersonically acute.

He put his great hand around one of his eyes so he could track the infinitesimally small pieces of blue dust as they traveled farther and farther away, and the other hand behind his ear so he could hear the speed at which they were traveling.

"Oh, those pieces of Wish are going far, very far," said the Great Toby. "There's one, halfway to the moon already. Another shot miles away and sank to the depths of the Atlantic Ocean. I lost sight of it when it dropped. Extraordinary, the power of the Magic of these very great Enchanters..."

"But she *will* come home?" said Bodkin in a very small voice indeed.

Hoola landed on Bodkin's shoulder and put her wing comfortingly on his cheek. "Sometimes the pieces of a person have gone so far, the center cannot hold."

Was this what the story had been about all along?

Did the stone really need this sacrifice?

Was this the death that Sychorax had seen in the adderstone?

Was this to be the price of a world that was rid of Witches?

Was this what being the person of destiny really meant?

"I should have been the person of destiny, all along!" said Xar, quite distraught. "I wanted it for the wrong reason. Then this would have been me instead of her."

Five minutes passed. Six. Half an hour.

She wasn't coming back.

Someone began to beat the big Drood drum, not angrily, but sadly, drumming to mourn a death.

Everyone was crying.

Apart from...

...Perdita.

Perdita wasn't crying yet.

She put her hand thoughtfully on the handle of the sword, driven with such force into the stone by Wish in the full height and strength of her magical powers.

Why had Wish done that?

Maybe Wish was wise beyond her years, thought Perdita.

She knew she would need that sword to come back.

"Everyone put your hands upon the sword," said Perdita suddenly. "These Wizard hands, these Warrior hands, werewolf pads, bear paws, troll trotters that have just fought the Droods and the Witches back-to-back. Put your hands upon the sword and promise that this is not just a single occasion, it will be the start of something *new*, a world where Wizards and Warriors work together side by side. You have to make a world worthy of Wish coming back to."

Sychorax blinked at Perdita uncomprehendingly.

"DO IT!" growled Perdita bearishly. "For so long it has been *she* who has had the belief in impossible things.

"WISH!
BELIEVE!"

Now it is *you* who has to believe. She believes in YOU ...why not believe in *her*? *PUT YOUR HANDS UPON THE SWORD!*"

Sychorax, Encanzo, Bodkin, Xar, Looter, every sprite, even Crusher the giant got fingertips on the handle of the Enchanted Sword. The Great Toby put his thumb on Crusher's head, and the people who could not get hands on the handle of the sword—Warriors, Wizards, giants—put their hands on those who *had*. Magical creatures crowded around. Squeezjoos wriggled into the center of everything and put one of his little hairy feet on the pommel. Everyone in that entire amphitheater wanted to join in.

"Leave a space for her to return to!" hooted Hoola. "Be *practical,* everyone...there has to be some room for her to come back."

The anxious crowd moved their hands and paws on the handle of the sword, and shuffled around so that there would be a space for a returning Wish, if that were even possible.

The sword with the love spell on it was calling out for its owner.

"And now, *WISH! BELIEVE!*" cried Perdita, calling up to the heavens above.

It takes a very great force indeed for tiny pieces of blue dust to be recalled from so very, very far away.

But the sword with the love spell on it was calling out for its owner. The power of the love spell was doing its work.

The sword in the stone began to shake. The love spell it had been dipped in was willing, wanting, *yearning* for the owner of the sword to return.

"Imagine her coming back! Bring her home!" sang Perdita.

All those hands, friendly hands, cooperative hands, loving hands, gentle paws, hairy feet, working together, holding on to the sword, longing to bring her back.

Wish was a very powerful Wizard, but she needed those friends on earth, on sea, up in space, to carry her home.

And from far, far away, and up in the distant most spaces of time, the little pieces of Wish were recalled. Twitching out of the numberless sands of a faraway beach. Tweaking out of the crook of a leaf deep in the tangles of a distant forest. Loosening out of the turn of a piece of dead coral half buried in the sands of a far-flung ocean.

A last little piece of blue dust, on its way to Mars, now traveling back, with the force of love.

"WISH! Wish with all your hearts and souls that Wish will come back!"

"I wish!"

"I wish!"

"I wish!"

"I wish!"

The universe held its breath.

WISH, reader of this story. Wish, with all your heart, for if you want those pieces of blue dust to return from the depths of the ocean, from the topmost reaches of space, it's going to take a lot of wishing. And I can't promise that even THAT will be enough.

But on this occasion…

…it was.

You must have wished HARD.

And that is the *only* way to wish, if you want something to happen.

As the little pieces returned from the distant reaches of the world that they had been blasted to, the outline of Wish began to reappear. It was first her hand, holding on to the space left for it on the handle of the sword. That came first. And then there was a sudden rush, a whirl of Magic so strong that it blasted everyone else's hands away as the rest of Wish was dragged back from the outmost reaches of the universe.

And there she was. Very limp, very weak, a little

pale and blurry at the edges at first, but growing stronger, firmer in front of Xar's and Bodkin's elated eyes. And her enchanted objects haltingly came to life once more, the frozen spoon warming magically on the cold ground, softening, and sitting up, the key and the fork uncurling themselves as if from sleep, the pins pricking upright. They hopped through the joyful, jubilating crowd and when the Enchanted Spoon curled himself lovingly around Wish's cheek the pink color slowly began to return to it, and as the fork, the key, the pins nuzzled themselves on her chest, making what sounded very like purring noises, Wish breathed deeper, the strength of life recurring.

In time with Wish's breathing, the sprite writing reappeared in blue, on either side of the blade of the sword that was still poking out of the stone.

Once there were Wishes . . .

. . . and they're still here.

"Love is weakness . . ." said Perdita, as the last little blue dusty piece of Wish returned, drifting down from above and settling right on the tip of her now-complete nose. "But what a very, very sweet weakness it is indeed."

21. In Which We Find Out the Price of the Story...

What ecstatic celebrations there then were in the great grim center of the dreadful Drood stronghold! That place of cold judgment, of sacrifice and tears had never seen anything like it.

Wolves capering, snowcats leaping, trolls stamping their trottered feet. Wizards dancing with Warriors, sprites shooting off spell after spell as they blazed like fireworks through the sky above, trailing sprite-writing in the sky that read: *She's alive! She's alive!*

The Greater Giants shuffling their feet and trying not to tread on anyone, but their faces smiling, thinking such deep thoughts that their heads were on fire and smoking.

A single werewolf, Lonesome, howling joyfully, "Owww oww oww!!!!"

Bodkin and Xar helping Wish to her feet, Xar punching the air and crowing like a rooster, Looter clapping Xar on the back in reluctant approval, Encanzo and Sychorax, those stern parents, crying tears of relief and embracing their children. It did, admittedly, take a moment for cold Queen Sychorax to lean in to the enthusiastic hug that Wish gave her. Initially, she gave a little start, as if she had been bitten, but she resolutely

Queen Sychorax took a MOMENT to get used to the hugging situation.

brought down her arms, saying proudly to her daughter, "I knew you'd be strong enough." As Xar showed his father his hand that no longer carried the Witch-stain, he glowed with pleasure when Encanzo said, "I knew you'd be good enough."

And Perdita gave Xar's trumpet a very severe look indeed, for it was quivering, ready to make a loud and

I knew you'd be strong enough.

rude noise at such fibbing on the part of the adults. Both parents may indeed have been lying, for they had never shown any such confidence, but they were good lies, and the children needed to hear these words from their parents. So the trumpet remained quiet, and Perdita put her big bear arms around Bodkin, who had no parent there, and growled, "And I knew you'd be brave enough, Bodkin."

And Perdita spoke the truth.

They stood there, joyfully celebrating for a while, the sprites whizzing above, the wolves howling happily, the giants stamping their feet, the Wizards shooting Magic from their staffs up into the sky, until Perdita reluctantly released Bodkin and halted the festivities.

Look, Father!
No Witch-stain!

"ROOOOOOOOOOARRRRRR!" bawled Perdita.

She lifted up onto her hind legs, three times the size of a normal bear, fangs showing in an enraged snarl, brown fur upraised in anger, and glowing spookily with a strange blue unnatural light, beating her great shaggy paws on her chest.

"ROOOOOOOOOOARRRRRR!"

There was a menace and a power in that roar that made the festivities abruptly halt. Even the disobedient sprites ceased their whizzing and their fidgeting through the air in respect for the bear's authority.

"ROOOOOOOOOOARRRRRR!"

Perdita roared for the third time, just to make it absolutely clear who was in charge.

And then she clomped back down onto her front legs, made a couple of grunting growls deep in the back of her great bear throat.

Her one-glassed monocle rolled grandly up her chin, over her nose, and settled in front of her Magic eye. She glared imperiously through the eyeglass around at the entire assembly of assorted creatures and humans, giving them all her hardest stare, and through the glass of the monocle the stare actually stung those it landed on, as if they were being pinched by fairies or bitten by midges, in order to make sure they were truly paying attention.

"Everyone!" growled Perdita, sorrowfully. "We must now take notice of Caliburn."

And finally...

...the old bear cried.

Big tears rolled down her bear cheeks and dropped slowly off her nose.

You see, you mustn't forget, dear reader, that try as you may, you cannot cheat the fate foretold. Someone in Xar's company was going to die. The story had demanded it.

It was not Squeezjoos or Xar, and it was not even Wish.

So it had to be *Caliburn*.

And none of them had even noticed.

They were all so busy worrying, wishing, begging the green gods to let Squeezjoos live, and then Xar, and then Wish, they had not noticed when the old bird was blasted by a spiteful stray piece of the Magic from the departing Kingwitch.

So now he was laid out quietly on the stone, with his breast bleeding.

"No, Caliburn, no!" said Wish, very distressed. "We did not wish hard enough for *you*!"

Xar picked the dying bird up carefully and cradled him in his Wizard hands.

"I order you not to grieve for me, any of you,"

croaked the old bird. "I am an old bird, and I will come back, I hope, as a human being, in my next life. We *all* saw death in the adderstones, and if someone had to die, I am glad that someone is me. For my time has come, and it is never sad to die when your time has come. It was a story that I started, and I saw it end happily, and what more than that can an old bird ask for? Even in bird years, I am very, very ancient, whereas *Wish* is only beginning. A life for a life, my life for hers.

"I leave you in the hands of my twin, and Ariel, you will have to be Xar's guardian for the both of us. My quest is complete."

The old bird was a little bag of bones, barely a feather on him.

It was as if all that worrying had taken all the life out of him, and as the final feather dropped, so did his life slip away.

"We only have this life on loan, so you must treasure every minute," said Caliburn. "Make merry for me, all of you. Promise me you will not cry. And I tell you, you must make a world worthy of my death and Wish coming back. Good-bye, everyone."

"But...but...but..." said Xar, bewildered, as if he did not really understand what was going on, "where are you going, Caliburn?"

"Well, I'm not going to die *here*!" said the bird in disgust, and even though he was dying, still managing to sound exasperated. "I'm going *home*, to where I was born. A hundred miles to the north...on a cliff top with the most beautiful view you have ever seen...Ahh...you can see forever from that nest..."

"There's a beautiful view *here*!" said Xar. "You're way too weak to make that journey!"

"Out of my way," said the bird, determined, lifting his weary featherless head.

"I said I would set you free when Xar became a wise and thoughtful adult," said Encanzo as Xar cradled the tiny little fragile body of Caliburn in his hands. "It is a

little early, but Xar has made definite progress. So, you are free to go, Caliburn. Ariel can even come with you, if you like. I make you free too, Ariel."

"No," said Caliburn, "I go alone."

"YOU MUST NOT GO! I forbid it!" said Xar, tears running down his face. "DON'T SET HIM FREE! He's

supposed to be looking after me, he's been with me all my life! How am I going to do without him?"

"Let him go, Xar," said Wish, who was crying too.

Xar lifted up his hands and threw Caliburn in the air.

For one terrible moment it looked as if the poor little dying bird was going to fall to the ground...but he stretched out his dying wings...

...his last words, very faint, over his old bird shoulder, were sweet ones.

"I love you, Xar...And you too, Wish and Bodkin."

...and weakly, but surely, Caliburn flew, off, off and away.

Out of this story, and into a new and unknown adventure.

22. Promises Have Been Made, Journeys Have Been Taken

As Caliburn flew off, a single one of his feathers drifted down into Wish's hand. Almost as if it were a gift.

Now the whole company went from rejoicing into the most heartrending tears, sobbing, as if their hearts would break, until Perdita stopped them by rearing onto her hind legs and ROARING once more, even though she was still crying herself.

"You are acting as if this were an ending," growled Perdita, the Magic of her tears trickling down her furry face and landing on the grass below, so that it grew fast and quick under her big bear feet. "And this is no ending. This is only the beginning. Caliburn asked us not to cry, and look at us!

"STOP IT, EVERYONE!"

A single one of Caliburn's feathers drifted down into Wish's hand, almost as if it were a gift.

Even the larger Gobtrolls (not noted for their sensitivity) were crying, but when Perdita reminded them of Caliburn's last wish, they wiped their noses on their sleeves and tried to listen.

"Pay attention!" said Perdita sternly. "For Caliburn's sake. As soon as you put your hands upon that sword, you made vows to the future that cannot be taken back. Promises have been made, journeys have been taken, things have happened that can never un-happen.

"Once-sprite," said Perdita. "You were the spell-raider who was in charge of the ingredients for the Spell to Undo Love Denied? I am hoping that Wish asked you to keep just a little bit back, just in case."

"I did!" sniffed Wish.

Perdita looked fondly down at her. "I thought you might have."

The little sprite hovering overhead on the back of the peregrine falcon urged the bird down and it landed on Perdita's shoulder. The Once-sprite sprang from the bird's back, in an impressive double somersault, onto Perdita's cupped palm. He gave a deep swaggering bow, and Perdita nodded respectfully in return, as the little sprite produced a vial from his back.

"The VERY LAST DROPS of the Spell to Undo Love Denied!" announced the Once-sprite, so small that he had to hold up the vial in both hands.

"Thank you, Once-sprite," said Perdita solemnly. "Spell-raiding is a dangerous job and you have guarded this well."

The Once-sprite pretended not to care about this compliment, but he went quite pink with pleasure as he leaped back onto the peregrine falcon.

"And now, Sychorax and Encanzo, it is *your* turn to make amends," said Perdita.

"My pronouncement is that twenty years ago, *you*,

Queen Sychorax, offended against the laws of love by taking the Spell of Love Denied in order to quash your affection for King Encanzo. And *you*, King Encanzo, offended against the laws of love, by turning your heart into a stone, in order to extinguish your love for Queen Sychorax. How do you plead?"

Queen Sychorax's pretty little nose was up in the air and her pretty little foot was tapping on the ground in annoyance, *tap, tap, tap*. This plump, badly dressed, middle-aged woman to stand in judgment over HER? Ridiculous! But then...what with one thing and another, the events of the last year had made her less sure of herself than normal.

"How dare you?" began Queen Sychorax. "I am the direct descendant of Brutal the Giant-Killer and to accuse ME of ever being in love with this poxy arrogance of a Wizard is treachery of the highest order and—"

But Queen Sychorax spoke without her usual freezing unshakable authority, and she was interrupted by the loudest raspberry Xar's trumpet had ever given, so loud, it made the queen jump.

PARRRRRRP!

"Oh all right then," said Queen Sychorax crossly. "We may once have had some slight affection for each other, but we were young and exceptionally foolish and unrealistic."

"How do you plead?" repeated Perdita sternly. And then she roared abruptly, right in the monarch's face. "TELL THE TRUTH!"

"Guilty," said Queen Sychorax, crosser than ever. "You really do need to do something about that bear breath of yours, Perdita. I have a cleansing mouthwash I can lend you."

"And I plead guilty too," said King Encanzo proudly, the storm clouds rising off his head in great churning crackling billows, but again, perhaps not entirely with the same bitter intransigence that he normally spoke. "But I was entirely deceived by this serpent of a Warrior woman into some temporary mild fascination and it would never have stood the test of time and..."

PARRRRRRP!

That trumpet of Xar's was really very irritating.

"Oh, cut it out, Tor!" said Queen Sychorax, accidentally using Encanzo's childhood name in her annoyance. "You were absolutely NUTS about me! Far more than I was about you!"

"*Lies*!" snapped Encanzo. "You loved me so passionately that you swore that you would give up those stupid Warrior knickknacks and run away with me to find a world where Wizards and Warriors could live and love in peace. And look where *that* little fantasy led us!"

Sychorax turned to him. "But there *is* no such world," she said, with just the beginnings of a hint of longing in her voice.

"There is indeed no such world," admitted Perdita, "*...unless you make that world yourself.* That's the only way such a world is going to happen."

Perdita paused a moment to let that sink in, and then she carried on.

"Firstly I'd like you to apologize to both your children..."

"Sorry..." mumbled Queen Sychorax, shuffling her feet.

"Sorry..." said King Encanzo, equally embarrassed.

"And then...you have both been found guilty of denying love, and that is a terrible thing to do," said Perdita. "So now you must make amends, by building this new world where Wizards and Warriors can live and love in peace yourselves, and you will begin by drinking these last drops of the Spell to Undo Love Denied."

There was a long, long silence.

"Tell you what," suggested Perdita, "I'll just sit down here and do a little bit of knitting, while you make up your minds what you want to do—knitting is so relaxing."

And she settled down on the edge of the stone with the sword in it and her knitting needles sailed out of her pockets and she began to knit, absentmindedly knitting some of the nearby grass into the knitting as she went, not to mention bits of her own shirt and some of Encanzo's cloak.

Encanzo and Sychorax could see the way the story was going now, but it didn't mean they had to *like* it. It is always difficult for older people, particularly proud monarchs such as these ones, to change course and admit they have been wrong, even when the road they have been taking has been leading them to misery and oblivion.

The Once-sprite, still sitting on the back of the peregrine falcon on Perdita's shoulder, began to sing the opening verse of "Tor's Song":

"I am young, I am poor, I can offer you nothing
All that I have is this bright pair of wings..."

"Oh, DO shut up!" snapped Queen Sychorax.

"Wrong moment," whispered Perdita to the Once-sprite. "Give them time. They're going to have to adjust."

The Once-sprite shut up, giving an injured sniff.

Really, some people.

He had only been trying to help.

"Drink it, Mother," urged Wish.

There were tears in Sychorax's eyes.

"It's a very powerful love spell," said Wish. "A spell so forceful it can undo the Spell of Love Denied..."

The two monarchs looked at one another.

Fierce blue eyes met wild gray eyes, and oh botheration, there was a sort of hiss and crackle and a fizzle in the air between them, a jarring in the universe, that familiar disturbance in the atmosphere that always happened when they met each other's gaze, and if it were possible for the air to thicken around them like thunderclouds forming, and for three of the candle-fires in the spellfight ring to spontaneously combust into life and flames again, well, then, that is what they did, and Sychorax and Encanzo could both feel themselves weakening.

"It's madness," whispered Sychorax. "Wizards and Warriors can never be together..."

"But perhaps, just perhaps," said Encanzo, "it is ONLY together that they can fight the might of evil now that we have Magic-mixed-with-iron in the world."

"So we'd be doing this as monarchs," said Sychorax, "on behalf of both our dominions?"

"Of course," said Perdita, knitting away merrily.

"And it would be a strictly business arrangement?" continued Encanzo suspiciously. "Just to get rid of the hatred between our two tribes? You can assure me that there would be absolutely no return of the beastly 'love' pestilence? After all, I had to go on an entire shadow quest to get rid of the 'love' disease last time...and I've got a slightly dodgy knee, nowadays, I can't go crawling around caves of Nuckalavees like I used to..."

"Oh, I'm sure not," said Perdita, now knitting what looked remarkably like a bit of Sychorax's sock into her knitting, goodness knows how that had wormed its way up Sychorax's leg and onto Perdita's needles, but there it was. "After all, you are both way too old for love, aren't you?"

"We're not THAT old," objected Encanzo, sucking his tummy in.

"People still fall in love with *me* all the time," added Sychorax waspishly, checking her reflection in the Chief Guard's shield and giving a satisfied sniff at the general freezing gorgeousness of it. "I'm beating them off with a stick, aren't I, Chief Guard?"

"Sometimes even literally," murmured the Chief Guard.

"But in this case," said Perdita hurriedly, "I'm sure it'll be strictly business. It'll just stop you wanting to kill each other, which is inconvenient in an ally."

"What exactly is in this love spell of yours, Wish?" said Sychorax.

"Forgiveness...desire...tenderness...courage...and endurance," said Wish.

"These are indeed powerful ingredients for those who wish to build a new world," admitted Encanzo thoughtfully. "I'll drink it if you'll drink it, Sychorax."

"You realize that if we do this," said Sychorax, "we will be forever at war with the Droods to the south, and the emperor to the east?"

Encanzo shrugged. "I never liked either of them," said Encanzo. "Did you? And you have to look at the alternatives. If we're not at war with them, then we're at war with each other. And these children…are not ready to be heroes. They need education, to be back at school, not chasing after Nuckalavees and climbing down mines, and fighting epic battles with Witches, they're way too young."

"Oh for goodness' sake, I know I'm going to regret this, but bring that spell here before I change my mind!" snapped Queen Sychorax.

Looter stepped forward with the cup and gave it to Perdita, who poured the remains of the spell into the cup.

The Enchanted Spoon bounced into the cup, where he stirred the last little drops of the Spell to Undo Love Denied with such energy that they frothed up and appeared to double, then triple in size.

"Now, Sychorax and Encanzo," said Perdita sternly. "All you have to do is drink it."

The two monarchs looked at the spell to reverse the Spell of Love Denied, stirred in a loving Cup of Second

Chances by the gentle tenderness of an Enchanted Spoon.

"What? Are you afraid?" taunted King Encanzo.

"Never!" cried Queen Sychorax, seizing the cup, and drinking half of the spell down.

"And forever!" cried King Encanzo, seizing the cup from Sychorax and drinking the other half and slamming the empty cup back down on the stone.

They both punched the air, shouting in unison: "SECOND CHANCES!"

The crowds of watching Warriors and the Wizards and the magical creatures and the trolls and the sprites all echoed the cry, shouting at the tops of their voices to the waters of the lake and the trees and the surrounding hills: "SECOND CHANCES! SECOND CHANCES! SECOND CHANCES!"

And then…

I am quite at a loss to explain exactly how this happened.

Because this was supposed to be strictly a business arrangement.

But…

…Queen Sychorax and King Encanzo kissed.

And we must avert our eyes, for it was a true love's kiss, which contained: forgiveness, desire, tenderness, courage, and endurance.

So it went on for a bit of a while.

The crowds of Warriors and Wizards fell silent in astonishment.

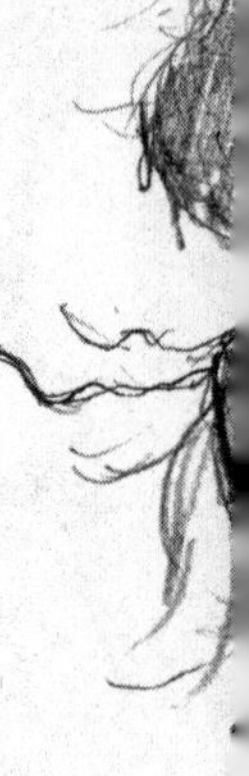

Xar's mouth dropped open in horror.

"They're *kissing*!" said Xar in disgust.

"YUCKY!" said Squeezjoos, making a face.

"Perdita!" cried Xar. "This is an emergency! This is a total, star-crossing, trouser-fraying, hair-pulling, Witch-infested disaster! They're *kissing*! Make them stop! Bring them DOWN!"

"I'm a spell-maker," replied Perdita, shrugging her shoulders. "Not a miracle worker."

"They're in love," explained Wish with a sigh of satisfaction, and spread her arms joyfully wide. "I knew it all along. They were always meant to be together, all this time. This is wonderful!"

They're kissing. YUCKY!

"It *is* quite sweet, actually," admitted Bodkin, who had his sentimental side.

"Just like you and me," cooed the key, nuzzling up to the spoon, before the fork tried to gently drag it

in its own direction, but instead accidentally tripped the spoon up and he fell off the stone and down into a troll poo.

From which he was rescued by a very noble pair of Perdita's eyeglasses.

And then the spoon promptly fell in love with the eyeglasses. (After all, wouldn't *you*, if someone had gallantly waded in to rescue you from a troll poo?) Which meant the spoon was in love with the eyeglasses and the key was in love with the spoon and the fork was in love with the key, and so on around and around, until eventually somebody somewhere at the end of all this would fall in love with the fork and then we would finish with a perfect circle.

Do keep up.

Oh, it's a bad business, the love business.

Everyone in love with everyone else.

And the possibility of heartache always lurking around the corner.

But people *will* keep on falling in love nonetheless.

And let us not think of heartache right now, for we have to enjoy this moment, which was really very sweet, with Queen Sychorax looking uncharacteristically soft, and even blushing a little, my goodness, not like herself at all, and Encanzo's face, normally stormy and sad with thunderclouds, now lit up like sunshine as he held her by the hand.

All around the amphitheater the crowds took up the cry, joyfully shouting, "They're in love! SECOND CHANCES!"

"This is appalling," said Xar, his hands on his hips, as if he were the adult and they were the errant children. "There is no other word for it. It is, quite simply, appalling. Is this what this has been all about? I've gone and gotten myself a STEPMOTHER, and, what's more, the worst stepmother in the world!" The power of Sychorax and Encanzo's kiss had carried them up into the air, but now they recollected themselves, floated gently back down to the ground, and Sychorax pulled away from Encanzo, straightened her breastplate, and sniffed.

"I will certainly bring a little order into your disorganized world," said Sychorax.

"Father!" scolded Xar. "You said you'd never love again... It's always a disaster! The shadow quest! Your knee! You argue all the time... admittedly she has got a really very pretty nose... I grant you that..."

"Thank you." Queen Sychorax smiled, with a peach of a smile so delightful it would have melted ice caps.

"But don't forget," warned Xar, "the rather more important fact that she's a treacherous, cold-hearted, wasp-tongued, multiheaded, forest-burning, frozen *nightmare* of a Warrior queen!"

Encanzo looked a little harassed. He ran a hand over his bald head. He seemed to have entirely forgotten about the jealousy, the arguing, the waiting in the hut for years, the riddling game with the Nuckalavee, the misery, and the heartache and all the other teeny little downsides of being in love with Sychorax.

"Yes, I know," said Encanzo. "But it is quite nice."

"*Why do people do this?*" howled Xar.

Encanzo put his hand in Sychorax's.

And then he turned to Xar and he grinned like a twelve-year-old.

"You'll understand when you're older," said Encanzo.

Sychorax laughed, really quite a *nice* laugh this time, not like rippling streams or tinkling glass or ringing bells, in the way Queen Sychorax generally laughed, but a nice normal laugh. "And maybe I'm not quite as bad as all that, after all," said Queen Sychorax.

She had only just finished saying these words when there was a loud popping noises from around her neck, as one of the beads of her necklace exploded.

POP!

There was a lot of smoke, and the bead disappeared, and lying on the ground was an extremely good-looking, sleeping, snoring, previous suitor to Queen Sychorax.

The beads on Queen Sychorax's necklace exploding...

"Who is this?" asked Encanzo with interest.

Queen Sychorax waved an airy hand.

She had the decency to look a little embarrassed. "Well, I did say, didn't I, that people are always falling in love with me? The emperor kept sending suitors for my hand, so I went on turning them into beads on my necklace. A lot kinder, really, than beating them off with a stick."

"I'll say," said the Chief Guard.

POP! POP! POP! POP! POP! POP! POP! POP!

Within the space of about a minute, all the other beads on the necklace apart from one had exploded, and the grass around about was simply a mass of splendid snoring menfolk.

"My goodness," admired Encanzo, "that really is quite a lot of suitors. One ... two ... three ... four ... five ... six ..." He ran out of fingers and carried on counting right up to twenty-four.

"Twenty-five, you've missed one behind the werewolf over there. I know," sighed Sychorax. "Is it my fault that I'm irresistible?"

"*ISN'T THIS TELLING YOU SOMETHING, FATHER?*" roared Xar.

But Encanzo wasn't listening. One of the nearest suitors, Thunderous Thighs Himself, was stretching and yawning in his sleep. "We should get them out of here before any of them wake up," said Encanzo, watching the suitors rippling their gorgeous muscles, absurdly long eyelashes fluttering as they dreamed, delightfully square jaws clenching.

Quite apart from anything else, it was rather spoiling the atmosphere to have so *very many* of Sychorax's handsome former suitors littered about the place.

Untidy.

They were in the way.

And their general superbness and their reek of dazzling male hormones was making the newly back-in-love Encanzo feel a little uneasy.

So Perdita hurriedly put a few more spells on the inconvenient former suitors, so they stayed fully asleep, and one of the Greater Giants helpfully filled his pockets with the good-looking young men, and gently carried them off, wading through the lake, and into the forest, to place them like little sleeping babes in the wood, in various different locations throughout the wildwoods, where they would wake in an hour or so's time, each of them all alone, and wondering what on earth had happened to them.

There was one last bead left on Sychorax's necklace.

And this was the important one.

Encanzo's heart that he had turned into a stone.

He had put it around the neck of the coldest woman in the wildwoods, in the knowledge that it was the one place where it would stay safely lost if he left it unattended.

Sychorax looked at Encanzo mischievously.

"Do you want your heart back again?" said Sychorax.

"I do," said Encanzo.

So Sychorax took the stone off her neck and warmed it in her cupped hands.

Sychorax had been wearing Encanzo's heart-turned-into-stone on a necklace around her neck.

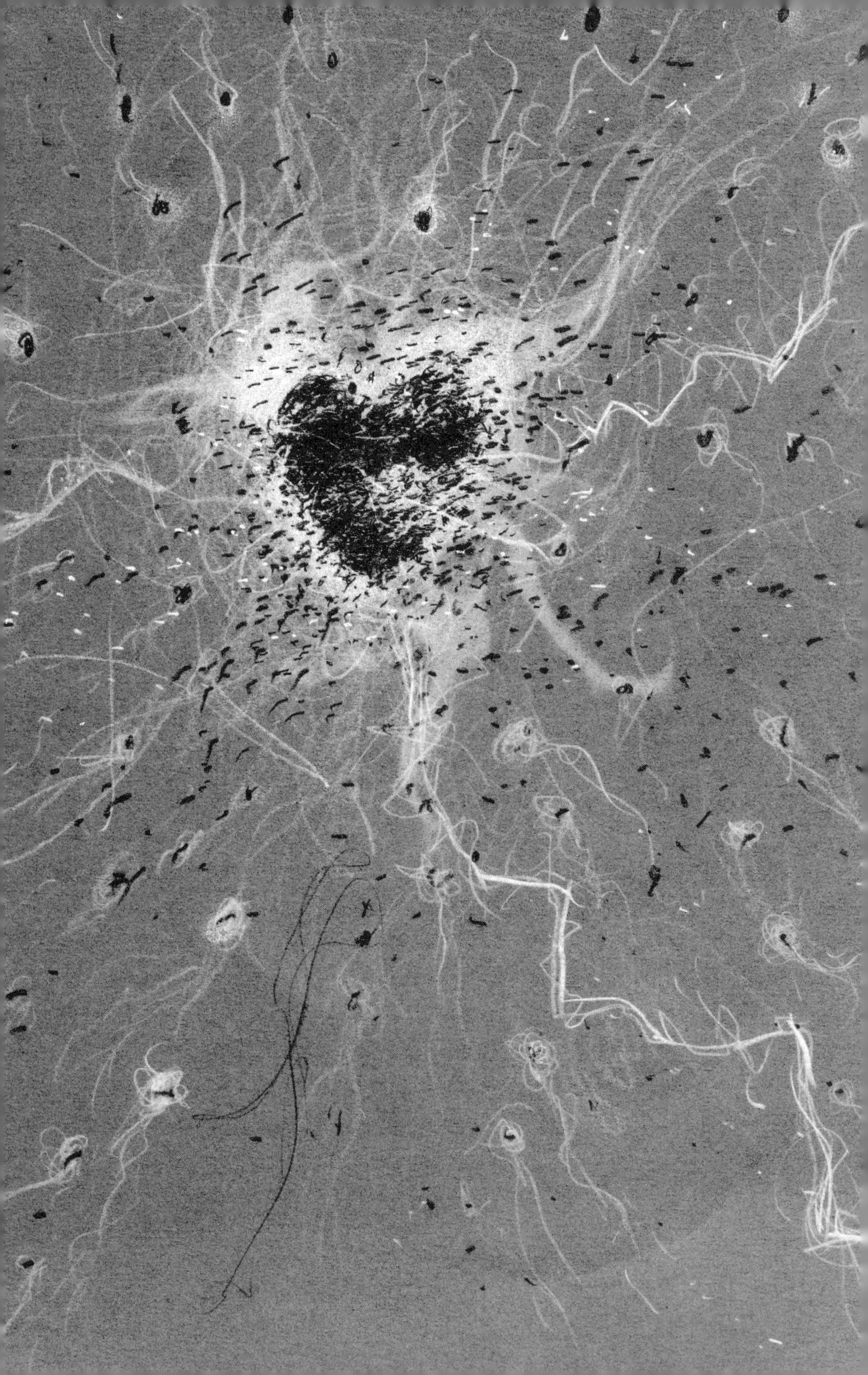

Encanzo's heart returning to its proper place.

And when she opened up her hands once more, the stone had disappeared.

Turned back into the spirit of a human heart, it sprang up from Sychorax's hands and floated in front of them like a ghostly miracle.

Melted from its adamantine impenetrable stone form.

Now the flying heart was…

vulnerable, fragile, beating.

Ready to love, and lie, and live, and break again, if needed.

They only saw the vision of the heart for a second, hanging in the air, before it plunged back into Encanzo's chest, and he let out a gasp of surprise, as if someone had brought him back to life again by a swift punch to the solar plexus.

In pain, he gasped, but smiled at the same time.

Before turning back to Sychorax and gazing fondly at her as if she had done him a great favor.

"We're DOOMED," said Xar gloomily.

But everyone else did not seem to share Xar's somber outlook.

Queen Sychorax made a very stirring speech.

"Warriors and Wizards! Giants and magical creatures, large and small! We are going to build a new kingdom, that will be, for the first time, Wizards and Warriors living together in peace and happiness in the forest!"

"HURRAH!" cried the Wizards and the Warriors, wildly overexcited.

"There will be no more tree burning," promised Queen Sychorax. "We will show how Warriors can protect the wildness of the forest, just as well as the Wizards..." (Now this was a huge concession on Queen Sychorax's part and showed that these adventures really had taught her something.) Perdita and the Greater

Giants positively beamed at this news, and the magical creatures of the forest cheered her so loudly that Queen Sychorax, very pink and pleased, could hardly be heard, and Crusher had to shush them all so they could hear the end of her speech.

"...and we will fight against the might of the Droods to the south and the Warrior Empire to the east...we will never surrender!" finished Queen Sychorax.

"Never surrender!" cried the Wizards and the Warriors, and the Greater Giants stamped their feet in excitement.

Encanzo took up the theme, crying, "Wizards and Warriors CAN live together!"

"We can!" the Wizards and Warriors shouted back.

"We will tear down the Wall..." promised Encanzo. "We will build here, for the very first time, in this place that has been cursed by the miserable power of the Droods, a great fort that is both overground and underground, that will be part tree and part stone. Its primary purpose will be EDUCATION. Education so that the great power of Magic-mixed-with-iron can be educated and controlled. Perdita and Ariel, you will be tutors-in-charge. Giants shall mix with Warriors, all shall learn together..."

All this was very well, but it did start the first little bickering between the two monarchs of this new kingdom, which threatened to spoil the mood for a moment.

"Oh no, hang on, we're not going to have Perdita running a learning place here, are we?" said Queen Sychorax, revolted. "We cannot have that woman in charge...you saw her back in Pook's Hill! Lessons in tree climbing...transforming into animals...bringing things to life...it's all entirely unsuitable..."

"I won't be in *charge*, exactly," said Perdita soothingly, "YOU'LL be in charge because you're the queen, aren't you, Sychorax? So you'll be giving all your wonderful orders and making all your magnificent commands, and we'll just have to do what you say. It'll be absolutely your queendom. Ariel and I will just be the *merest* employees...There's a lovely view over the lake from this hilltop; it's an excellent site for a learning place. I think I'll have my Lair of the Bear right here. It will be a great spot for sunsets..."

Seeing Sychorax beginning to fume, Perdita hurriedly changed the subject, because this looked like it might become a full-blown argument, and it wouldn't do for the new kingdom to start off on the wrong foot.

"...but that's all for tomorrow...a learning place can't be built in a day. In the meantime," said Perdita, "don't you think we should be having a celebration banquet?"

"A banquet? Hurrah!" cried the Wizards and the Warriors and the magical creatures, always delighted to have an excuse for a celebration.

23. The Banquet

And so began the most magnificent banquet held in that part of the world for many a long year.

They had a lot to celebrate. The saving of Xar and of Squeezjoos. The return of Wish from the brink of annihilation. The ending of the burning of the forest, and of the evil reign of the Droods.

And most of all, the last defeat of the Witches.

Wizards and Warriors had partied once before together, on Midwinter's End Eve, back in Castle Death, but that had been a one-off, one night out of time, a temporary truce.

This particular jollification was a much more significant one, intended to mark a whole fresh beginning, the merging of their two kingdoms, the looking-forward to a brave new world.

So they were determined to make a magnificent hullaballoo of it.

The Greater Giants gathered fallen trees of immense size and built a bonfire that would be seen for a hundred miles. The fire was lit with the flame that Ariel had carried in his firebox for Perdita, that contained bits of hearth fires from east, south, west, and north, to symbolize the new joining of their world, and it burned so many different colors that it hurt the eyes to look at it.

The sprites got out their most explosive spells and whacked them up into the sky like rockets and firecrackers, where they erupted in glorious rainbow showers, making the most wonderful, hopeful smells. One spell smelled of baking bread, another of daffodils, another the sweet delicious fragrance of cinnamon-flavored milk. Encanzo's fiddles hung in the air, playing themselves with such joyous tunes the legs itched to dance to them. Lonesome the werewolf, no longer lonesome now that he had found this pack to run with, howled a happy howl to the full moon above.

The Greater Giants jigged their slow jigs, ankle deep, in the Lake of the Lost, singing haunting songs so low they seemed to vibrate through your chest when you heard them. Songs of ways they had wandered, of the call of the Western Seas, where a giant could really be a giant, and follow his calling, wading out to the horizon and over where the sun dips to see what happened at world's end.

Crusher was thrilled to be able to have conversations with Toby Tobunder, a Greater Giant who seemed to know everything about everything Crusher had ever wondered about. So they talked excitedly about brains, and whether the universe had an edge, and they made up sentences like:

"Is it bizarre how saying sentences backward creates backward sentences saying how bizarre it is?"

Squeezjoos enchanted Xar's teacher Ranter's underpants so that they had an iron grip on his buttocks and were impossible to take off. Worse still, they were levitating just ever so slightly off the ground and carrying Ranter up with them. It is very, very difficult to look dignified while hovering just a couple of inches above floor level, your tiptoes just scraping the ground, suspended by your underpants. Rather uncomfortable too.

Mustardthought put a spell on Wish's teacher, Madam Dreadlock, so that every three minutes she quacked like a duck and waggled her bottom as if she were about to lay an egg, and then burst into singing the Warrior War Song which went something like this:

"Kill the giants one by one! Burn the trees and scorch them down! Stuff your pillows with the beards of trolls! That's the WARRIOR WAY!"

Which is really quite a loud and jolly Warrior song, one of Madam Dreadlock's favorites, in fact, meant to be sung full throttle with every ounce of wind from a splendid Warrior chest, and you have to give her credit, Madam Dreadlock was really giving it some effort as she belted it out at the top of her considerable lung capacity. But it wasn't quite in the spirit of the Reconciliation Banquet, so every time she launched into another bloodthirsty verse of:

"Drag the mermaids by their hair! Drive the werewolves from the woods! Throw the snowcats into jail! That's the WARRIOR WAY! *Quack*!"—not only was she surrounded by a furiously growling mob of snowcats and wolves, and mermaids rising from the lake, who had to be physically restrained by Xar and Wish and Bodkin from going ahead and eating her, but also, Queen Sychorax would give Madam Dreadlock her most toe-curlingly chilling stare, and say in a voice like the sourest of lemons, "Will you STOP that, Dreadlock? Why can't you control yourself? These Wizards are supposed to be our *friends* now..."

"I'm so sorry, Your Highness, I don't know what's come over me," wept poor Madam Dreadlock, giving a squeal as one tricksome mermaid shot out of the water, slipped through Bodkin's fingers (mermaids are awfully slippery), and sank her fangs into Madam Dreadlock's left buttock before Bodkin could catch her and throw her back in the lake.

Mermaids can be very vicious if you insult them.

Now that the adventure was over, Looter was almost back to his old pleased-with-himself self again. And with his cronies clustering around him once more, his arrogant confidence was returning like a comfortable old coat. It would take more than an adventure like this one to substantially change Looter. A snowcat does not change its spots so easily.

"See how I'm going to impress these girls," Looter said to his leering cronies. "These Warriors will need to learn their place. All girls love a guy who is a natural leader and who makes them laugh. Watch and learn, guys, watch and learn."

And then he strolled over to where Drama and Unforgiving were picking their noses with their daggers (REALLY don't try this at home—it is a bad Warrior habit and actually quite dangerous) and disdainfully watching everyone dancing.

"It was quite simple really," boasted Looter to his friends, in a very loud voice, as if they were in the middle of a conversation, "No one has ever escaped from the Mine of Happiness before, but that never puts a truly great future leader like me off, does it, Leafsong?"

Leafsong and Looter's other cronies—who had arrived during the battle, along with Wish's stepsisters—nodded their heads sycophantically. Drama and Unforgiving were less impressed. "*You?????*" asked Drama, with nearly as much splendidly withering scorn as Queen Sychorax herself. (She *had* learned from an expert, after all.) "You're a bit on the smelly side to be a great future leader, aren't you? Pooh! What a whiff...don't you Wizards ever use deodorant? *We* find a spot of porridge under the armpits works wonders..."*

But Looter had a thick skin and mistook their scorn for interest.

"Yes, the richness of my scent is actually a sign of my future greatness," explained Looter kindly, and absolutely dead seriously. "The potency of my pong not only frightens away predators,** it is also an indication of my manliness and the strength of my Magic. Xar may have drawn a lot of attention to himself in this recent adventure, but *I* am the elder and more talented and more pungent son, and therefore *I* will be the future king of Wizards. I know you mean well, girls, but like a lot of females, you're talking too much, so do shut up a moment, will you, while I tell you this interesting story about myself? I had been planning a breakout from the Mine of Happiness for weeks..." continued Looter, admiring his reflection in the Lake of the Lost. "My annoying little baby brother and that ridiculous weird stepsister of yours nearly thwarted my plan, but

* The ancient Egyptians are thought to have sometimes used porridge as a deodorant but this is the first reference to it being used in this way in Bronze Age Britain.

** Seriously, in the Bronze Age some people did think human stench frightened away wild animals.

luckily, my own arrangements were foolproof. I knew I had to keep the Cup of Second Chances a secret in case Witches tried to get hold of it…the cup was safe with me…"

Drama and Unforgiving were just pondering whether to give him a quick punch on the nose to get him to stop talking, or whether a strategic shove in the midriff area to land him in the lake would be better, when…

POOF!

Bumbleboozle waved her wand and the sweat glands opened up instantly all over Looter's scalp, pouring out perspiration, and Looter's splendid quiff collapsed like snow in a heat wave, in a greasy, slimy, yucky mess.

Wish's stepsisters loved that, and laughed loud and long.

"Ooh, is that a sign of the strength of your Magic as well?" jeered Unforgiving. "Or does all this slime mean you're *such* a powerful Wizard you're about to turn into a frog?"

"You will regret this, Warrior girls," said Looter from between gritted teeth. "You wait. In no time you will be begging for my protection and my leadership."

It is difficult, however, to sound all that impressive with your cheeks running with grease, your fringe plastered in front of your eyes, and your mouth full of hair, and I'm afraid Wish's stepsisters only laughed louder and harder.

You see, it would take some time for these ancient enemies to get used to living with one another, and there would be plenty of battles ahead about who-was-going-to-boss-whom.

But despite little altercations such as this one going on between Wizards and Warriors all over the Drood stronghold, even on that first evening, this place was beginning to feel like it might indeed be their new home.

The pixies were already buzzing about in great golden clouds, welcoming everyone at the tops of their voices and whizzing out into the forest to inform the fairy communication network of this unusual and fresh alliance, despite Hoola saying sternly that they must keep this a secret until they had built up the fortifications that would defend their new establishment.

"Oowewon'ttellwewon'ttell!" hummed the pixies excitedly, zooming out to the forest and immediately whispering the exciting news to any wild Wood-sprites or Moonrakers basking in the moonlight of the uppermost tree canopy, who would listen, before dashing back again, chanting the following song, with some of the words muttered under their breaths:

"You're HOME! You're HOME! Welcome to your HO-O-OME!

Countlesslovelygiantssnowcatswolvesandbearsand troopsofWizards...

And also...

Multiple*horrible*numbersof

Dwarf-bashing, ogre-murdering, forest-burning, sprite-killing...turnipsintincansthatcallthemselves...

Warriors!

Not to mention the...

bossyblondgirlswhoputporridgeundertheirarms...

Wonderful stepdaughters of Queen Sychorax!

And don't forget the...*FrozenQueenwholikestelling everyonewhattodo...andusedtokeepastoneinherdungeonsthat tookawayeveryone'sMagic butwe'reallsupposedtohave MAGICALLYforgottenaboutthat...*

Glorious Queen Sychorax herself!

WELCOME!

...to your iron-receptive,
steel-accepting, *(it'llneverwork, Igiveitthreeweeksbeforetheystarttotryandkilleachotheragain)...*

...magical, marvelous, MAG-NI-FICENT, new HO-O-O-OME!!!"

The Wizards and the Warriors ate heartily as they sang the old songs together.

The "Wizards of Once" song was particularly appropriate for this occasion.

Once there Was Magic...

Wandering free
In roads of sky and paths of sea
And in that timeless long-gone hour
Words of nonsense still had power.
Doors still flew and birds still talked
Witches grinned and giants walked
We had Magic wands and Magic wings
And we lost our hearts to impossible things
Unbelievable thoughts! Unsensible ends!
For Wizards and Warriors might be friends

In a world where impossible things are true.
I don't know why we forgot the spell
When we lost the way, how the forest fell.
But now we are old, we can vanish too.

And I see once more the invisible track
That will lead us home and take us back.
So find your wands and spread your wings
I'll sing our love of impossible things
And when you take my vanished hand
We'll both go back to that Magic land
Where we lost our hearts
Several lifetimes ago
When we were Wizards
Once.

And then there were so many other songs, sad ones, happy ones, warring ones, regretful ones, all muddled up together, so the effect was quite confusing, sometimes sweetly harmonious, and sometimes the songs seemed almost to be battling each other, like various different bird species singing in a wood.

"Let me lead a GIANT'S life
No little STEPS, no holding back!"

Then the crooning, yearning, hopeless song of the mermaids...

"There's a world you can't see, a life you can't know, a song you can't hear, a love that won't grow, there's a color of mind that you'll never smell and an undersea heaven curled up in a shell..."

Perhaps Encanzo and Sychorax were singing their own song together, but we couldn't hear that either because they had flown up into the air and disappeared for a while on their own private adventure.

So, Wish and Xar were singing their song, the "Never and Forever Song," for them:

"I promise you gales and a merry adventure,
We'll fly on forever and never will part
I am young, I am poor, I can offer you nothing...
Nothing but love and the beat of my heart."

24. Which Contains a Sting in the Tale

Much, much later, deep into the night, when everyone had partied so hard they had exhausted themselves and the full moon was high in the sky, the companions were settling down to sleep. Perdita had said good-bye, regretfully, to the Greater Giants who had wandered off to the north once more, and indeed, to her own walking boots, who had insisted on going after them.

"I know we were supposed to be retiring, Hoola," said Perdita longingly, "going a-vagabonding, the wind in our hair…but now these children need us. We can join the boots later…"

Perdita had now turned herself into bear form, so that she would be a gigantic, warm, shaggy, and comforting presence to snuggle up to through the rest of the night. Her brown fur was glowing spookily and yet comfortingly blue.

Most of the smaller sprites and hairy fairies were already asleep, having laughed themselves silly at Ranter and the underpants joke, and the pixies had joined them. (Pixies like to sleep on top of one another, so they formed a sort of little anthill of glowing, snoring people, their crazy haircuts sticking out all over the place.) Squeezjoos was still awake, even though it was way past his bedtime, but it is hard to fall asleep when you are so thoroughly overexcited you are turning somersaults in the air. The snowcats and wolves were snoring away, and everyone else was discussing between themselves what might have been the moral of this adventure, now that they had finally come to the end of it.

Wish sighed with the satisfaction of a quest completed—she, the most unlikely hero, had been strong enough to control her power after all. She was looking forward to this school of Perdita's. And better still…

Wish was staring at the feather she had caught when

"What does this mean?" asked Wish.

Caliburn flew away. "It's turning gold!" she said in awe. Sure enough, the dark edges of the feather were shining bright in her hand. "It's a sign," explained Perdita. "Caliburn is a bird who has lived many lifetimes. It is a promise from Caliburn that one day he will return."

"What have we learned from this adventure?" mused Bodkin. "I've learned that rules really can be broken in pursuit of a higher good, the Warrior Code isn't everything, and that a bodyguard can still be a hero, as long as they stay awake."

"I've learned that Wizards and Warriors can live and work together," said Wish. "But I knew that in my heart of hearts already."

"HA!" said Xar. "We'll have to see about that...I get a bad feeling about this learning place thingy they're proposing to build here when your mother is involved."

"We learned that love is the greatest force in the world, and it should never be denied," said a very sleepy Perdita. "And, try as my brother Caliburn might have done, the child who has Magic-mixed-with-iron was born anyway, despite his interference, so you meddle with fate at your own (and everyone else's) peril. What have *you* learned, Xar?"

"I've learned that it's so hard," said Xar sadly, "so, so hard NOT to be Magic in a world that is full of it."

Xar's companions and sprites were full of consolation.

"I have gone there before you," said the Once-sprite. "I too lost my Magic. But look! See here...I have learned to fly on borrowed wings, higher and swifter than I ever did before."

"We will do all your spelling!" sang the larger sprites eagerly.

"We will carry you wherever you want to go..." the snowcats said with their snores.

"I will frighten enemies and howl at the moon for you!" howled Lonesome.

"And I will be yours favorite sprite, yours everloving Squeezjoos," said Squeezjoos, flying down, and laying his head on Xar's cheek. "I'lls do everything for you, Master. We's don't care if you're not Magic. You're still...

"the…

"best…

"master…

"in…

"the…

"world!"

"Thank you, everyone," said Xar, genuinely grateful. "You're the finest companions a Wizard could have."

"Anyway, it still may be that you do actually have Magic that will eventually come in. You may be just a very late developer," said Perdita. "The Witch Magic blocked your real Magic. It's like a tooth. The big tooth can't come through until the baby tooth comes out. And if that's the case, it's a very good thing your Magic waited this long, or the Kingwitch would have taken all of it."

"Really?" said Xar, eagerly, eyes like stars. "You think, even after all this, I still could have Magic that hasn't come through?"

"Maybe not," warned Perdita. "Don't get your hopes up. But yes, it still might be possible. You just have to learn to be patient, and not mind if it never happens."

Too late.

Xar was already planning and getting excited and dreaming up the next step before he'd even got to the one before.

"Maybe the reason why my Magic has taken

such a long time is that it's a really strong powerful Magic...it's going to make me the most powerful Wizard ever...where I walk the ground will shake...maybe it will be Magic-that-parts-the-oceans...maybe it will be Magic-that-controls-the-heavens...maybe it will be *Magic-that-works-on-gold*!" said Xar.

"*All* Magic works on gold, Xar," said Wish.

"Yes, but this will be different, it will turn everything I touch into real gold!" said Xar. "Nobody has ever had that Magic before."

"That's because anybody who had that Magic would very quickly be *dead,*" said Bodkin. "As soon as you tried to eat so much as an apple, it would turn into gold on your lips. You'd starve—you can't eat gold, Xar, you really do have to be careful what you wish for."

But Xar wasn't listening. He was already on to the next thought.

"I'm going to have the biggest, most extravagant, coming-into-my-Magic party EVER," said Xar. "I'm going to change my name like my father Tor became Encanzo, and my brother Bore becoming Looter. I'm going to change my name and make my own destiny, just like my father before me.

"But if I'm going to make my own destiny with this new name, it's going to have to be something really, really good.

"So…what shall I call myself?"

"Choose *wisely*, Xar," warned Perdita sleepily. "Names are important."

Xar thought for a good minute, which was a long time for Xar, and showed how much he had grown up in the last year.

He could choose any name.

Any name under the sun.

But as happens sometimes, when you're trying very hard to think of something, his mind went completely blank.

And then Tiffinstorm sneezed.

"A-A-A-A-A…*FUR!!!!!*"

So, inspired by the sound of the sneeze, Xar chose a name that he had never heard of before, a name, in fact, that he had just made up on the spot.

He turned to Perdita and the others with a great happy smile.

"The name I have chosen," said Xar proudly,

"…is…"

He waited for Perdita and the others to be hanging on his words.

"…*Arthur*," said Xar.

"Brilliant!" squeaked Squeezjoos.

"It is not brilliant," said Timeloss disapprovingly. "It doesn't *mean* anything. It sounds like a sneeze."

"A-A-A-A-A...*FUR!!!!*" said Tiffinstorm, sneezing again, in agreement with Timeloss.

"Arthur?" said Perdita, opening both of her bright bear eyes wide, because this particular name had woken her right up, and she was suddenly very awake indeed.

She did not know why, but she felt the first stirrings of unease. "No...don't call yourself Arthur..." urged Perdita.

"Why not?" argued Xar.

In fact, until that moment, Xar had not completely decided upon Arthur. He was about to change his mind and go for *Gargantua*, as having a suitably splendid kind of ring, but of course as soon as Perdita didn't *want* him to be Arthur, well, the die was cast, the game was won and lost all at the same time, and Xar had to be Arthur at all costs, and hang the consequences.

"So, why not Arthur?" demanded Xar belligerently. "I'm going to be a king one day, and 'King Arthur' sounds great, don't you think?"

"I thought your brother, Looter, was going to be king because he is the eldest?" said Bodkin.

Xar waved an airy hand. "HA! That's what he thinks. *I* know it's ME who is going to be the king."

Perdita searched through her many lifetimes, and one of her lookings into the future was definitely telling her that "King Arthur" was a bad choice of name for someone who wanted to forge his own destiny. Some trembling quivering in her fur, some distant prospective memory in her ancient bear brain, said that the name "Arthur" had its fate already written for it, in large, golden, yet tragically darkening, letters of fiery stars and time.

"It's just...I think that *particular* name rings a bell..."

"It can't ring a bell, Perdita, I just made it up," said Xar, with all the enthusiasm and innocence of a young person for whom everything was happening for the first and last time. "It's a great name for an Enchanter, don't you think? OR a Warrior. I could be *anything*, Perdita, that's the beauty of it. King Arthur the Enchanter...Arthur the Knight of the Wildest Western Woods...High Chief Arthur! Oooh, I like that one. Arthur the Giant-Leader...Arthur the Elf-Wrangler..."

"Xar! You can't wrangle elves—the elves are our *friends*..." said Wish.

"Okay, Drood-Wrangler...Iron-Empire-Wrestler..." said Xar. "Whatever...the opportunities are endless..."

"Nonetheless, I would urge you to think of something else," said Perdita.

Perdita searched her mind rather desperately for alternatives. "I mean, it's a little *tame* for you, don't you think?" said Perdita cunningly. "There are far more glamorous names. How about Swaggerfist? Gallantstar? The Dark Knight? Goldenbritches? That sounds good...anything...Xar...anything...just not Arthur...there's something about that name that tells me there may be trouble ahead..."

"Oh, Perdita, I don't know what you're worrying about..." scolded Xar. "There's ALWAYS trouble ahead. And what's in a name? It can't REALLY change my destiny, you know, in true life. It's unlike you to be so irrational."

"Well, I know it's not logical," said Perdita. "But couldn't you just try something else? As it makes no difference anyway? Just to humor me, you know?"

"No, I'm sorry, Perdita, I've made up my mind. Arthur it is," said Xar stubbornly.

And Perdita sighed because she knew from Xar's tone of voice that there wasn't a hope of Xar changing his course now he had set his mind on it.

"You could forbid it," suggested Hoola sternly.

"No, Hoola, the boy must be allowed to choose his own name, wherever that name may take him," said Perdita. "If this last set of adventures has taught us anything it is that we shouldn't interfere. It wouldn't work if we tried, anyway."

"What adult name were *you* thinking of taking, Wish?" said Hoola, hoping to distract Perdita's attention, for Perdita was looking rather distressed and holding her head in her paws as if she was beginning to get a migraine. "*You* deserve to have an adult name, now, Wish, for you have most certainly come into your Magic in a big way."

"I was thinking of something to do with the sea, because I love the sea," said Wish enthusiastically, "and then something that means 'circle,' because circles are such a great shape, I love the idea of everybody being equal, and you're always equal if you're sitting around a circle."

" 'Morgana' means 'sseacircle'?" hissed Tiffinstorm helpfully.

"Mor-ga-na . . ." said Wish thoughtfully, rolling the syllables around in her mouth as if she was tasting them. "Mor-ga-na. Yes! I like it!"

"*Noooooooooooooo* . . ." moaned Perdita to herself, clutching her forehead.

Should I call myself Lance-a-loads?

Her migraine seemed to be getting worse.

"How about you, Bodkin?" said Wish. "What do *you* want to call yourself?"

"Well, I want something very Warriorlike," said Bodkin, "that shows off how much I've improved with my bodyguarding, and my weapon skills. So I was thinking of something like, Shaking-spear-masses or Waving-sword-galore or maybe even Lance-a-something after that new weapon I invented…" said Bodkin thoughtfully. "Sounds very impressively 'bodyguard hero,' don't you think? Lance-a-loads? Lance-a-plenty? Lance-a-reams?"

"Lance-a-legion?" suggested Wish.

"No, too long…" said Bodkin. "Something a little snappier, perhaps?

"…Lance-a-*much*?"

"STOOOOOOP!" roared Perdita, to Bodkin's surprise, and then adding, for he looked a little hurt, "You can tell us tomorrow, Bodkin, there's plenty of time for you to think up your adult name."

And then Perdita carried on, almost as if she were talking to herself, trying to reassure them all about something that only she could see. "This could all be a coincidence...for here is the thing about stories. They get splintered and fragmented and fractured along the way, until there is no *knowing* what they mean. And there must be loads of Morganas and Arthurs and even Lance-a-somethings in the future. Wish and Xar and Bodkin may not be the Morgana and Arthur and Lance-a-something I am thinking of..."

"Well of COURSE I'll be the one you're thinking of!" said Xar, very offended. "*I'm* going to be the one you're thinking of, because *I'M* THE BEST! I'm always the best, Perdita..."

"Yes," said Perdita, a little sadly. "You're the best."

"But there won't be any problems because I just made that name up!" said Xar joyously. "I'm going to be the only Arthur in the entire world! So don't worry, Perdita...there's nothing to worry about...everyone really does worry

"WAY

"TOO

"MUCH...

"Look!" said Xar, pointing upward. "Squeezjoos is writing the moral of the adventure up in the air in sprite-writing..."

"'Love is greater than Witches...'" read Xar. "And...I can't quite read the next bit..."

Love is greater than witches…

... and true love lasts Forever

"'And true love lasts forever ...'"
finished Wish with satisfaction.

"Finally!" sniffed Perdita. "Out of the mouths of sprites ...Now THERE'S a moral to go to sleep on."

And the big bear closed her eyes.

The End

Epilogue

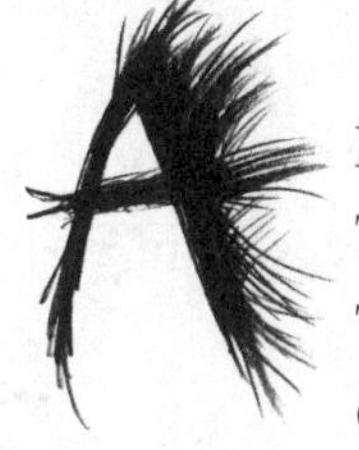

NYONE WHO HAS SKIPPED TO THIS EPILOGUE BEFORE READING THE REST OF THE STORY IS A BIG CHEAT AND SHOULD GO RIGHT BACK TO CHAPTER 1 OR I WILL GET REALLY QUITE UPSET.

And that is where we will leave the heroes, for the moment.

Tired but happy, with an adventure completed, and a whole new world opening up in front of them.

Who knows if Xar really was the Arthur that Perdita was thinking of? Many baby boys in the future would be named Arthur in honor of the heroic exploits of Xar.

And of course there would be trouble ahead.

Xar was right—there is *always* trouble ahead.

There would be trouble with Looter. There would be trouble with the Tatzelwurm. There would be trouble with Queen Sychorax's suitors. There would be trouble with the iron emperor, and the Droods, and even the mermaids have been mortally offended in the course of this story.

People would fall in love with the wrong people, like

the fork falling in love with the spoon. Round tables and shining castles would be built and maybe they would fall.

Though the Witches were defeated, there were other evils in the wildwoods, perhaps even worse than Witches, if worse can be thought of. These evils would wake, and our heroes must fight them.

That is the way with stories, you see.

Sometimes things that look like endings aren't really endings at all, they're just the start of a new and even more interesting adventure.

Because here is the thing about stories, and human beings.

History is a set of repeating circles, like the tide. Human beings make the same mistakes, again and again. But things do get better over time.

The same elements come into play, so many, many times. The same conflicts, the same names, the same struggles, repeated throughout history, in echoes, like the ringing of the ghost-axes in Sychorax's indestructible-and-yet-destroyed prison.

That is why you have to listen to the stories...

...for stories always mean something.

The question is...and this has always interested me...

What *do* they mean?

And by my question, you will know who I am.

(It is often by our questions that we are known.)

For this has been a story in search of its own narrator, who did not even know that she had gotten lost in the wildwoods.

I am the narrator of this story.

And my name is…

…*PERDITA*.

Yes, I bet that surprised you.

HA!

Shake me by the paw and admit that you were startled.

"Perdita," you see, is another name for someone who is lost.

But see how I have found her!

As soon as I saw her name, I knew that *I* was *her*.

I am the bear, the creator, the protector, and the conscience of the island.

It was *I* who became the advisor to Wish and Xar, it was *I* who had the wise eyes that guided them, it was *I* who was the tutor who took them into adulthood.

So if you guessed the narrator was *Caliburn*…

…and I bet a lot of you did, you clever readers…

…you were very nearly right.

(But not quite.)

For I am also the raven, the trickster, and Caliburn is my twin.

Caliburn looked like he started the story, didn't he?

But it was always me all along, hidden, Magic, and invisible in the quiet still darkness of the sheltering trees, before I stepped forward and revealed myself to myself.

I am sorry if that is tricksy.

But a story IS tricksy.

The crucible of the story changes those who listen to it, those who are within it, and the person who is telling it, all at the same time.

Why is it important that *I*, Perdita, am the narrator and not Caliburn?

There is hardly any difference between Caliburn and me.

We are *twins*, after all.

And Caliburn was a wise and wonderful storyteller, and such a part of myself that it was almost as if we were the same person.

But the distinction between us is an important one.

Caliburn is male and I am female.

And although of course that should not matter…

…I can look into the future sufficiently to know that the story a *woman* tells may be lost over time.

For it really does matter who is narrating the story.

You may have been told that *King Arthur, also known as Xar*, was the child of destiny. But I was there too, a shapeshifter, down the mine, in the castle, although you could not see me, and I can tell you that the child of destiny was actually *Morgana le Fay, also known as Wish.*

And she was not a sidekick but a hero.

How Wish's and Xar's destinies played out, and how their fates were intertwined with the child-Bodkin-who-we-now-know-as-Lancelot, and let alone, the child-we-haven't-even-met-yet-who-is-really-rather-amazing-and-is-going-to-be-called-Guinevere, well...

...that is all in the future, and that is all another story, and it may be a different one than the one you have heard before.

All I can tell you *now* is the truth about the story so far, in the everlasting hope that the future story might change.

Tomorrow, the Round Table may rise again.

Tomorrow, Camelot may be built once more, and the shining towers stand glorious forever.

In the meantime...

In the imperfect mess and tangle and wildwoods of the present...

I am the narrator, and my name is PERDITA.

In my bear form, I am friend to heroes and the voice of omen. I am associated with the goddess Cerridwen and the great star constellation known as "Arthur's plough," and my poetic cauldron is one of change and rebirth and transformation.

In my raven form, I am associated with the giant Bran, the sword Excalibur, Caliban, and the witches in *Macbeth*, the god Odin, and the faraway tribes in the new world that is yet to be discovered.

But I might as well not only be the bear and the raven, but also Ariel and Encanzo the Great Enchanter, and Sychorax the Warrior Queen, and the dark and dreadful Kingwitch himself all rolled up into one.

For I am both a weapon and a downfall.

I have lived many lifetimes, witnessed many battles, eavesdropped on tragedy and comedy and everything in between, which is the joy and the grief and the curse of a storyteller.

Heed my

broken voice.

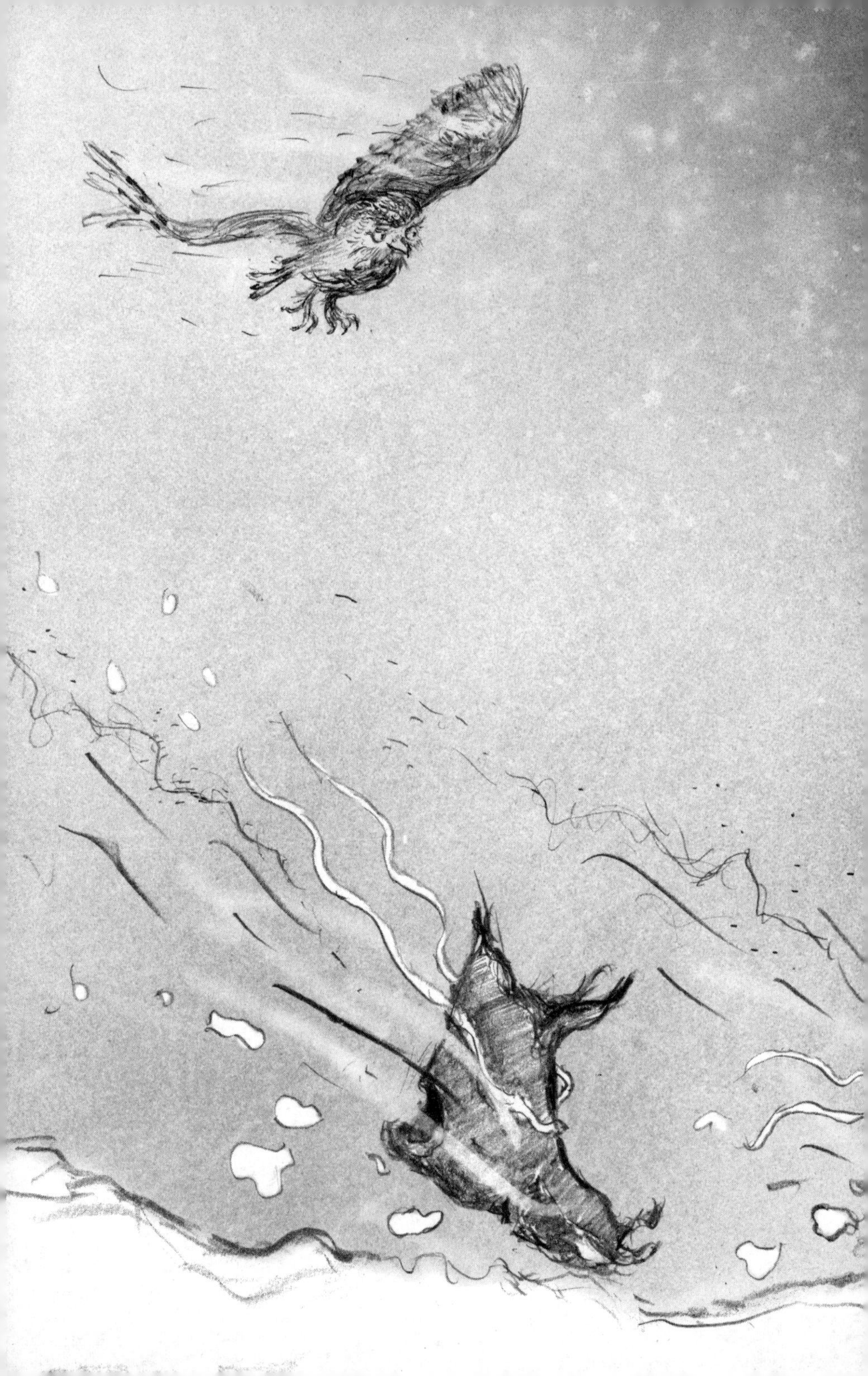

Perdita's old
crusty walking boots
following after the
Greater Giants on
their own...

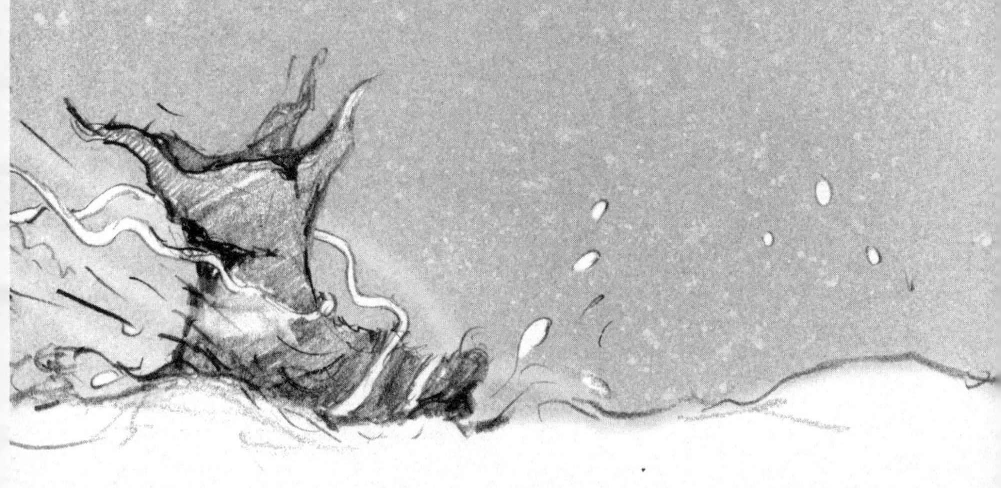

ACKNOWLEDGMENTS
(thank-yous)

A whole team of people have
helped me write this book.

Thank you to my wonderful editor,
Anne McNeil, and my
magnificent agent, Caroline Walsh.

A special big thanks to Samuel Perrett,
Polly Lyall Grant, Rebecca Logan, and Camilla Leask.

And to everyone else at Hachette Children's Group,
Hilary Murray Hill, Tracy Phillips, Emma Martinez
Valentina Fazio, Beth McWilliams, Katy Cattell,
Kelly Llewellyn, Nicola Goode,
Katherine Fox, Jennifer Hudson,
Alison Padley, Rebecca Livingstone.

Thanks to all at Little Brown,
Megan Tingley, Jackie Engel,
Lisa Yoskowitz, Marisa Finkelstein.

And most important of all,
Maisie, Clemmie, Xanny.

And SIMON for his excellent
advice on absolutely everything.

I couldn't do it without you.

Discover the Magic of Cressida Cowell
visit
cressidacowell.com
to find out all about her books,
events, and lots more!
/CressidaCowellBooks
@CressidaCowellAuthor
@CressidaCowell

You're never alone if you have an Enchanted Spoon.

Debra Hurford Brown

Cressida Cowell

is the #1 internationally bestselling author and illustrator of the Wizards of Once and the How to Train Your Dragon series. She grew up in London and on a small, uninhabited island off the west coast of Scotland, where she spent her time writing stories, fishing for things to eat, and exploring the island. She now lives in Hammersmith, England, with her husband, three children, and a dog named Pigeon.